A Wizard Scorned

Patricia White

Hard Shell Word Factory

Another one for you, Bill

© 1998 Patricia White
ISBN: 0-7599-0283-6
Trade Paperback
Published August 2001

Ebook ISBN: 1-58200-021-2
Published 1998

Hard Shell Word Factory
PO Box 161
Amherst Jct. WI 54407
books@hardshell.com
http://www.hardshell.com
Cover art © 1998 Dirk A. Wolf
All rights reserved.

All characters in this book have no existence outside the imagination of the author, and have no relation whatever to anyone bearing the same name or names. These characters are not even distantly inspired by any individual(s) known or unknown to the author, and all incidents are pure invention.

Prologue

THE HUGE CAT stretched, yawned widely, showing an impressive set of fangs, and rearranged his wealth of sleek, black fur, and an even sleeker wealth of underlying muscle, on the dark, sun-warmed surface of an old lava flow. He did it all, and with great deliberation, before he even attempted to answer the young man's question.

"Since, this once, you have the brain to ask my advice before you end up fire-dancing in your bare-feet, I'll give it. Youth, they say, is curable by time and experience; if rash acts don't do you in beforehand. But, it would seem to me, and my motives may not be the same as yours, that you'd be making a very large mistake if you do not accept the task these men have offered you. You have the knowledge and the magic to see it to its end."

The cat's words were plain in his mind, as they always were. The wizard took a deep breath, tried to marshal and somehow dispel his doubts, to rationalize his fear that the task was beyond his doing. That the men who had offered him gold had somehow twisted their words, had let their dreams and needs speak louder than the truth. He couldn't.

To others, Sojourner, the great cat that must forever wander, might be a myth, a winter tale told when the fire was burned to ashes and embers and the wind sang a sad lament outside the walls. But not to Will. Will knew the truth; or as much of the truth that could be known. And if this deed was important to Sojourner, then it had to be— if Will could make it so.

"Your quest?" Will asked, leaning against the side of the stone, pushing his fingers through his disordered hair, trying to fight off the memories Sojourner, probably without malice but certainly with purpose, had invoked. It was a useless battle.

The hot sun blazed in the summer sky, but Will shivered with another cold. The icy cold of a small boy who stood in the snow and watched, young and helpless, tears of sorrow freezing on his gaunt face, as his world ended in a roaring fire and the screams of his dying parents. And the great, silver-eyed cat, coming from nowhere, curling around the child, warming him, guiding him, saving him from...

It had happened long ago, but was eternally bright in Will's memory. It was all there, the grief and the fear and, above all else, the debt he owned Sojourner. A debt that would not be paid until That Which Was Lost could be found or Sojourner was somehow freed from the terrible burden he...

"Young wizard," the big cat's rumbling voice, audible only in Will's mind, sounded infinitely weary as he said, "time runs too fast. It must be soon or all will be for naught."

"And me fetching the brides will help...."

THERE WAS NO real answer to the wizard's hesitant question. So many paths spread before them, but only one would lead to Sojourner's freedom, lifting the dark spell that made him both more and less than he had been. He sighed.

"Young wizard, all was tangled at my changing, my magic and my memory were torn by the spell. I cannot see clearly, but, yes, this much I know: the off-world brides have a place in what must be. One of them is terribly important. How that can be, I know not. Only that she..."

Laying his massive head on his forepaws, he closed his silvery eyes. Sorrow was heavy around him, but Sojourner was a cat. That, too, was his eternal bane. Grief was a raw and bleeding wound in his soul, but cats do not weep. They cannot.

"I know not the outcome, young wizard," he said softly," but whether it be for good or ill, this bride fetching must be done and very soon. That much I can see, well and truly."

It was Will's turn to sigh, but the wizard didn't even try to argue.

Chapter 1

"A WIZARD? Gathering brides to take to some alternate earth? Really, Maggie! The whole concept is positively ridiculous! The man is obviously a fraud!" However much the truth rankled in her orderly mind, Jane Murdock carefully refrained from adding, "And only a fool would believe such blatant hogwash. A silly romantic fool."

Instead, she sighed—rather heavily and, if the truth be known, with a strong undertone of irritation. Taking off her black-rimmed reading glasses, Jane placed them, with rather too much care, on top of the small stack of file folders on her Queen Anne desk. Then, she switched off the computer, took a deep breath, and walked, marched might better describe her mode of locomotion, across the wide expanse of thick white carpet to where her secretary, Maggie Hilton, was standing. The white-and-gold credenza was to her left, the door to the outer office behind her.

With an effort visible to even the most disinterested of observers, Maggie stood her ground. Trying not to twist her short-nailed hands together, or not to take a step back or even flee the scene entirely, or not to betray her great and still growing unease, her breath came a little too fast. No matter her feelings, she waited for Jane, looking for all the world like a fear-petrified mouse about to be devoured by a very large, very hungry snake.

"Maggie, listen to me," Jane said quietly, wanting nothing more than to continue her work session, to complete the presentation for the Morris job. That's what she wanted but she knew, full well and not a whit happy with the knowledge, that absolutely nothing would be accomplished until she had convinced the younger woman that what she was planning to do was incredibly stupid . Indeed, it was quite possibly dangerous as well. "The things this man has promised you can't possibly be true, and, if you'll just use your head for a moment, think this idiotic premise through, you'll have to concede that. I'm sure that you will be able to find the flaws this whole silly scheme, if you will just examine carefully what this man, this... this...ah...so-called wizard has told you."

Red mouth set, unyielding, eyes filled with stubborn resolve, Maggie didn't looked convinced, so Jane took a new approach. "You are what? Twenty-two? Twenty-three?"

"Twenty-three, almost twenty-four," Maggie said, her chin betraying the slightest of quivers. She took a quick breath, swallowed hard, blinked, and even sniffled a little, but she still refused to back down, even an inch.

Jane asked her next question, "And, I assume, since you are very competent in your rather demanding job as my personal secretary, you are reasonably well-educated? High school? Business school?"

Maggie nodded.

"Then, you must know that wizards do not exist, have never actually existed. Given that, why would you, a modern woman, a presumably liberated woman of the 90's, even come close to believing this man can wave his magic wand, or whatever it is he's going to do. He's not going to transport you to some wonderful world. Take you to some utopia in some perfect country on some other earth, where men want wives and aren't afraid of love, commitment, marriage, and all the rest of that garbage he's been feeding you. Don't you know that he's handing you a line of bull big enough to..."

Several inches too wide in the hips, brown hair wisping down from what was supposed to be a French roll, brown eyes large in their fringe of dark lashes, olive complexion smooth, but not in the conventional sense truly attractive, Maggie blushed hotly. Then she gave her employer what could only be described as a pitying look. And she took in a little hissing breath before she said, sounding both sad and slightly embarrassed and stubborn enough to give a mule pause, "Ms. Murdock, I didn't really expect you to believe me. But it is true. Will, he's the wizard, warned us about talking to other people about this. He told us what they'd think and all. But, that doesn't really matter. It's just that you've been awfully good to me since I came to work here, and I couldn't just up and leave without telling you where I was going and why."

More red rushed up to burn crimson spots on her round cheeks and her voice quavered, just a little, but Maggie went doggedly on, finishing what she intended to say in a rush of words. "If I just disappeared, you know, just went out to lunch today and never came back, I was afraid you might worry that I'd had an accident, or been kidnapped by terrorists, or something bad like that. I like you too much to make you worry about me over nothing. It just wouldn't have been right to leave without telling you the truth."

Jane hadn't gone out of her way to be nice to her secretary. They had been terribly busy for the past several months and had spent many long days working in each other's company, which led to a certain superficial intimacy. It wasn't a relationship that Jane had, in any way, fostered.

Her position as Vice President of Smith, Smith, and Melrose, a Fortune 500 management consulting firm, engendered a lifestyle that was high-powered, demanding, and time-devouring. It was also a lifestyle that had no room for friendships, casual or otherwise.

Not that Jane had ever had that many friends; her aunt, the one who raised her and cast her out as soon as humanly possible, had seen to that. She had done it for Jane's own good, or so she said, rather often and with great sincerity. According to her, work was the only way out of poverty, work coupled with education and driving ambition. Knowing poverty only too well, Jane had taken her aunt's teaching to heart—some, mostly disgruntled competitors, said she had learned the lesson far too well.

Now, for the most part, Jane didn't care what others thought or said about her. Their talk couldn't actually change anything. She was already on the upper rungs of the ladder to success and had no doubt that within the next few years she would reach the top. It was a goal, it seemed, she had been working toward since her parents' death when she was almost four, the time she had gone to live with her aunt in a walk-up flat in the poorer part of town.

The thirty-three years stretching between the time of her parent's untimely deaths and the present hadn't, for the most part, been what anyone would call easy or enjoyable. Still, now her bank account was growing, her stock portfolio was thick and diversified, and she was already a force in her chosen field. Granted, all the work, dedication, and achievement hadn't left room for much else in her rather hectic schedule; except maybe a frozen dinner tossed in the microwave and a few hours of sleep.

But, it did have its rewards. A personal shopper bought and coordinated her designer wardrobe. Her hairdresser, the Jean-Claud of Jean-Claud Salons, made weekly office calls to keep her shorn locks chic and fashionably gilded. There were drawbacks also; even if they were, at least as far as Jane was concerned, minor. She had never been in love. The men in her life were strictly clients of the firm, with business alone on their minds. Jane knew that she was rather lacking in the sex appeal department and liked it that way; it posed far fewer complications in her work universe. What she considered the worst drawback to her current position had nothing at all to do with men, or ticking biological clocks, or babies: Jane didn't even have time for a cat and she'd always dreamed of having one.

At the thought of the cat a ripple of sadness touched her, but only for the moment. She was too busy to feel sorry for herself. Far to busy to allow the best personal secretary she had ever had to go haring off with a self-proclaimed wizard. The kind who, supposedly, worked real magic, the sort of sizzle-and-crackle, wishes-come-true magic that only existed in children's minds and adults' fantasy books.

Real wizards, had such a thing actually existed, certainly wouldn't have done what Maggie claimed and advertised for brides in the classified section of the *New York Times*. The whole notion was ridiculous. Totally ridiculous.

Irritated by the delay, the disruption it was causing in her well-planned day, she was determined to prove Maggie, and the rest of the so-called "brides" were being conned. But, Jane knew, with only a whisper of guilt, that her concern was more centered on the fact that she would have to hire and train a new secretary than on anything else; including Maggie's future happiness or lack thereof. Taking care of people, and straightening out their incredibly messy lives, wasn't real high on Jane's list of priorities; especially when they acted, as Maggie was certainly doing, from total stupidity, not reason.

Maggie cleared her throat, made a little gulping sound. "Will is still looking for brides, Ms. Murdock. I thought maybe you might like to come with me...ah...us," she said softly. She looked at the floor, not at Jane, and blushed fire engine red, a burning red that brought little drops of sweat to her brow and upper lip.

Her words were so completely unexpected that Jane was caught off guard, if only for a moment. "Me? Why on earth would you...I can't believe that you would even imagine that I would even consider such an asinine proposal, let alone have...."

Despite her excellent secretarial skills, Maggie certainly wasn't listening to her boss' sputter of protest at that moment.

She seemed to listening to her own heart's needs rather than to anything that even smacked of sanity. Her eyes fixed on some inner vision, her blush faded to a becoming pink and she smiled. It lit up her face, made her appear far prettier than her usual wont. It wasn't the smile but the tone of her voice, the longing in her words that gave Jane an almost irresistible urge to grab her by the shoulders and shake some sense back into her silly head. She was, however, too disciplined to give in to urges. She gritted her teeth instead. And listened to soppy, romantic words that were little more than drivel; at least as far as Jane was concerned.

"Babies," Maggie said softly. "I'm going to have a husband that loves me and babies, lots of babies. We'll have a house, a log house, with a fenced yard and yellow roses climbing all over the big front porch. Horses. We'll have a herd of horses, and a dog, a big, happy dog. It'll be just like in the old days. You know, when men loved and protected the women who worked beside them to realize a dream...."

It was too much. Jane snorted in disbelief. "Instead of sounding like a dreamy-eyed I-don't-know-what, you'd better go to the police and see what you can do about getting your money, whatever it was you gave this..."

Still smiling, Maggie shook her head. "It isn't like that at all. We didn't give Will any money or anything else. The men from Will's earth, the ones who ordered brides, did that. They paid for everything. You know, like Will's magic to get us there and our new wardrobes for there and..."

Grinding her teeth together until the cords stood out in her thin neck, Jane clenched her hands into fists. Then she counted to ten. Took five deep breaths. And finally allowed herself to say, with a little less sharpness in her voice than would have actually taken the other woman's head off, but not much less, "Maggie, how can you be so damned stupid about this? Wizards do *not* exist. Magic only happens at magic shows. It's an illusion, a trick carefully designed to fool the mind into believing something that isn't true. Your so-called magician is a crook, a charlatan, a real phony, and he's getting something out of this. And whatever it is, you're the one who is being took. And not to some alternative earth either."

Raising her head to look directly at Jane and taking a huge liberty, Maggie put her hand on the sleeve of Jane's watermelon-red silk jacket. She didn't exactly beg, but there was definitely a note of pleading in her voice when she said, "Ms.

Murdock, even if you are rich and famous and all that, you're still a woman. You have a woman's dreams and a woman's heart. And I know you have to want more out of life than you're getting now, something real and lasting, like love, instead of all this cold-blooded business junk. Please, won't you just come with me and talk to Will and..." Her voice wavered, died. Her hand tightened for just a second before it dropped away from Jane's arm, but Maggie's eyes never wavered—and neither did the pity and concern and real caring that was so apparent in their depths.

Perhaps it was her own irritation simmering into something very close to fury. It certainly wasn't the younger woman's misplaced pity that made Jane say, "I can see that we aren't going to accomplish a thing until this is settled. Go get your purse, re-schedule my luncheon appointment, and leave word with the receptionist that we will be out of the office for an hour or so. If anything important comes up, she can beep me."

Her secretary, beaming happily, was scarcely out the door before Jane, falling prey to a marauding band of second thoughts, opened her mouth to call Maggie back, to cancel the wizard visit. But Jane had never backed out on a promise in her life. And, even if this current venture was an exercise in futility, she had no intention of starting now.

Straightening her shoulders, she walked, with unyielding determination in every step, to her desk. After she cleared the top of folders, Jane retrieved her own surprisingly large bag from the desk drawer, added her reading glasses to the diverse and multitudinous collection of things inside, and was ready to go.

Or almost. Holding the black purse by the shoulder strap, she took a moment to look around the sunny office. She admired the lush ferns, the view of New York from the sixty-third floor, the clean, uncluttered expanse of very expensive carpeting and even more expensive furnishings. Fighting off the odd feeling that she was bidding the whole place a final farewell, Jane slid the bag onto her shoulder, stepped into Maggie's office, and firmly closed the door to her own private domain behind her.

Their cab was fighting the traffic on Fifth Avenue before Jane said a word, and then she only asked, "Are you sure you want to go through with this, Maggie? You could save us both a lot of trouble if you'd just forget all this nonsense. If we go on, I can assure you it won't be pleasant. Men, like this phony wizard of yours, who prey on women aren't exactly the most savory..."

Jane shook her head.

Smiling gently, Maggie didn't try to argue, she just said, "Please, don't worry about being hurt or anything, Ms. Murdock. Will isn't at all like you think. He's different than any man I've ever...I don't know. He's got brown hair that sort of flops down in his eyes. It makes you want to brush it back and...His smile is...well, he isn't handsome exactly, but he is somebody that you can really trust. He's...You'll see."

Jane considered herself a master at reading faces, voices, and what she heard in Maggie's gave her pause. The young woman was obviously enamored with Will, and that fact alone was enough to cause even more complications. The man was not only a phony, but if she was getting all the clues, he was also a bounder and a cad, a man who was intent on leading a whole group of young women astray.

"You'll like him," Maggie said again. "I know you don't trust him now, but you will. You'll see."

She saw all right, but what Jane saw certainly wasn't what she had expected when she followed Maggie up to the door of a tall, narrow, brownstone on Forty-Second Street. At least, that's where Jane thought it was, but for some reason the actual location kept eluding her mind— not that it mattered, she certainly didn't need to find it again.

According to the few fantasy flicks Jane had seen, and regarded not only as a waste of time but also as a waste of film, Maggie's wizard wasn't exactly dressed-for-success in his chosen profession. Jane's expectations of flowing gowns, peaked hats, and long white beards weren't met. Will was wearing shiny black cowboy boots, faded blue jeans (the cheap kind with no labels), and a western shirt, blue-plaid with pearl snaps down the front, when he opened the door.

Jane blinked, but nothing changed as he stepped back and invited them in. The a room was nearly filled with chalky symbols drawn on a shabby brown carpet and a plethora of flaming candles and burning incense. There were, at least, twenty young women, not a single one of whom would ever grace the cover of Vogue. But each and every one of them had a look of anticipation, of energy, eagerness, aliveness that made them far more than just pretty.

It was a look that Jane Murdock came very close to envying— and would never, not even in the hidden places in her own mind, have admitted.

Chapter 2

LANKY, NOT-QUITE-FINISHED-LOOKING, taller than Jane, but not by more than a scant inch, and, at the very least, a good decade younger, Will, the so-called *wizard*, smiled and waved Jane and Maggie toward two unoccupied chairs. Ignoring the soft-voiced whispering of the other brides, and Jane, he said, his approving gaze for Maggie alone, "Maggie, I was afraid you weren't going...I'm glad you're here. We'll be leaving shortly—as soon as the last two of the wizard-order brides arrive."

He paused for breath before he asked, with a bare, disinterested glance in Jane's direction, "Is this a friend come to see you off?"

Blushing, rather prettily, Maggie shook her head, gnawed on her lower lip, and said, guilt tingeing her explanation, "I know you said not to tell anyone we were leaving, Will, but, I couldn't just...I don't have any family, but Ms. Murdock, Jane, is my boss. She came with me to...to...she thinks you are doing something wrong. I let her come because I wanted her to go with us to your world. She doesn't believe that you're who you said were, or anything like that, but I thought if she just met you, listened to you talk, then she'd know you were telling the truth about the other world and everything...."

"Shhh, Maggie, it's all right. You've done nothing wrong," he said, forgiveness in every syllable, before he turned to face Jane who was standing several steps closer to the front door than was her contrite secretary.

It was then that Jane got her second really good look at him. He might not fit her mental image of a wizard, but he damned sure wasn't handsome either—not unless your tastes, which Jane's didn't, ran to callow boys. By a narrow stretch of the imagination, he might be considered wholesome-looking, but only after he got his mop of rough-looking, brownish hair cut and styled and conditioned. His eyes, blue and piercing, might pass muster—they even had an honest, somewhat worried look, which didn't quite fit with his con.

Unless, of course, Jane thought, he was just the front man in a larger scheme—one that boded no good for the young women involved.

WILL DIDN'T WANT to look at Ms. Murdock, not when just looking at Maggie gave him so much pleasure, but there was something about the woman that demanded his attention. What, he didn't really know, but her figure would have put a bean pole to shame and her face, especially those burning black eyes, wouldn't find her a husband even in a place as woman-starved as...

He shook his head and, surprisingly, really meant it when he said,
"I'm really sorry, ma'am, but I can't take you with us. I'd like to, but I'm afraid you don't meet the specifications."

Maggie came close, the light, flowery fragrance of her perfume tickled the inside of his nostrils, her nearness made him almost breathless—and it certainly diminished Ms. Murdock's importance in his own particular scheme of things.

"She's only thirty-six or so, not nearly as old as she looks," Maggie said softly. "And she's not sick or anything, you know, like anorexic. She'd fatten up if she just would just stop working long enough to eat. Her hair is really...It'll grow and..."

He wanted to please Maggie—far more than he had any right to—but magic, even if it was by his own doing, had its rules. His particular preference couldn't come into play—if it did, Maggie would never marry one of...

Will wouldn't allow himself to finish that thought. He was just a struggling young wizard with nothing to offer in the way of a home or worldly goods or even...And that's why Maggie was going with him, that's what she wanted: a loving husband, a home, and babies. That's what he had promised, on his wizard's honor, to give her.

Strangely, and certainly against his better judgment, he was already more than half in love with her, so he knew he could give her one of the three easy enough, but not the others, not a home and babies. Not now, possibly not ever. Will sighed, but he was intent on doing his duty and doing it as painlessly as possible. And doing his duty meant letting Ms. Murdock down as quickly as he could, without hurting her feelings, or making her angry, and getting on with activating the travel spell that was almost ready to go.

"I'm truly sorry, ma'am," Will said, reaching out to pat Jane's silk-clad shoulder, "but my employers gave me a fairly rigid set of qualifications and you just don't..."

Fire ran from her shoulder up his hand and arm, and for just an instant he saw a pair of silver eyes, looking not at him, but at her, and a longing that transcended time and space, was...

Jane jerked away.

Will shook his head and rubbed at the burning that still ached in his fingers. She couldn't be the one Sojourner had foreseen. She just flat-out couldn't be. Jane Murdock was tall, gaunt, nearly ugly, and as arrogant and self-centered as anyone it had ever been his displeasure to meet.

But, despite all that, there was something about her, something..

HIS TOUCH STILL smarting and burning on her shoulder, Jane blinked away what had had to be a hallucination. She took another step away from Will and said, fury making her voice cold, enunciating each word clearly, making sure that both Will and Maggie understood exactly what she was saying, "My looks, or lack thereof, are not a matter up for discussion. I am not here to become one of your...your *women*. I neither need nor want babies, a husband, or whatever else you're pretending to peddle to complete my life.

"I *am* here to tell you that if you don't quit whatever it is you are doing with Maggie and the rest of these young women, I am going to the police. I will have you arrested for white slavery or pimping or procuring or pandering or..."

Consternation, mixed with what too closely resembled pity, was written plainly on his young face, giving him an almost comic look. Will took a step back, then two more, stopping when the outer edge of a small, dusty piecrust table, its top fairly covered with burning candles, touched his thigh. "I am deeply sorry that I have offended you, ma'am, but you don't honestly understand what it is you're planning on doing. I have given these women my word of honor, and that means a good deal to a wizard, that they will find love, marriages, and homes in my land. That is important to them and me, so I can't allow you to..."

"Will, or whatever your real name is, you don't have any say in the matter," Jane snapped. "Con artists like you make me sick, promising these gullible women the world and then having them end up in some house of..."

He ran his fingers through his hair, disrupting what little order it possessed. But his voice held only puzzlement when he said, "I know it must be difficult to have reached your age without acquiring a husband and a family, ma'am, but I truly don't understand why you're reacting this way. I didn't mean to hurt your feelings—I really didn't draw up the list of requirements. The men who hired me to bring back the brides were adamant in their need for healthy, pretty young women of childbearing..."

"What you're doing is illegal!" Jane all but shouted. "You can't just waltz in here and..."

"Ma'am," he answered, bowing ever so slightly, acting as if she were well over-the-hill and in need of cosseting, humoring, and careful explanations, given in words she should have no trouble understanding, even in her state of advanced senility. "I assure you that what I am doing is well within the laws of your land. If you care to examine them, I have a business license and all the necessary export permits.

"Besides, this particular business has a long history in your country. In fact, it was a very respectable thing when your own West was still young and untamed and good women were beyond price."

The door opened, two young women hurried in, stepping around Jane, smiling at Will, murmuring apologies for being late, causing a whirl and billow of incense and a bending of candle flames.

While Will was greeting the newcomers and seating them and Maggie in the three empty chairs left in the circle, Jane began edging toward the closed door to the outer, saner world of honking horns, screaming sirens, and roaring subways. She fully intended to escape from the madhouse, and the madman in charge, and run, not walk, to the nearest police station.

Will reached the door before Jane did. Although how that was possible, she didn't know. He put his hand on the knob, held it tight as he confronted her, tried to finish his rather feeble explanation of what he was doing in New York.

"Mail-order brides have long been a tradition in your land, ma'am. Just because a regular mail route hasn't been established between my land and yours doesn't mean that what I am trying to do is illegal. And, I can assure you it will not be detrimental to either the morals or..."

Whatever else he intended to say was lost in the theatrical and, in Jane's estimation, totally overdone, billow-of-smoke, spectral-blue- light, crash-of-thunder entrance—from out of the nowhere into here—of one of the most beautiful women Jane had ever seen.

The woman was dressed in what looked to be

state-of-the-art wizard robes. They were complete with cabalistic designs in a shimmering gold and a tall, peaked hat—it, like the robe, was of the purest of whites and sort of glimmered and gleamed with inner light.

Dainty as an angel, waist-length hair so fair it only hinted at being yellow, she stepped into the middle of the room, carrying a long, bark-peeled, willow switch. Her smile was anything but angelic when she looked from Will to the seated brides—her green-eyed gaze passing over Jane as if she were some slick-tailed, smelly rodent too insignificant for existence, and too repugnant to be stomped.

"I am Cordelia," she said, acting as if the pronouncement should mean something—it didn't to Jane, and as far she could tell, it didn't seem to be making a big dent in Will's memory either.

He gave the newcomer an awkward bow and said, sounding polite but more than a little apprehensive, "Pleased, Cordelia. I am Will. How may I serve you?"

"So, Will," she said, her voice as smoky as the room and heavily ladened with scorn, "ignorant fools that they are, they actually thought a no-talent, freshly hatched wizard like *you* could circumvent my spell? I can assure you that it is not going to happen. Not now, not ever; unless Max comes to his senses. And then, the interdict will no longer exist, so it really makes no difference. Does it?"

The woman smiled and Jane was hard put not to shiver.

Will gave his head a slight shake, as if he were trying to make sense out of odd bits of nonsense. "Who's Max?" he asked.

Not bothering to answer, Cordelia raised her switch, brought it slashing down, whistling with power, sparkling with some sort of glowing dust.

"Cordelia, don't!" Will shouted, lunging toward the intruder, and knocking Jane down and falling on top of her in his headlong rush to prevent whatever it was Cordelia was going to do. "My transport spell is set. If you're not careful you'll kill the brides and..."

Jane landed flat on her back, and not without pain, loss of breath, and a sudden, brief but very curious blurring of her vision. And an odd feeling that someone, or some silver-eyed something, was watching and, just maybe, reaching out to her, whispering a name that might have been hers. But couldn't have been, of course. Any reasonable person knew better than to rely on feelings when reason was a much more reliable tool.

She wasn't frightened; Jane was too furious for that, furious at both Will and Cordelia. But most of her anger was directed at the man who seemed all elbows and knees as he lay where he had landed on top of her. He couldn't seem to be able to do anything but struggle fruitlessly, poking Jane in various of her body parts in the process of trying to regain his footing.

"Damn it, get off me!" Fighting to catch her breath, she pushed at the self-proclaimed wizard, and tried not to see what was going on, tried to believe that the scene beyond Will's shoulder was all smoke and mirrors, stage magic, illusion. It had to be.

What was happening couldn't be real, not in New York City, not in a run-down brownstone. The brides, Maggie included, couldn't, positively could not be popping out of existence, one by one, like blips on an old video game. Cordelia couldn't be lifting the switch to bring it down on Will's unprotected back.

Acting on instinct, not on any deep-seated need to protect the man, Jane's right hand went up to ward off the blow. The stinging switch struck them both.

Cordelia's cold, mocking laughter and anything but fond farewell were ringing in her ears when Jane, and the young man sprawled on top of her, did some existence popping on their own. It was not an illusion.

SOJOURNER LOOKED deep, caught a single glimpse of a woman's face and ice ran through his veins, froze him in place, stole his breath. She was all fire, black fire, shot with green, to his seeing, and he longed for her as he never longed for another human. And even before the seeing broke, fragmented, leaving him alone, the great cat knew her name, whispered it once in his mind. *Jane.* And with the naming came the fear—for her, or for himself? Sojourner didn't know—and not even the warm sun could take the cold from his bones, from his heart.

She was coming. He wasn't ready—perhaps he would never be ready. He tried to look again, to probe the future for what-would-be. It yielded nothing.

JANE DIDN'T KNOW exactly what had happened to her, but she doubted, most sincerely, it was a magical illusion. She didn't know what to think of the silvery-eyed presence that had haunted her dreams. If that had actually happened. But she did know that the smelly bed that cradled her when she woke, thankfully alone, was only too real.

Nose wrinkling at the musty, musky odor, Jane wasted no time scrambling out of the bed and brushing bits of lint and other specks of unknown nastiness off her jacket and knee-length skirt. That done, she took stock.

She had been asleep; that was a given. Although she felt no after-effects and her clothes betrayed no evidence of any great time period having passed, she still concluded she must somehow have been drugged and transported to some third-world country or something.

And, from the looks of things, she was not only going to have to rescue herself but Maggie as well; that's presuming she could even find her secretary. But first, she had to assess the situation and try to make some plans. She had to know what she was going to do. It certainly wasn't the moment to turn into Chicken-Little and run around screaming her head off. Even if she did feel like the sky had fallen right in the middle of her tidy, ordered life and that a good scream or two wouldn't be entirely amiss.

Her modest heels catching in the braided rug, Jane began a cautious circuit of the small room, stopping frequently to rub her eyes and shake her head. It was like a room in a museum of Old West artifacts—one that had been setup as a very life-like diorama, accurate to the last tawdry detail. Mentally, she ticked off the items that had no place in her real life. The slop jar, for used wash water, perched on the lower shelf in the rough wood washstand which was topped with a plain white pitcher and a basin to match. The lidded chamber pot, the so-called thunder mug of yore, under the edge of the iron bedstead.

The soiled, and rather racy-looking, wrappers hanging on a row of wooden pegs beside the curtained doorway. The oil lamp, with a yellow flame burning inside its smoked glass globe, on a stand beside the bed. The billowing muslin that was the ceiling. The moss-and-mud chinking between the huge logs that formed two walls of the room.

But strange as her surroundings were, it was the stack of dingy towels on the wash stand and the bowl of what looked like lard on the bedside table that made her realize where she was. And it afforded her no satisfaction to know that her suspicions of Will were all true.

The young man had, indeed, been lying to the women he had recruited in New York. There were no husbands waiting for

them, no rose-covered picket fences, no cooing babies; there were only places like this.
Houses of ill-repute.

Chapter 3

DEPENDING ON her mind, her powers of logic and reason, as she had done her entire life, Jane wasn't one to jump to hasty conclusions. Especially those based on too little evidence, but this was one conclusion that didn't require that sort of effort on her part. It was a house of ill-repute, or, to be perfectly accurate, a room in a bawdy house. Given the givens, that's all it could be.

Added to that was another irrefutable fact—she, Jane Murdock, was the tawdry room's present occupant, the resident whore, as it were. And, despite the odd jumps and descents in whimsy her mind seemed to be taking, Jane was far from being amused.

And, judging from the loud shouts and drunken laughter coming from somewhere beyond the curtained doorway, the room was very much in service. Jane, with a shudder of revulsion, knew she was, more than probably, on the current bill of fare. It had all the aspects of a melodrama, but there was no noble hero waiting off stage to save her.

Indeed, what would a noble, virtuous, and lily-pure hero be doing in a place like this? Hell, heroes weren't even supposed to know places like this even existed, were they?

Making herself take a deep breath, of not exactly pollution free air, Jane straightened her back and tried to straighten her errant thoughts, to make them stop skittering and jumping, making weird connections, and flittering on to something else. It wasn't something she could allow, especially under the present circumstances.

If she was going to get out of this particular predicament, she was going to have to do what she had always done and save herself. And if the sound of feet climbing up a creaking stair was a viable indication, she was going to have to do her saving pretty damned quick.

But how? There wasn't a single window in the room; the only light came from the flickering flame in the oil lamp. She turned abruptly, feeling the solid thump of her black shoulder bag against the jut of her hip, and walked to the door. She pulled aside the curtain to peek into a shadowy hallway before she took a tentative step out of the room. Despite the oddly pooled areas of dark, there was still light enough—and it seemed to have no real source—for her to see the man who had ascended the stair.

Every smear of dirt on his whiskery face, every patch on his filthy shirt, every speck of dried sweat and ingrained grime on the man himself grew increasingly plain as he came toward her. He rubbed his hands together in obvious glee while he grinned in what could only be described as anticipatory delight.

Jane stood her ground. His grin faded when he got his first glimpse of her.

Stopping short, he stared at her, shook his head. "I might'a knowed. Cordelia said she brought us a present, but...."

He pulled a flat, brown bottle from his hip pocket, lifted it to his mouth, and took a healthy swig of what had to be, from the smell that was joining the general stench in the air, rot-gut whiskey.

"Oh, well," he said, more to himself than to Jane, "I won the toss, and to my thinking, a skinny old whore is better'n nothing. 'Sides that, Cordelia gets a mite riled iffen her presents ain't rightly appreciated and it's a right chancy thing to rile a wizard. 'Deed it is."

After taking another pull from the bottle, he staggered toward Jane, arms outstretched, evidently intending to embrace her or to do something equally repulsive.

Disbelief and growing horror smothering the swarm of questions in her mind, Jane backed through the doorway and into the bedroom. She knew full well it wasn't the smartest move to make, but not seeing any other way out of the present confrontation.

Jerking aside the soiled curtain, he followed her into the small room, pausing just inside the doorway to lean forward and peer at her. "You be more'n a sight peaked. You ain't be having the whore pox or nothing bad like that, be you?"

She didn't know what whore pox was, but she wasn't about to demand an explanation. Explanations weren't first on her list of priorities, getting away from him was. "Certainly not! Get away from me!"

Jane took another step back, fumbled in her purse, trying to find one of the cans of pepper spray she knew was in there somewhere. She'd bought two canisters yesterday, or what seemed like yesterday, and dropped them both in her purse. She was certain she had done exactly that, but she couldn't seem to find either of them in the welter of objects inside the large purse.

"Nah, I ain't going nowhere. I paid my two-bits just like the rest of 'em, and I won first shot at you fair and square. From the looks of you, I reckon I ain't gonna get my money's worth, but, by damn, I ain't gonna do nothing to make Cordelia mad neither. Wizards take offense mighty easy, and she's a mite unhappy already."

Scratching at an itch on his backside, he said, "Well, you'd best just flop on your back and let's get going. I ain't got all night." He guzzled down what was left in the bottle, tossed it into a corner, and motioned toward the bed as he staggered in that direction himself.

It was too much. Jane wanted, more than she would have thought possible, to scream something totally inane, like, "Damn it all to hell, women aren't wizards, they're witches or something." And then blast the drunken idiot with a full-faced spray from one of the cans; the pepper spray cans her scrabbling fingers absolutely could not seem to find.

Instead, feigning a calmness she wasn't even close to possessing, she said, in her most authoritarian voice, "Get out of here and leave me alone. Wizard or not, your Cordelia has made a big mistake this time and that's all there is to it."

"Come on. It ain't right for an old, wore-out whore like you to be acting like a scardy-cat girl what's never been bedded. 'Sides that, like I done told you, I ain't got much time. We ain't had us a whore for a right long spell and the rest of them horny devils do be a-waiting. They'll do be climbing up the stairs in three shakes of a lamb's tail, howling for their turn to ride you and..." He pulled down his suspenders and started to unbutton his pants.

"The rest of them?" Jane didn't know if she had spoken the words aloud, the same words that were circling round and round inside her head, making her sicker by the minute. It was beyond reason. It couldn't be happening. And whether she wanted to believe it or not, it was true. Jane Murdock was in a parlor house and men, who had already paid their service fee, were standing in line, waiting, as this drunk had so crudely expressed it, for their turn to ride her.

"Awww, come on. There ain't no sense playing them kinda games. I paid my two-bits and I gotta right to..." he whined as he unbuttoned another button on his pants, exposing his soiled underwear and all too obvious intent, and took several unsteady steps toward her.

The oil lamp flickered, flared, sent up a cloud of acrid smoke to cloud the globe. It tinted the shadows a darker hue, and added to the overpowering stench of old sweat, old lust, and too new whiskey. Within her purse, Jane's hand dug frantically, discarded item after item, and, when she had almost given up hope, found one of the cylinders of pepper spray.

Now she was armed, and if her anger was any gauge, very, very dangerous. She pulled the can from her purse, trigger finger at the ready. "That's far enough," Jane said, unconsciously assuming what could best be described as a gun-fighter's stance: feet slightly apart, knees bent, eyes narrow, the business end of the spray aimed straight at his bewhiskered face.

Possibly he was too drunk to understand her warning, or possibly he was so horny that he just plain didn't care what happened to him in the process of getting what he had purchased with his two-bits. Jane didn't know which, nor did she actually care.

Arms outspread to grab his paid-for doxy, grinning, he took another step forward, straight into a hot, burning, choking cloud of mist. Coughing, wheezing, gasping in more of the burning spray, he went down to his knees and started to cry.

Tears running down his face, sort of choking and whimpering at the same time, he moaned, "You blinded me. Damn it, ma'am, why didn't you say you was a wizard? I ain't got me no hankering to bed no wizard. Or to get me in the middle of no bedamned wizard quarrels neither. Swear to God, I ain't."

For a very fleeting instant, Jane felt sorry for the man, but the pity wasn't strong enough to keep her from threatening him with another dose of the same medicine. As to the blubbering accusations he was making, she didn't have a clue as to what he meant, or why he was even saying it.

She certainly wasn't a wizard, and, as far as that went, she had very serious doubts as to their existence. Discounting his blabber as nothing more than drunk-talk, Jane asked one of the questions that was important to her at the moment, "Where are we?"

"Jake's. Brummelville."

"No, the country, or state, or whatever it is?"

"The Great Northwest," he mumbled, rubbing his eyes with the heels of his hands, hiccoughing, and sort of wiggling back and away from where she stood. "Please, ma'am, let me go. I ain't no good to you. Hell, I'm a-blubbering like a babe and I can't see a blamed thing. Ain't that hurt enough for what I do be trying to do to you? Seeing as how I ain't gonna have me no woman and I ain't gonna get to see the lynching neither?"

The smoke from the guttering lamp mixed with the spray, burned the inside of her nose, stung her eyes, and tickled the lining of her throat. Jane ignored it. The man was either a fool or thought she was one. *The Great Northwest* indeed! There was no such place, and she knew it. She had to, in her business, geography could be very important.

Jane started to demand an immediate explanation, but something else he had said finally found its way into the receptors in her brain, added up the evidence at hand, and formed some very far-fetched conclusions. Sincerely hoping she was wrong, that a horse thief, or a bank robber, or even a cattle rustler was going to be the guest of honor at the necktie party, she asked, "Who, exactly, is being hanged?"

"That lying son-of-a...'scuse me, ma'am. I meant that lying wizard, Will. The one Cordelia drug in and tossed on the card table downstairs in the saloon. Afore she told us you was up here waiting to pleasure the rest of us what hadn't tried to break spell against having wives and such."

He rubbed his eyes a little harder, tried to pull his foot out of his mouth, so he could talk without offending Jane still more. She was already beyond being offended and was verging on pure rage. "Who is being hanged?" she asked, lifting the spray again.

"You know, ma'am, the wizard who came prissing into town a-driving that purty red wagon and a-promising to bring in a passel of brides to... Hell, ma'am, I don't reckon you need me to tell you anything about..." He squirmed his way backward until he was almost at the curtained doorway.

Anger still burned in her chest, but fear was beginning to pinch and writhe in her flat stomach. Jane took a deep breath before she asked, trying her best to sound meaner than a snake, "Where is he now? Where's Will?"

"Ma'am, I didn't have nothing to do with that. Honest. I didn't send for no bride. No siree-bob. Whores are good enough for... Oh, God, ma'am, I didn't mean that you..."

His trembling hand clutched the curtain and he tried to scoot back under it, to escape what he obviously thought was a wizard's wrath. Although Jane wasn't sure what had given him that particular idea unless it was the blast of pepper spray he had taken full-face.

As unwizardly as was humanly possible, Jane's wrath was probably greater than the drunken lecher knew, but her fear—that Will was going to swing before he could get her out of whatever it was he had gotten her into—was what made her ask, "Tell me where Will is, or I swear I'll..." She lifted the pepper spray canister a little higher.

Perhaps he could see the fury on her face, or perhaps the threat in her voice was enough. Whatever the cause, the man gulped mightily, hunkered down a little lower, and his voice was almost a whisper when he said, "After they judged him, they put him in Nell's room. She was a right good madam, but she vanished with the rest of her girls when Cordelia got on her high-horse and hexed the whole damned country all on account of that bedamned Max Farrel."

He gulped again and whimpered deep in his throat. Trying, once again, to escaped from Jane and her pepper, he tangled himself in the curtain, pulled in down, rolled out into the hall, and started to crawl toward the head of the stair. His unbuttoned pants slid down, tangled around his knees, and sent him into a nose-dive.

Jane followed him through the doorway, into the oddly shadowed hall, and stopped his floundering flight with a question, "Where is Nell's room?"

"That one." He pointed to a closed door on the other side of the hall. "Please, ma'am, that's all I know. I gotta go down and...Hear 'em? They be having a fit for me to hurry, so's they can have a shot at the whore what Cordelia done brung for..."

Not even daring a single furtive glance in her direction, the man gulped loudly. He reached down and tried to pull up his pants. He managing to do so only after he had clawed his way up the rough, splintery boards of the unfinished wall and stood, owl-eyed and swaying, as he restored something of his rather drunken dignity. It was a dignity short-lived.

Either his fear of Jane, or the rot-gut he had swilled, or a combination of the two took the starch from his bones and the teaspoon of sense remaining in his brain and left him limp and mindless. Snoring softly, he sort of melted down, in slow-motion, until he looked like nothing more than a sprawled heap of soiled clothing lying against the base of the wall.

Some part of her wanted to kick him good and hard in a very meaningful place, and maybe do it more than once, but despite her fear and anger, Jane's reason still had the upper-hand. Prodding him with her toe, to make sure he was really passed-out and wasn't just pretending in order to escape from the terrible wizard he thought she was, Jane took in a quick breath. She tensed, ready to jump back at his slightest response.

His only response was to take another rasping, snoring breath.

Letting out her pent breath in silence, she eased around him, and cautiously made her way to Will's prison. Her hand closed on the door knob, tried, unsuccessfully, to turn it. "Locked," she muttered, "I should have been smart enough to realize they would..."

Then, Jane Murdock, who was far from being a frivolous lady, grinned like a kid at Christmas. The randy dolts had left the key in the keyhole.

It took next to no time for her to open the door. Having the foresight to take the key with her, she looked into a small, smelly room that greatly resembled the one she had just vacated. Except this one had a small window high in one wall. It let in a pale shaft of daylight to fall across a man. His face hidden by his arm, he lay sprawled on the soiled and spotted, black-and-white striped mattress that covered a truly saggy bed. One that had clearly seen too much use, most of it unkind and unclean.

She couldn't tell for sure, but, as far as Jane could deduce, the sprawled figure had to be Will. This man was wearing the same cowboy regalia, even if it was slightly the worse for wear, that Will had worn when she had seen him in the New York brownstone. And, even if every nuance of his posture shouted defeat, he was still lanky, young-looking, and everything else he had been to her last seeing, as unpleasant as it had been.

Angry, sorely tempted to let him hang, Jane sighed. As much as the so-called wizard deserved his punishment, she couldn't allow him to hang, not when she needed him to get her out of this place and get her home.

Working on the adage, nothing ventured, nothing gained, Jane swallowed hard, squared her narrow shoulders, and stepped into the room as if she owned it. Will, if that's who it was and not something else set up to trick her, didn't move when she closed the door behind her. She walked, with no attempt to conceal the sound, across the creaking floor boards, stopping at the foot of the filthy bed, staring down at the not much cleaner occupant. She frowned a little, gnawed at her lower lip and tried to puzzle out why the occupant was so still, so unresponsive.

It was as if he was being held in place by unseen chains, bonds that restricted not just his movement, but also stopped his ears, blinded his eyes, kept him from all knowing. It was a frightening thought, one she absolutely didn't want to pursue. If Cordelia had done something terrible to him, what was Jane going to do?

It was a false worry. His arm fell back to his side and his head, with its mop of floppy brown hair and too young face, came up in an instant when she whispered, "Will? Wizard Will?"

Chapter 4

EARLIER THAT afternoon, Cordelia and the angry, shouting men in Jake's saloon had left no doubt in Will's mind about what they intended to do to him, and now he wasn't entirely sure he could stop them. Cordelia was a very strong wizard indeed. So strong, in fact, that whatever prisoning spell she had set on the him controlled him completely. And not just his body.

His mind, especially that part that communicated with Sojourner, was blocked. It was as if Sojourner had ceased to exist—and even the thought of that happening made Will sick, not body sick, but soul sick. The great cat was his family, his friend, his...

Swallowing down the thickness that was crowding his throat, Will shook his head. That couldn't have happened. Sojourner was stronger, in all ways, both magically and physically, than the irate, vindictive woman. Cordelia, even is she was proving the truth of the saying, Hell has no fury like a wizard scorned, was no match for Sojourner; and never would be. She probably wasn't even aware that he actually existed.

Sojourner was hidden away with the spelled wizard wagon and was, in all probability, still safe. It was only Will who had run afoul of Cordelia's magical edict, an edict he hadn't been aware of, and now, when he did know, it was too late to...

That thought led him to another worry. He might know about Cordelia and her thwarted love life now, but he didn't know what had happened to Maggie and the rest of the brides. He was incredibly weary—using their magical powers did that to wizards—but weary or not, the brides were still his responsibility.

They had given him their trust, and there had to be a way to live up to that trust, to save them from whatever fate Cordelia was planning to push onto them. He had to rescue them. He just had to; especially when one of the young women might be the one to free Sojourner from the curse that kept him a cat and...

One further worry slid into his mind, one that shouldn't even be there, nagging at him, tugging at emotions he wasn't free to have. But it didn't matter what he wanted, the worry remained, told him in doom-struck tones, "Maggie is with the rest and she, too, is in danger." It made him ache, but it couldn't release him from Cordelia's spell.

"Will? Wizard Will?"

The woman's voice interrupted his scurrying thoughts, brought him back to the present.

"Who?" He jerked his arm away from his face, sat up, stared at her, but it was a long moment before he recognized her. And the recognition gave him no relief; it only added a new responsibility to his already heavy burden.

What was her name? The tall, skinny woman was Maggie's boss, but...Finally the name came to him, bringing with it a whole chattering flock of questions, each demanding an instant answer.

"Ms. Murdock? How did you get here? Where are the others? Is Maggie, I mean, are the brides all right? Did Cordelia hurt..." Watching her face, seeing, only too clearly the mixture of anger and fear that were warring within her, he stopped, swiped his fingers through his messy hair, trying to push it into some sort of order, and giving himself a moment to think.

"Listen, Will," she said, interrupting his confused thinking and his ineffectual grooming, "we have to get out of here. The men downstairs, your...ah...disappointed bridegrooms, I would guess, are planning on hanging you very soon. I would prefer being on a plane, heading for New York, before that rather untidy business occurs. And, the way I see it, you are my ticket for that much anticipated journey. So, come on, damn it, let's get going before it's too late for either of us to get out of this place."

He already knew he had been named guest of honor at the lynching party. And that one of the women, probably Ms. Jane Murdock, had been chosen as the designated whore, but it didn't seem the right time to say so. Not when this skinny, arrogant woman in red, a woman from another world who didn't believe in magic, had opened the door without much effort and somehow disrupted the prisoning spell that Cordelia had set around him.

Maybe everything wasn't lost after all. Wanting to grin, or laugh, or maybe just give the stick of a woman a big hug; not that he would ever dare do something like that, Will was on his feet and heading for the door almost before Jane had finished her sentence.

"No planes here," he said, stepping around her and cautiously opening the door to the hall, letting a high volume of noise, mostly men shouting, blast in through the opening.

"What's going on down there?" he asked. "It sounds like they're mad at somebody else besides me."

Finally, almost sure that no one was coming up the stairs or lurking in the mage-lit hall, he stepped out of the room and took two steps toward the rear of the building. He stopped short when he saw the drunk sprawled on the floor. "What happened? Did you..."

NOT ENTIRELY sure she trusted him, and not wanting to give Will any advantage in whatever sick game he was playing, Jane said, "Yes."

"Why?"

"Because I'm worth a hell of a lot more than two-bits," she snapped. And was instantly horrified at the words that had come from her mouth. "I mean he was drunk and trying to get what he thought he had..."

She had followed him into the hall. Will turned to face her. "So, it's you they're calling for down in the saloon?"

He wasn't smiling. In fact, he looked terribly embarrassed, like a boy who had just heard a new dirty word, one used in conjunction with his elderly aunt. But Jane didn't take kindly to his implication, especially when the single word that was being chanted, coming up from below the stairs far too clearly for her peace of mind, was whore.

"Listen, Will, or whatever your name is, you got me into this, and I want out." Knowing the present situation was at least partly her own fault, if she had stayed in her nice clean, beautiful office and kept her nose out of the wizard business, she wouldn't have run afoul of whatever evil he had engineered. But, the way Jane saw it, knowing her own fault in the matter didn't erase his guilt either.

Jane waved the pepper spray in his face, to show him she meant what she was saying. "No matter what you or your filthy friends may think, I am not a prostitute, nor do I intend to become one. So, get me out of here, and do it now!" Her thumb tightened on the release valve of the gas cylinder.

The noise coming from below eased a trifle, enough to allow Will to be saved by a single voice. A querulous, demanding voice that was already too close, climbing the stair, and coming closer by the second.

"Dang yer mangy hide, Jobe. You be a-taking too damned much time. It be my turn to ride the whore and I be a-coming to do it."

"Damn!" Will muttered. "I thought we'd have...This way. Hurry." Disregarding the pepper spray, he grabbed Jane's wrist and started tugging her toward the shadow-dark at the far end of the hall, moving away from the sound of climbing feet and complaining man.

Under the circumstances, it seemed a prudent and reasonable act. Jane didn't try to escape from his gripping fingers; not when there was a chance to escape from what seemed a far greater threat to her continued physical well-being. Becoming a lady of the night had never been one of her career goals; and, if she could help it, she had no intention of embarking on a new career at this point in her life.

She went with him willingly enough, but she kept her thumb on the trigger and the spray at ready. She had no intention of being ambushed again. Will might be playing the hero at the moment, but he still had a lot to answer for; and most of the lot didn't come close to adding any shine to his hero image.

"Where?" she whispered when he pulled her into a dark, narrow nook at the very end of the hall.

"Outside stair. We'll..."

Again the other voice interrupted, and by his words they knew the stair-climber had found the unconscious man slumped in the hall.

"Jobe? What ails ya?" A long moment of silence followed, then the thud of running feet, and a shouted, "The damned whore is gone!"

Jane and Will didn't wait for whatever answer the shouter got from below the stair. Slipping through the doorway at the back of the nook, going from shadow to late afternoon sunshine, they ran. With Will in front and Jane not a step behind, they ran down the steep and somewhat unstable stair that was attached to the back of the two-story log building.

At the bottom, Will whispered, "This way," and led her into an unsavory-looking alley, trying each door along the way until he found one that was unlocked. Almost jerking her inside, he closed the door behind them and thumbed an iron latch into place, locking them in a place that smelled, rather badly, of smoke, steam, and sweat, all old, all rank, none pleasant.

It was a near thing.

The pursuit was hot on their heels and definitely not taking care to keep its mission quiet. Men were shouting angrily, yelling orders at each other, arguing, pounding on doors—and if such a thing were possible, the anger seemed to increase when a deep-voiced man shouted, "We got to swear us in a posse. The stinking wizard be gone, too!"

"The miserable bastard stole our whore?" It was a howl of protest, fury, and it carried an implicit threat of vengeance, deadly vengeance. "Get the damned rope!"

The voiced threats were frightening enough, but when the pounding and doorknob rattling started on their own door, Jane's heart tried to crawl up her throat and choke her. She made a small sound— not from choice—and felt the trembles attack her long legs, threatening to fell her like a logger fells a tree. Will's arm was around her almost before she knew she needed its support—and she was too scared to even think of pulling away.

And even if he was just a boy, and a crook at that, she was oddly chilled, terribly aware of her own aloneness when the hunters had passed and Will released her and turned to examine their new shelter. Or what of it he could actually see in the murky light that was filtering in from somewhere in the front of the long, high-ceilinged room.

Evidently, he could see better than she could.

"This way," he whispered. Jane, because protesting would have served no useful purpose, followed him without a word.

SOJOURNER PACED back and forth, tail lashing, top lip drawn back in a snarl of frustration. Will was still blocked away, chopped free from their bond by some dastardly spell. The great cat needed to talk to the young wizard, needed to know more about the black-eyed woman of fire who had come from another world. The woman who wasn't a bride, but was...

Even if his growl was just a soft rumble in his chest, Sojourner fought hard, fought against the magic that had been raised, selfish magic, cruel magic, raised by a woman. A woman who intended real harm to Will and his female companion.

"Come quickly!" He sent the thought out into the night, added enough magic to keep them safe from all things arcane, all curses and be-damns wrought by the love-blind wizard. Then, without thought or effort, he leaped the ten feet separating him from the top of the wizard's wagon and sat down, in outward calm, to await their coming.

And once more he was afraid, afraid of the morrow and the gifts it had in its keeping. Gifts long promised, writ in the stars, but they were gifts of love for a man; never for a cat.

ALTHOUGH MEEKNESS wasn't in her genetic makeup, Jane followed Will without question. And to her credit, even if she had to post it to her own account, she didn't even whimper when she banged her shin, painfully hard, against an immovable object. Stumbled sideways, she plunged her left hand into a small vat filled with some very slimy something or other. She had no way of knowing what it was, but it carried a disgusting odor, like drain cleaner mixed with old, dirty bath water and essence of gym socks, all over-ripe and unpleasant to begin with and gaining nothing good from the mixing.

Not wanting to soil her silk suit, but afraid the stuff would eat holes in her opal ring, the twin to the one on her right hand, Jane shook the drippy goo off her hand as she tried to thread her way through the maze of objects that filled the room. A room, or so she was beginning to conclude, that housed both a laundry and a bath house. And if the smell was any indication, the inhabitants of wherever she was were sorely in need of both.

One part of her guess was verified when she came to where Will was standing at some sort of table. He was pawing through a wicker basket of clean, folded clothing, selecting a handful of items that he shoved at her as soon as she was close enough to take them.

"Put these on."

She didn't like arbitrary orders and had no intention of following them—especially when they were given by a man who, from the looks of him, was practically young enough to be her son. Still, she hadn't succeeded in her life without applying a liberal amount of common sense to all issues, and now didn't seem a particularly good time to change. Trying to keep all signs of her irritation out of her voice, she asked, hoping she sounded only curious, "Why?"

The light, coming in through two small windows in the front of the building, wasn't much more than grayish, thick-looking murk, hiding much more than it revealed, but Jane stood there, trying to see his face when he said, "Because those men out there are looking for...for a..." He sounded red-faced and sweating, embarrassed, but after a brief hesitation he went doggedly on, completing what he had started. "They're looking for a woman in red, not a scrawny, consumptive- looking man."

"I'm not scrawny!" It was an automatic protest—one that wasn't strictly true. Jane knew she was too thin, but there were too many other things in her life, time-demanding things that left her no time for such trivial pursuits as eating. Besides that, thin was in, wasn't it? She glared and him and refused to even look at the bundle of clothes she held in her hands.

She still couldn't see him, but she knew Will wasn't even close to grinning when he asked, sounding harassed and end-of-his-patience-ish, "You're not a two-bit whore either, are you, Ms. Murdock?"

It was a question that had already been answered and she intended to add nothing to the concept. However, she was completely aware of the surliness in her own voice when she asked, "What about you? What are you going to do?"

"I won't look!"

Offended dignity was strong in his voice, but she didn't care. Business first had always ruled her life—and, at the moment, her business was trying to get out of the present situation with her chastity reasonably intact and then get home, more or less, safe and sound. In order to accomplish those goals, she needed Will, and she needed him—unhanged. And after she, and Maggie if they could find her and the other brides, were on a plane heading for New York City, the irate husbands-to-be could hang Will twice for all she cared. But the now had to be taken care of first, and she seemed to be the one to do it.

"Your own clothes," she said, patience fairly exuding from every word, explaining what should have been readily apparent to even an ignorant boy such as he. "Are they consistent with this particular neighborhood? Or are they something you acquired in New York so you could blend in with the rest of the phonies?"

"I'll change right now," Will said, his voice sounding suspiciously meek.

"Good," Jane snapped, relishing the small victory. "You do that, and I, in turn, will promise not to look."

Apparently willing to give Jane her due, Will was chuckling softly as he grabbed more garments out of the basket and they retired to their separate corners and donned the borrowed finery. Not that there was anything fine about Jane's rough-dried pants and shirt, one of some stiff canvas-like material, the other of what might possibly be some sort of flannel.

And, although she didn't take time to examine them too closely, from what little she could see, both garments were faded to an indeterminate shade of grayish-brown. But then, she thought wryly, the town's absconding whore really didn't need to make much of a fashion statement, did she?

Chapter 5

IF WILL HAD been amused earlier, his laughter had vanished, had been replaced by a practical reality when they returned to the clothes table and he got his first look at her. Mouth pursed, eyes narrow, he finally nodded. "I think it will work, ma'am, but you'll have to have some boots. And a hat. That'll do the trick. That is, if nobody gets too close a look and we can get out of town as soon as it's dark."

She looked down at her sensible shoes, medium-heeled, unadorned, black leather, expensive Italian pumps, that looked far from sensible, almost frivolous, sticking out of the too short trouser legs. Jane knew Will was right, but she wasn't especially interested in admitting it without a quibble or two.

"Boots? Just how are we going to go about getting them with everybody in town planning on stretching your neck and sending me back to that rather unsavory place of...ah...business?"

"*We* aren't, ma'am. *I* am. And, no matter what you say to the contrary, I'm going to do it alone."

"How?"

Will sighed, but after a tiny pause, he said, again speaking to her as if she were learning impaired or else not exactly playing with a full deck. "Ma'am, I was in this town for almost a week before I came to your world to fetch the brides. This is a frontier town without many niceties, but there is a cobbler shop down the street. He's probably got something there—I'll go see after things calm down a bit."

He looked at her again before he said, "And, well, maybe if we take a look-see around here we'll find a hat some waddie threw away when he came to town with his paycheck in his pocket and a bath, whiskey, and...ah...soiled doves on his mind."

The euphemism had a rather pleasant ring. Besides that Jane had no time for feeling insulted, or getting an attack of the vapors, or whatever it was that women did in situations like this one. Presuming there actually were women who had been in a like situation, which Jane sincerely doubted.

She did, however, have one objection to using someone else's discarded headgear. "What about lice?"

He turned to look at her, a puzzled frown wrinkling his face. "What?"

"Little bugs that get in your hair and bite and lay eggs and itch like crazy and..." She didn't say she knew, only too well, the symptoms, but a strong echo of her childhood humiliation was beneath every single word, at least, to Jane's ears, and it wasn't an experience she cared to repeat.

"They sound nasty. I'm glad they don't exist on this world." He came close, patted her shoulder, as if he were trying to soothe the irrational fears of a shrinking older woman, much older, practically doddering.

Jane stiffened at his touch and stepped away, but not before she said, meaning every single word, "Cut the sympathy crap, Will, and just get with the program. As soon as we get out of this mess, you are going to see to it that I catch the first plane out here that will get me anywhere near New York. Until that time, which I can assure you we are going to spend together, I am not going to listen to any of your lies about alternate worlds and/or you being a wizard or any of the rest of the crap you are trying to peddle.

"Neither am I going to allow you to treat me like some sort of Victorian spinster, a senile old woman who swallows every half-baked crumb of nonsense tossed in her direction. Do you understand what I am saying? You might have had the rest of those idiot women fooled, but I'm not one of them and I do not enjoy being cosseted and soothed and generally belittled."

His tone sounded a little huffy, a little dander-up-ish, but his actual answer was nothing but polite agreement. It held only a touch of I'll-humor-her-misconceptions. "Whatever you say, Ms. Murdock, but before we have any major confrontations about truth and fiction and mental abilities, we need to deal with the matter at hand. Such as boots for your..."

He was stating the obvious. Jane ignored him, turned away while he was still talking, rather pompously, and embarked on a search for a trashed hat of some description. What she found, in a trash bin in the back of the bathhouse, wasn't all that pleasing to either the eye or her sense of smell. But Jane barely wrinkled her nose when she clapped the dilapidated, droopy-brimmed, greenish-black hat on her head. She stomped back to where Will was standing, and modeled it, with rather more elan and modish posturing than the occasion called for, before asking, "Now what?"

With a small nod of approval at her find, he said, "We'd

better wait awhile before I go on a boot-napping expedition. The men from Jake's are still roaming the streets and, judging from the yelling and cursing, are no less riled. From the way it sounds, not that I'd say it's real flattering, they're madder about losing you than they are about me escaping."

He smiled at her, seemed to be actually trying to inject some levity into their situation. "Still, you have to admit, as outlaws we make an interesting combination: disgraced wizard and town whore."

"Oh, sure," Jane said, sarcasm fairly oozing from her words, "the raw material from which TV movies-of-the-week are made."

"What's that?"

It sounded like an honest question, but Jane wasn't deceived, not one iota, by his apparent innocence. The man, for all of his youthful facade, was a bounder, a cad, not to mention a panderer and a procurer, and now he was trying to pull another of his scams. She wasn't about to be taken in.

"Like I told you before," she said, snarling out the words, "I'm not a believer. I don't believe anything about you, except the truth of it, that you are a con artist working some kind of nasty scam on love-hungry, trusting young women. So, don't try to pull any of that innocent junk on me. You know what TV movies are as well as I do."

Jane could have added "Probably even better since I rarely have time to watch any," but she didn't. She just gave him one of her better glares and let it go at that.

"Yes," he said slowly, apparently choosing his answer with care, "I know a little about the movies on TV, but I..."

Someone walked, with echoing footsteps, down the boardwalk in front of the building, stopped at the door, and the fugitives heard the scrape of metal against metal as a key turned in the lock.

"Hide!" Will hissed.

Jane needed no second invitation. She was on her knees behind a pile of some kind of coarsely woven sacks before the warning was completely out of his mouth. And he wasn't an eye-blink slower in scurrying for the same cover. Side by side, they huddled in the shadows, scarcely daring to breath, straining their ears to hear what was happening, expecting the worst.

All they heard were hoarse mutters, interspersed with some fairly inventive cursing, and the crash and bang of unseen articles being tossed hither and yon. "Damned fools wanting to ride out this time of... I got me laundry to dry and...Ain't nobody gonna make me do no hanging. By damn, they ain't. I got me a business to run, I can't go chasing off after a whore, especially a damned whore what done in old Jobe and left him lying there, dead to the world, and a snoring something fierce. No damned posse can..."

"Tige, ya'd better get a wiggle on. Get yer ass out here. We's ready to ride." The shouted order came from outside the building.

The shop owner ignored the voice for a long moment before he said, "Go without me, you miserable, no-good, son-of-a-sow." But he said it under his breath, far too softly for the man outside to have heard. When he raised his voice to answer the command, all he said was, "Be with ya in a minute. I can't find me damned sword."

"Come without it! We's riding now. And we's gonna have us a time before morning."

"Okay! Okay!" Still muttering something that sounded like, "Buncha damned fools chasin' off after wizards and whores right at dinner time. No sense, no sense at all," he left the laundry/bath house, carefully locking the door behind him before he went marching off to meet with his impatient companions.

After the man was gone, and Jane's heart rate had returned to something approximating normal, she got to her feet and stretched, trying to get the kinks out of her tense muscles. Will did the same, but they didn't have much to say to each other. There were a few things Jane intended to get cleared up, but it didn't seem to be the time or place to start making her grievances public—but she would.

And she would make sure he understood just exactly how she felt about everything—just as soon as they were out of town and...

Jane didn't know what came after *and* but she didn't let that worry her either. Gathering up her silk suit, nylons, and shoes, she rolled them inside one of the empty, coarsely woven bags. But she kept her large purse, with its cargo of pepper spray and a myriad of other things, close at hand.

Will was sitting on the table, swinging his legs, looking otherly; that was the only word that seemed to explain his appearance. When Jane finished her preparations, she asked, "Where are your clothes?"

He jumped, looked around a bit wildly, and finally asked,

"Why?"

"We'd better take them with us when we leave. If the laundry owner finds them here, everyone will know we changed and they'll be looking for us in our new garments."

"Clever! Very clever." He fetched his own discards, formed his bundle; and, if anything, it was neater than hers. He even found a length of twine and tied the roll before handing her the remainder of the string to secure her own bundle.

"Thanks," Jane said, using her hunk of twine as a belt rather than a package fastener. "Just what I needed. These pants are a bit on the large size."

"Good."

"What?"

He explained. "Baggy will help hide who and what you are."

There seemed to be the seeds of an insult in the statement, but it made too much sense for her to argue. She didn't pursue the matter any further. She just found a comfortable place to relax, on top of one the bags, telling herself that the sacking, even if it looked entirely different, had to be some form of burlap. It was filled with, judging from the smell alone, dirty laundry, but Jane was well passed fretting the small stuff.

All she wanted to do was not think about anything, to just wait until it was dark enough to escape from wherever it was they were. Next, to find Maggie and get back to her own busy, well-ordered life and forget all about being an escaped whore, on the lam, as it were, from the pre-paid customers at Jake's.

She must have relaxed more than she would have thought possible because she woke with a start. And with a curious impression that her sleep had been guarded by a silvery-eyed man, a tall, lean man with black hair who watched and waited with infinite patience.

But, the nebulous impression fled when Will dropped a pair of high-topped, thick-soled, yellowish boots in her lap and said, "They're all I could find. I'm afraid they're plenty big but I grabbed a couple of pairs of thick wool socks to go with them. They should help with the fit."

They did—if not too much—and Jane had the socks and the lace-up work boots on and tied before she asked, "Now, what do we do?"

"From the looks of things, every man in town rode out with the posse, but..."

"What about the women and kids? Won't they..."

"There are no women and children in The Great Northwest."

"That's ridiculous! Are you trying to tell..."

He managed to evade the question by saying, "What I'm trying to tell you is: now comes the hard part. The livery stable is at the far end of town."

"So?"

Will glanced at her out of the corner of his eyes and began a very cautious explanation. "I hid my wagon in a...well, it's a safe place quite a little distance away. Sojou...the cat is with the rest of the team, waiting for us, but I left two of my unicorns with the blacksmith to be shod before I world-traveled. He was going to put them in the livery when he was finished and I can't just go off and leave them here. They're part of the team and we need them to pull the wagon."

Unicorns? He must be mad, no sane person would possibly believe that she was ignorant enough, or stupid enough, to believe in some mythical creature that had its only existence in the minds of gullible fools. A description of Jane Murdock that wasn't in her resume; nor would ever be. She could personally guarantee that.

Taking a deep breath, fighting down the fury that was threatening to overwhelm her reason, Jane dug her blunt fingernails into the palms of her hands, glared at him, and didn't say a single word. But her heart was stuttering and kicking against her ribs when she followed the self-proclaimed wizard and unicorn-owner out the back door and into the gloom preceding the dark of night.

The town, which looked like the movie set for a really bad western, was shrouded in shadow, smelled like garbage and worse, and far too quiet to be believed. There wasn't a sound, not even the faint whisper of the wind, or crickets singing, or anything else. It was goose-bump-making eerie.

"Be careful," Will whispered.

It was a needless warning. She was already scared enough to have a bad case of the dry-mouthed heebie-jeebies. But Jane, the fingers of one hand barely touching the false fronts of the darkened buildings, stayed close behind him as they made their slow, cautious way down the boardwalk. She didn't utter a sound, not even when one shadow detached itself from a deeper pool of black and moved stealthily down the center of the rutted street, heading directly toward them.

The thing, whatever it was, moved slowly closer. Hunched,

misshapen, more shadow than reality, it shuffled down the center of the street. Whatever else it looked like, it didn't come anywhere close to looking like a man.

Or maybe Jane's own heart-pounding and totally unreasoning fear was painting it too large and too evil. Whatever the reason, whatever it was, the thing terrified her, turned her sweat into sudden ice, shuddered in her very bones.

Nearly unable to draw air into her constricted lungs, Jane froze in place. Will caught her by the sleeve, jerked her against him, and with his right arm wrapped around her rib cage, he half-carried, half-dragged her into a recessed doorway several steps further down the walk. His left hand was firm and unyielding as iron over her mouth. Her back was tight against his chest when the snuffling, blubbering thing sort of slithered passed their meager shelter without even turning its head in their direction. That's presuming it even had a head.

The odor trailing along behind it was curiously pleasant, beguiling to her senses, enticing enough for her to lean away from the young wizard, struggle a little in his... She didn't know exactly what to call it, but Jane knew it was far nearer a wrestling hold than it was a brotherly embrace.

"Shhh, don't move yet. I can't see it very well, but I think it's a *were*."

Will's hand was too solidly clamped over her mouth for to ask, "What's that?" And, after a few seconds the alluring fragrance dissipated, leaving Jane strangely disconcerted. She was almost embarrassed by her terrible, and incomprehensible, need to go where the odor led, to follow the thing at any cost, even if it led to her own destruction. It wasn't a compulsion she could either understand or explain. Whatever its hold on her had been, her response hadn't been intelligent, or even logical.

All her life she had thought she was both. But at that moment, Jane Murdock wouldn't have bet a dime on anything having to do with who or what she was. Except maybe scared. She knew she was that, a whole lot of that—and steadily growing more so. And not without cause, but she knew that fear was only an emotion. Emotions had no place in her world, the real world. And as far as she could tell, emotions weren't doing much to get her back to New York either.

Chapter 6

WILL RELEASED her and made a cautious move in the direction they had been traveling before the advent of the so-called *were*, whatever that was supposed to be. Jane stood in the recessed doorway a moment longer, trying to still the sick quivers in her stomach and the unnerving wobbles in her legs. When she had gathered together enough strength she followed him out into the *were*-infested hell hole of a town.

"Get with it," she told herself, as sternly as her mental state would allow, which wasn't very. "Don't just stand here. Move!"

He was back at her side before she could convince her reluctant body to do much more than stand there and twitch.

She was surprised by the touch of real-sounding panic in his voice when he asked, "Ms. Murdock, Jane, are you all right? I mean, did its breath touch you? I thought we were far enough away to be safe from that, but you're an off-worlder and a woman at that, so I don't know how much exposure you'd have to have to..."

The young wizard might just as well have been speaking a foreign language for all the sense she was garnering from his low-voiced, hesitant questioning—which was beginning to add to her already considerable irritation. "What on earth are you muttering about now?" Jane heard the snap in her voice and was glad it was there, glad she hadn't turned completely into a whimpering ninny.

She had already had more than enough of his flim-flam, his crazy assertions, and she certainly had no intention of falling for whatever new con game he was trying to pull now. Jane Murdock was too smart for that, and she was going to prove it one way or another. And, in the doing, she was going to get rid of that odd feeling of being watched over, protected by some invisible something, a fiercely gentle something with silvery eyes.

"The *were*," Will said, leaning close, looking at her even more closely. "It's breath is supposed to be poison for anyone who breathes too deeply of its sweet perfume."

"Oh, great! What's a thing like that doing roaming the streets?" Sudden and totally unreasoning fear pushed a good share of the sarcasm out of her voice, but left in the chill and the disbelief.

Will seemed to disregard every thing but the question, treated it like a request for information. "It's probably a town watch *were*. While killing isn't usually part of their job, they can be deadly under certain circumstances. Ma'am, you have to realize that *weres* aren't truly alive, and they're dumb as dirt.

"Wizards make them out of protoplasm, zinc, and a drop or two of water from the Fountains of Youth. They sell them to isolated communities like Brummelville for very little. Most wizards see it as a public service."

Jane expelled her breath through her nose and started to say something less that complimentary—to either the wizard or the town, but Will went on with his explanation as if she hadn't made a sound.

"It's probably spelled to obey the city marshal and to protect the town from hydrophobic griffins and near-sighted wyverns and other natural dangers. My guess is, the marshal turned it loose when everyone went riding out to catch us. That way, if the posse didn't get us, the *were* would."

"Stop it! Just stop talking like a..." Shaking her head, hoping to dislodge some sense from the tangle inside her brain, Jane fought back a stupid little niggling thought that wanted to ask if Will had made the thing. Which, of course, was just plainly ridiculous. Wasn't it? He had to be lying. Didn't he?

Giving herself a large number of demerits for even thinking the question, Jane took a deep breath before she said, "Please, Will, let's just go get your horses and get out of this terrible place. I don't care what that thing is, or why it's prowling the street, I just want to find Maggie and go..."

She stopped herself before she said, "Home," and substituted, "back to New York," before the self-styled wizard hustled in a yellow brick road or tried to sell her some ruby slippers.

Sighing rather heavily, as he had been doing more and frequently since she rescued him from the madam's room at Jake's, Will reached over, took hold of her wrist, and tried to pull her out of the recessed doorway.

Not about to be manhandled, by him or anyone else, Jane jerked free.

He sighed again before he said, speaking very softly, "It might not be that easy to do what you want done. And it won't happen at all if we don't make it to the livery stable before sunrise—which doesn't seem very likely if you aren't willing to move."

"I'll move. Just keep your hands off me! I'm not in my dotage, crippled, or senile—I am still quite capable of walking unaided."

"Yes, ma'am," he said, his voice carefully expressionless, but if it hadn't gotten too dark to see his features, Jane was sure the young man was, if not actually laughing at her, then smiling far too broadly. She didn't enjoy that feeling one bit. But she said nothing more as he turned away. Still mute, she followed him down the echoing boardwalk, hoping the *were*, whatever it was, wasn't going to come back and gobble them up or do whatever it was *weres* were supposed to do to their hapless victims.

Turning off that thought before it could grow any larger, she settled the strap of her heavy bag a little more firmly on her shoulder. Hugging the bundled clothing against her chest, she absolutely refused to allow her fear to master her common sense. *Weres*, whatever Will had tried to feed her, didn't exist any more than real wizards did. Just because a big dog or something went snuffling by in the dark, there was no reason for her to turn into marshmallow creme. Was there?

Again the feeling of protection wrapped around her, held her, soothed her fears. Jane's chin came up. Her eyes narrowed. And, if the darkness had been a little less threatening, the young man a little less of a stranger, she would have answered her own question, would have shouted, "No!" at the top of her usually well-modulated voice.

SOUNDS, NOT EXACTLY furtive, but certainly threatening, drifted in from the outer darkness. Men sounds. Sounds of danger—not just for himself, but for the off-world woman and for Will.

Sojourner gathered his muscles, sprang to the rough ground, and vanished with nothing more than a vague whisper of displaced air to mark his going. Events were moving too quickly, there wasn't time to plan, to set the old spells. He took another silent step toward a rocky outcropping, staggered, almost fell, as a vision, a seeing, clearer than he had seen in years, flashed, full-bright and searing, into his brain.

If he had had the proper equipment, Sojourner would have smiled, albeit grimly. At long last, when it was too late, the foretelling was coming into being. The woman in the flames, the woman with the midnight eyes...She was...

The seeing faded, was gone, leaving only a scattered memory of what he had seen and the heart-breaking knowledge that it was too late. It had always been too late—for him, and for her, for the love-magic that was destined between them. And on him alone rested the blame, his were the acts that had doomed them to loneliness and despair.

He raised his head, and great white fangs gleaming in the cold starlight, he flung his man-grief, his man-guilt, and his man-anguish into the sky. It was a cry of loss torn from his very soul, but only the bone-chilling scream of a great cat clawed bleeding holes in the heart of the night.

LARGE PURSE swinging from her shoulder, Jane Murdock, liberated woman, followed behind Will, as docile and meekly obedient as any well-trained slave. And, as things stood at the moment, she didn't have any more choice in the matter than her unliberated, don't-think, do-as-you-are-told foremothers.

It galled her, wore at what little patience she had left to do so, but she had to at least pretend to go along with some of Will's nonsense until she could get to an airport. Once there, she would flash her gold Visa card, and catch a plane to some place that was civilized. A place where lynchings weren't public entertainment and she wasn't the merchandise for sale in the upstairs room.

According to her value system, if some man bought a part of her body, it was going to be her brain. And he wasn't going to get it for any measly twenty-five cents either. That was for damned sure. Jane was nodding in agreement with her interior monologue when Will, only scant inches in front of her, stopped.

Turning slightly toward her, his face only a lighter glimmer in the darkness, he leaned close and whispered, "The livery is across the street—I think. At least, it should be. Give me your hand."

"Why?"

"Because I can see quite a bit better than you can."

When she still didn't comply with his order, Will said, with just a bare hint of testy exasperation in his voice, "Please, Ms. Murdock. We have to hurry, and I know you don't want to hear me say it, but night-sight is one of the first things young wizards learn at Wizardholm, the Arcane Academy in the Middlethorn Mountains. It's the class taught right after snapping fire from the tips of the fingers and before devising specific love potions for the emotionally challenged."

He was doing it again. Anger twisted in Jane's empty stomach, but she mastered it. Will was her ticket home and, no matter what she believed to the contrary, she wasn't going to do a single thing to jeopardize her future. Even if he was, she added silently, the biggest liar she had ever met; a boy without class or manners.

Swallowing her pride was a bitter potion, but she did it and extended her hand, both without a word. His fingers closed around hers, and they were, which surprised her no end, firm and somehow comforting, like the hand of a younger brother, or a caring friend; not that she had ever had either.

Will led her down some steps at the end of the boardwalk and forced her long legs to really step out as he practically ran across the dusty street.

She couldn't see a bat in front of her face—not that she actually tried; she was too busy trying to keep her footing to do any vain looking. Especially for low-flying rodents and other creatures of the night. But, despite what she could or couldn't see, even though she had never even seen a livery stable, she would have recognized her surroundings for what they were by the odor. An odor which, oddly enough, wasn't particularly unpleasant.

Hay and grain and warm animal smells combined, tickled the inside of her nose, making her want to sneeze. She didn't, but only because she tucked the bundle of clothes under her arm and pinched her nose between her thumb and forefinger of her freed hand, breathing through her mouth as Will led her deeper into the building.

He paused. "Wait here," he whispered. "Don't move." He released her hand, placed it on what felt like a rough, upright post of some description. He was gone before she could protest or question.

Content to obey, for that moment at least, Jane stood in the darkness, listening for any sound that might foretell approaching danger. Nothing actually broke the silence except the movements of unseen animals. And, then Will's soft crooning as he found his horses and began to reassure them that he had, indeed, returned for them, that all was well, and other soothing bits of nonsense.

Jane wasn't at all prepared to obey when Will, accompanied by, from the sounds of them, two giant beasts of burden, came to where she waited and voiced a new, and totally unreasonable, demand. And it was a demand, even if he did make it in a soft voice.

He named them when he said, "Ma'am, Clyde and Cleo have never carried anyone on their backs before. They are good and willing creatures usually, but...I think it would be best if we lead them out of town before we even try to mount. They're wearing halters, so you shouldn't have any problem leading Cleo." He pushed a slick, braided something-or-other into Jane's unwilling hand.

"Come on. She'll follow Clyde. All you have to do is hold the lead rope and walk with your other hand on her shoulder, she'll be your guide. Unico...ah...Cleo can see in the dark."

A horse! He actually expected her to touch a horse! Well, he could just think that one through again. Horses had no place in her life. She had never even been within smelling distance of one, but Jane knew they were big and dangerous. Really dangerous.

And there were two of the beasts right beside her. Fear shuddered in her muscles, brain, and tongue, making her swallowing hard before she squeaked out, "I...I..." The words of denial caught in her throat.

"There's really nothing to be afraid of, ma'am," Will said softly, his tone too damned soothing not to be hiding something.

"I'm not!" The deferential concern in his voice, sounding far too much like a young man's slightly patronizing attitude toward an elderly, and mentally frail, relative, infuriated Jane. "And stop calling me *ma'am*, I'm a long way from being your dying grandmother!" Her voice rose too high, too shrill, echoed in the upper reaches of the livery stable.

Will's response was immediate—and not at all gentle, but still young-sounding and strained to the breaking point. "No, you're a fool, a stubborn, opinionated fool. There's a posse chasing after us. There's a were prowling the streets. And you're acting like it's a Sunday in the park with genteel companions. Well, let me tell you, it's not!

"Whatever you may or may not believe about me and this earth, that posse means business. Ms. Murdock, if you want to return to service the drunks at Jake's or to swing by your neck from the nearest oak, that's your affair. I've done my best to keep you...Not even Sojourner would ask me to..." Sputtering into silence, he snatched the rope from her hand and started leading both of the horses away.

She didn't have a clue as to who Sojourner might be, or

even what his interest was in their current dilemma, and she might be opinionated and stubborn, but Jane Murdock was far from stupid. Well aware that she had provoked his outburst, and that what he had said was nothing more than the truth—for once—Jane acted accordingly. "I was wrong. I'll..."

He stopped, but he said nothing, just stood there in the dark and waited for her to go on. She didn't keep him waiting. "I'm sorry. I'll do what you want. Give me the rope." And after a second's reflection, she added, "Please." And it was a sincere request for forgiveness, even if it did come out rather harsh-toned and stilted.

Rustling sounds in the ankle-deep hay announced his passage as Will came back to where she still clung to the post, took her by the wrist, and led her to the horse, Cleo.

"Here!" Lifting it above shoulder-high, he placed her sweating hand on the animal's smooth hide. The hair under her hand was soft and warm, but when the beast's muscle twitched, it was all Jane could do to keep from screaming at the top of her voice. Somehow, and she wasn't entirely sure where she got the strength, she managed to hold her reaction to a whimper. And if she had never been quite so fearful in her who life, Jane Murdock stood stock still and did not jerk her hand away.

If he could actually see in the dark, which she was beginning to believe, but not the wizard part of it, Will didn't laugh at her fear. Instead he said, and it certainly, given the time and the circumstance, seemed a *non sequitur*, "You'll have to get rid of your clothes."

"What?" Her answer bristled with hostility. "Listen, you'd may think I'm at your mercy, but..."

"I'm sure that there are men who would be tempted by...Ms. Murdock, whatever lewd behavior the folks on your world exhibit in stressful times, I can assure you that, even if you were twenty-one and lush, this is neither the time nor the place for hanky-panky, or public nudity." His voice was deadly serious, and sounded almost angry that she would even suspect him of having such seamy ulterior motives.

"So, ma'am, what I'm asking for is not the clothes you're wearing. I want your other garments, the ones in the bundle. I regret the necessity of depriving you of your off-world garments, but you're going to need both hands free before the night is over."

"Okay, but I'm keeping my purse," she said, and then added, "Jane."

"What?"

"My name's Jane. Why don't you call me that instead of that infernal *ma'am*?"

This time he did chuckle. "Sounds good to me." Taking the clothes from her, Will said, "I'll stick them under a pile of hay in the back. By the time somebody finds them, we'll be so long gone it won't make any difference one way or the other."

It was a reasonable assumption, one she could find no fault with, so Jane did what he asked, took Cleo's lead rope in exchange for her eight-hundred-dollar, watermelon-red silk suit. When he returned, she squared her shoulders and said, with a confidence that was ninety-nine percent sham, "I'm with you. Let's get these horses going and get out of this terrible town."

Chapter 7

THE NIGHT WIND, like some soft-spoken ghost, prowled and murmured around the outside of the large building. Within it was all warm darkness and slight sounds, sounds of huge horses moving restlessly, burrowing rodents, Will doing a little restless moving of his own, and Jane's own heart sounding too loud inside her ears. Will was taking too long in his clothes-burying and she was growing antsy, more than antsy, dry-mouthed scared. And it wasn't going away.

The lead rope in her sweaty hand, she waited for an eternity or two, but she wanted to move, to leave the stable, the town. She knew, full well, that if she didn't do it soon, she might not have enough courage to do it at all.

Fear galloped in her chest, pounded in her head, whispered dire warnings. She was alone in a strange land with a stranger. Horses were big and dangerous and she standing right beside one of the monsters, standing there with dark all around her, waiting for a man who might still go off and leave her.

"Aren't you ready yet?" she asked sourly, hoping the sourness would conceal the fear lurking just beneath its surface.

There was an unreadable something in Will's voice, a doubt, a hesitation, when he said, "Yes, I'm coming, but, Jane, when we go out, please, just let Cleo do the leading. Like I told you, unicorns can..."

"You just can't give up, can you?" Jane muttered, her fear of the animal beside her somewhat tempered by the irritation she was feeling toward the man.

His irritation was certainly no less; and his voice was as sour and angry-sounding as her own, maybe more so. "If it makes you feel better to think Cleo is a horse, I'm sure she won't mind at all. Just think what you will, but do it quietly, and do it on the move."

Whether or not Will and the horses could see was a moot point, but for Jane there was only night and sound. She heard Will and his own big horse move away, felt Cleo follow after them, stepping out slowly enough that Jane had no real difficulty walking along at her side. Although it racked her nerves, made her jump at every wind-whisper, it actually wasn't long, maybe a half-hour, maybe a bit more, until they had left the small town far behind. Only then did they pause for a moment, to breathe in sagey-smelling air and to regroup.

Or, as Will said, to consult with the animals. Jane flatly refused to think of them as anything but horses, but Will still called Clyde and Cleo unicorns. Which they weren't, couldn't be, had never been; Jane was flatly certain of that.

The huge draft horses had refused, very politely, or so Will said after he had, supposedly, asked them if they would be willing to accommodate riders. Jane didn't believe a single word of it, but Will's silly lie didn't hurt Jane's feelings one little bit. Just the thought of trying to climb on top of one of the enormous creatures, let alone trying to ride it, gave Jane cold-chills and made her hyperventilate until she was light-headed.

But the horses' refusal, or Will's lie about their unwillingness, had made for a long, slow walk through a velvety darkness, lit only by a billion shiny stars that had been flung, with a lavish hand, across the firmament. And those only until clouds, unseen but towering, hid every sparkling particle of light from view.

Their night travel was fraught, at least to Jane's way of thinking, with frequent alarms and sudden pauses. None of which proved to be anything of import. Except for the wild, fierce thunderstorm which had drenched them, pelted them, and iced them, all with raindrops and/or hail half as big as hen's eggs.

It, too, had its benefits, or so Will informed her when she muttered an imprecation against the storm. The very violence of it had washed out their tracks, leaving no evidence of their passage. Jane wasn't entirely sure that that bit of help made up for the storm terrifying her and the big horses, but it was a start. Maybe now she could get out of this godforsaken wilderness and get back to civilization—which she intended to do just as soon as they could find Maggie. If the younger woman was even in this place, wherever or whatever it was.

The worry raced round and round inside her head until it wore a groove, repeated itself over and over, and until her mind grew numb and Jane stopped caring much what happened. All she could do was plod along beside the big horse half-asleep, half-scared, half-uncaring, and another half-plotting dire revenge against the young man. It was all his fault, wasn't it?

Regardless of what she thought or felt, they had journeyed far. Despite Will's low-voiced encouragements, given more to the animals than to her, they could have spent the going in circles for all she knew. Even after the storm had passed, the sky and the wilderness around them was black dark, and it gave Jane more shivers than city lights, muggers, and screaming police cars had ever done. She was so spooked by whine of the winds, the howl of unseen beasts, the creaking and rustling of trees, and heaven alone knows what else, that she was actually glad the big draft horse was walking along beside her.

But she didn't ask Will to stop, not even for a moment's rest. She was determined to stick it out as long as he did. She'd show him who was a doddery grandmother and who was a callow youth.

Dawn was faint and barely silver in the eastern sky when Will said, sounding as if he were extremely thankful it was so, "We're here."

Tired, her feet blistered from the over-large boots, dirty, wet, hungry, and probably suffering from any number of other maladies, Jane was in no mood to be civil. "Where, exactly, is here?" She looked in the direction he was facing.

Dawn slowly spread an argent sheen across most of the sky, but there was still only a faint light. Enough to touch the surface of things, more than enough to begin to distinguish objects, presuming there were any objects, other than what usually constituted scenery, to see. The small valley, shadows pooled near a stand of tall, dark-needled trees, was clearly just a tiny bit of green meadow, surrounded by hills and forest. And it was just as clearly an empty meadow.

Will's self-satisfied chuckle did nothing to improve her mood. Neither did his words. "It's a concealing spell. Simple to set and impossible to detect usually."

Not waiting for her comments, he started walking a little faster, gesturing as he continued his explanation. "The wagon is over there, on this side of the spring, not far from the stone outcropping. The rest of the unicor...that is, the rest of the team are grazing on the far side of the meadow. I don't know where Soj...ah...where the cat is right now. He doesn't go far, and...uh...he's so big that nothing much bothers him. He's..."

Looking in the general direction indicated by his pointing finger, Jane narrowed her eyes, stared into the massed shadows as they walked a winding, invisible way through huge trees and shrubs and into the valley itself. They followed nothing that she could see, but presumably Will could because he walked with increasing eagerness.

Still, Jane wasn't convinced. Giving lie to his tale of spells and such, she finally saw a large, ornate vehicle. It was, as far as she could tell, the product of a misalliance formed by the mating of a circus wagon, a Gypsy wagon, and a wagon belonging to a snake-oil salesman straight out of the Old West. The gilt-touched carvings, on the side and back that she could see, were touched with fire by the first light. The rest of the large, high-wheeled conveyance was some dark shade that might, when the light got brighter, resolve itself into fire-engine red.

It was too gaudy by far, but Jane didn't give a hoot what it looked like as long as it gave a promise of food and a place for her to rest her weary body. What's more, she could totally disregard his talk of spells. They had to be errant nonsense, the spoutings of a madman, or out and out lies, because she could see his precious wagon. Which made it fairly reasonable for her to assume that what she could see would be equally visible to anyone else interested in doing a little looking. Wouldn't it?

She received an unexpected answer to her unvoiced question. And the answer wasn't nearly as welcome as the sight of the wagon had been. Especially when it was punctuated by the flash of drawn swords and a harsh-voiced order to get their hands in the air and to keep them there.

Will obeyed far more quickly than she did; not that she was lax or tardy in her own act of obedience.

"What now?" she muttered, holding the big horse's lead rope well above her head. She wasn't actually afraid. She was too tired to feel anything but irritation. Jane glowered at the seven dusty men, each one with a drawn sword, who stepped out of the shelter of the grove of tall evergreens to surround her and Will. They took the horses into their own keeping and prodded the captive humans toward the wagon, doing it all with a single explanation.

One of the men, a short, heavy-set man with a villainous, black mustache of epic proportions, tipped his hat back with the tip of his thumb and said, "We've been waiting for you for a time and a time, wizard. The boss wants to see you."

"How did you find my wagon and..."

Will's question was interrupted by laughter. The same man who spoke before looked Will up and down, shook his head, and said, "Lordy, wizard, I reckon you must be fresh out of that college of yours, that place over in the Middlethorns. Seeing as how you, like most of them bare-weaned wizards, ain't got a lick of sense or you'd be knowing the how of it. This little valley do be the boss' land, do you think, knowing what he's been through, that he wouldn't have bought the best and had it right proper spelled and warded against trespassers? Especially them that are up to magic doings."

Will's answering, "Oh," sounded sheepish and not a little crestfallen, and the red that burned his face scarlet made him look even younger than he usually did.

Jane didn't join the general laughter; she didn't think any of it was funny—especially the part about magic. She lowered her arms and glared again, at the world in general, no one man in particular.

The speaker quit laughing, narrowed his eyes, and came close enough to poke at Jane's midsection with the tip of his sword. "Looks like you fellas have been breaking a few more laws, too. That shirt you're a-wearing looks mightily like one of mine. The very one my good mother made with her own two hands, the last thing before that she-devil sent her off with the rest of the females. You reckon that might be the truth of it? That you do be a-wearing what's rightfully mine?" The pointed sword poked a little harder.

"Yes." Will's answer held no fear. But he wasn't the one getting jabbed with the business end of a sword either. Still, it was heavily seasoned with sincerity and leavened with gratitude. "And, we owe your dear mother a debt of thanks. Her labor of love helped keep us off the wrong end of a hangman's noose. I will be eternally in her debt."

"We've wasted enough time, wizard. You can discuss hangings and the like with the boss. But, I'll be taking my shirt back..."

Jane made a small, and much too feminine, sound of denial. The man looked at her with a wary eye, cleared his throat, removed the sword from her immediate vicinity, and said, "We'll find out the straight of this later. For now, it would be best if the pair of you just climb, real peaceful like, into that purty red wagon. Find yourself a place to rest for a time and a time. And make damned sure that you don't make a whole lot of noise doing it. You understand what I'm saying, wizard?"

"Certainly," Will answered, pushing Jane before him, doing exactly what the man had ordered. Then, after Jane was safely through the door that was set dead-center in the back of the wagon, he stood in the doorway for a second or two. Then he looked back, and asked, as politely as a boy at a tea party, "If you don't mind my asking, just who is your boss?"

"Max. Max Farrel," the man answered, stepping up on the broad folding-step and closing the door, before calling to his companions, "Round up the rest of 'corns and hitch 'em. It's a long haul back to the ranch, so let's get this thing rolling."

"So," Jane said, "what do we do now?" The interior of the wagon was sooty black, and smelled faintly musty, sort of stale, but not dirty. Maybe just unused. And there was the faintest hint of another odor, spicy, almost remembered. It tickled the inside of her head, enticed her, but Jane was far to weary, and too reasonable, to give in to fancies. Instead she stumbled, fell against one side of the wagon, bruising her shoulder on what seemed an inordinate amount of cupboards and drawers.

"We're going to do exactly as we were told," Will said, answering the question Jane had asked before he added, "Jane, there's a bunk just ahead of you and on your left. Why don't you just rest for a little while? You'll feel better after I find us something to eat."

"Yeah, sure."

Will put his hands on her shoulders, guided her toward the narrow bed built into the side of the wagon. "Jane, I know it's been hard on you, but they aren't going to do us any ill. As long as we do as they say, they're harmless."

Unable to contain her sarcasm, Jane snapped, "That's apparent. They're carrying swords just for the fun of it, right?"

"Sabers."

"What?" Shaking her head, trying to clear some of the haze from her thoughts, Jane's groping hand found the bunk. She eased her body around, sat down abruptly, but she didn't relax. She couldn't. Not yet. Not until... She shook her head again, fighting back a feeling, one she couldn't identify—and wasn't sure she wanted to.

"Sabers," Will said, hesitation readily apparent in his voice, hesitation and a broad stripe of underlying worry. "The men out there, the waddies, are carrying sabers. They all do when they are out on the range."

His words came very close to being pure gibberish, but Jane's feeling of growing unease, anticipation, foreboding, or whatever it was had gotten stronger. It added to her discomfort. Muttering a expletive of scatological derivation, Jane sat up a little straighter, and growled, "Okay, Mr. Know-it-all, just exactly what is going on around here? Who is Max Farrel? Isn't that the name your friend Cordelia mentioned before she drugged us and dragged us off to...to wherever the hell we are?"

"I...Jane, Cordelia isn't exactly what you'd call a friend. She's a... You aren't going to like or believe any of what I have to tell you, so why don't you eat first and..."

"No! You talk. And this time, you tell me the truth or..."

"That's what I'm trying to do, but...Cordelia is a wizard, and she fell madly in love with Max Farrel. Or so I learned after Cordelia had her way with us. What she did isn't right, power isn't to be misused...It can backfire, take the doer and...What I'm trying to say is: love and wizards can be..."

Taking off the droopy-brimmed hat, twisting it in her hands, Jane took a deep breath. She fought back the urge to scream at the top of her voice, and said, all things considered, rather mildly, "What in blazes are you talking about? There's a posse hot on our heels, these saber-rattling waddies—whatever that is supposed to mean—are hauling us in as trespassers and will probably behead us, and you stand around spouting crap about love. What's love got to do with anything?"

Her voice was harsh with fury. It was an anger made worse by the constriction in her chest, the pounding of her heart, and her terrible certainty that something was going to happen. Something momentous, destined, beyond all time and all doubt, something that was going to change her life completely.

"Everything."

"What?"

Will, his voice flat, without expression, said, "Love. It's the cause of everything that happened to us. To you. To me. I don't know, maybe even to Sojourner."

Jane had had more than enough, she wanted to lie back on the bunk, close her eyes, and rest for a century or two, but she couldn't, something made her ask, "Who, pray tell, is Sojourner? And what does he have to do with any of this?"

Chapter 8

"SOJOURNER IS..." Will hesitated. "Jane, I can't come close to telling you that tale without giving you information that you really don't want to hear."

"Try," she snapped.

It might be daybreak outside, but it was so dark inside the wagon that Jane couldn't see a blasted thing, but she could hear Will opening cupboard doors, rummaging around, and muttering to himself long before he said, "There's some apples that aren't too wrinkled, some cheese, and...Do you want to eat something before I try to explain how love, a wizard scorned, and a couple of other things got us both into this mess?"

He just wouldn't quit, but Jane, as tired as she was—and almost smothered by an odd sense of foreboding—wasn't about to let him get away with it. "I told you before, I'm not interested in any of your lies. I don't want to know anything about scorned wizards, or love gone awry, or any of the rest of that junk, all I want is to..."

She was interrupted by a man's hoarse shout of fear, a shout all tangled and intermixed with the high-pitched, heart-stopping squall of some unknown and unknowable beast.

"Kill it!" another man ordered.

"Sojourner!" Will's whisper was heavy with fear. He was on the move in an instant. Taking a running leap, he hit the back door with his shoulder, flew out into the daylight, not slowing until he was well into a shifting, yelling, saber-swinging ring of waddies. Waddies intent, from the looks of it, on chopping to bloody bits whatever was hidden by their moving bodies.

Caught in the fist of a compulsion she couldn't even come close to understanding, Jane ran after Will. She paused, if only for a second, in the doorway, just long enough to toss all reason and caution aside. Then she plunged down into the melee, fought her way to the center of the ring and saw what was lying there.

"No!" Jane Murdock screamed just once, a cry torn straight from her heart, and the pepper spray was in her hand, shooting waddie after waddie as she fought, like a demon, to save the downed and bloody cat.

Weeping and cursing, the saber-carrying waddies backed

away from her, fear, of her, replacing their blood-lust.

"Sorry," one said, "We didn't know he belonged..."

Ignoring them all, Jane dropped the empty canister and knelt beside the great cat. Tears welled up in her eyes, clogged her throat, and she didn't know why she wept.

Or why there was, suddenly, no fear in her.

In agony, she reached out with both hands, wanting to heal, to embrace, to protect the great black cat, a cat that might have been a huge leopard, but wasn't. But was something more, so much more.

She touched him, cradled his massive head in her arms, and her tears, the tears of a hard-headed, hard-hearted businesswoman who never wept, fell on his sleek black fur, glistening like diamonds in the morning sunlight. Her fingers caressed him.

Silver eyes opened, looked up at her.

Under her fingers, to her eyes, the cat was gone, replaced by what could only be a vision, a dream—a dream she barely remembered from a time that had never been. "Who are you?" Her awed whisper was scarcely more than a breath, but it took what strength was left in her body, left her weak, vulnerable, and somehow wanting.

When the answer came, gentle and sorrowing, inside her head, Jane fainted.

BLOOD AND TEARS were everywhere. Men were weeping and coughing. Sojourner and Jane were lying, huddled together, on the bloodstained meadow grass, and Will's mind was moving in slow motion. He honestly didn't know what to do—but his first thought, as always, was of the big cat.

It was to Sojourner Will went first, fearfully, scarcely daring to breathe he was so afraid the saber wound in the cat's shoulder was mortal. Will was equally afraid his own relatively untried magic couldn't staunch the flow of blood, couldn't heal the torn flesh, couldn't make the cat whole again.

He dropped to his knees, cudgeled his brain, finally found the proper ritual for stopping blood and bringing healing sleep. Forcing himself into a state of outward calm, Will said the words slowly, making sure each syllable, each tiny nuance was correctly pronounced, each hand motion exact, as he set the spell. It was a powerful spell and it drained what strength he had left, stole energy from his mind, heart, and soul, but Will didn't care if the effort crippled him for life. He couldn't let Sojourner die.

"Young wizard, I beg you, save the woman with midnight eyes, save Jane."

The thought was weak, but it came clear in his mind, and Will, acting at Sojourner's command, extended his sleep spell to include Jane. There was nothing more he could do in that direction. She was tired and, from the looks of her, she had been starving herself for years. Rest, and good food, would probably do Jane Murdock more good than anything. It might, he thought wryly, even take the edge off her tongue.

Will's own weariness was held at bay by his fear for the cat, but neither weariness nor fear kept out the thought: Sojourner doesn't know what he's getting into with that one. But on the heels of that came a grudging, but honest, admiration. Jane Murdock, as arrogant and bossy as she was, had rescued him before he was hanged. She had walked through the night without complaint. And, she had practically saved Sojourner single-handedly, she and her wild shooting had sent the attackers into in an eye-burning, coughing retreat that had saved the big cat, if not his life, at least from further injuries.

She was a real pain, in the neck and various other body parts, there was no getting around that, but...Will shook his head as he set the last bits of the spell into place and got, stiffly and slowly, to his feet, and looked around for aid in getting his two patients into the wagon. He didn't have to say much, just that Sojourner and Jane both belonged to him, and unless they were treated properly, he would be forced to do something the unicorn wranglers would regret for an eternity or longer. He had no idea what that would be—he was far and away too tired to even snap fire from his fingertips, but they didn't know that.

The red-eyed, sniffling waddies, seemingly as fearful of the off-world woman as they were of the great cat, followed Will's directions with dispatch. But there was more eye-rolling and quick breathing than was strictly necessary, even if they had been thoroughly pepper-sprayed and were still feeling the after-effects. It took six of the men to lift the cat, but they carried both Sojourner and Jane into the wagon, one at a time, placed the limp bodies on the two bunks before beating a hasty retreat.

The one with the mustache, Will guessed him to be the ranch foreman, stopped at the door, waited until the others were out of earshot before he asked, "She ain't being that Cordelia, be she?"

Will shook his head.

The other man blew out a quick breath, one that lifted his huge mustache and set it a-flutter before he asked another question, "Right powerful wizard though, ain't she? Has to be, making the men cry like that? I reckon she ain't rightly one to tangle with, ain't that being the straight of it?"

He knew Jane Murdock didn't even believe magic existed, let alone practice its ways, but Will wasn't about to say so. Her use of the pepper spray had given them the upper hand and probably saved Sojourner from a death by saber wounds, if the big cat could actually die, but she wasn't a wizard. He knew that, or thought he did, but figuring a lie wouldn't come amiss, Will nodded again.

After a quick glance toward the outdoors, the man came a step closer to where Will was standing, spoke quieter and with real meaning. "The posse rode through here long about midnight, looking for the lying wizard what stole the town whore, or so they be saying. That be you and her, ain't it? That be why she's rigged out like a man, to hide her from the likes of them?"

The light was dim inside the wagon, and so was Will's wizard sight, so he couldn't read the expression on the other man's face, didn't know whether to agree or lie again.

The foreman, if that's what he was, saved Will from all decision making. "The boss be telling me to bring you in—they," he pointed toward Jane and Sojourner, "be with you. The boss be first in his wanting—iffen he no be wanting them, then he'll be calling the posse. I be having no say—it be the boss' call."

"Thank you."

The words were barely out of Will's mouth before the waddie turned, jumped down to the ground, and shut the door to the wagon, leaving the wizard alone with a swooned female and a bloodied cat. And, for the first time in their long association, Sojourner needed him, for more than just bodily hurt, and Will was afraid. In his heart of hearts, he knew he couldn't come close to filling the need. And, from what he'd seen of her so far, he wasn't sure Jane would even try.

THE BED MOVED beneath her, swaying, sort of bouncing, jouncing, and jolting, in several directions at once. The movement troubled her, brought her back from some hazy place, made her aware of the rumble and crunch of slow-moving wheels, of voices just barely audible, and of someone whistling a strangely mournful tune. It didn't exactly sound like the train. A train? To where? Why was she on a train? She hated trains, always flew, never....

Unwillingly, Jane opened her eyes, tried to reduce the strangeness she saw, to make it recognizable, acceptable. Even in the dim light that filtered through closed shutters, Jane couldn't turn the varnished interior of the jolting wagon into a sleeping compartment on the Orient Express, the only train she had ever dreamed about boarding. And it certainly wasn't her New York apartment.

What's more, she couldn't dismiss the spicy odor that was as old as time, as new as tomorrow. The spicy smell that had haunted her forever, tantalized her, lived in her mind, her soul, and couldn't exist at all.

But it did. Memory socked her a good one, right between the eyes, and then it gave her a one-two punch in the stomach, came exceedingly close to knocking her back into nothing. Jane held back her gasp, caught her lower lip between her teeth to keep from whimpering like a lost child, and turned her head with the greatest of cautions. None of it made any difference.

He was there, across the narrow aisle, watching her with tarnished-silver eyes, sorrowing eyes. And he was cat, not a man, a huge, black cat. But her brain and her hands remembered otherwise and her lips framed a question, "Who are you?"

There was no answer, no deep, sad voice inside her head, no whisper that said only, "My love." The two words filled too full of recognition and regret, deep, abiding regret.

It couldn't actually be happening; it must be a dream. Jane wanted to wake up, to know she was dreaming, but she couldn't. She could only lie on the narrow padded bunk and stare at the cat until his silver eyes closed, setting her free from his spell.

Her own eyes closed, but she didn't sleep, not with sweat dampening her hair, her feet burning inside her purloined boots, and cramps trying to knot in the over-used muscles of her calves. But most of all she couldn't sleep because of the questions that rattled around inside her head. They were annoying questions that she damned sure didn't want to ask, questions that somehow found their way to her tongue and escaped without her consent.

"What is going on around here? Where are they taking us? The cat, who is he? What's wrong with him? Why is he there, inside..." That particular question hadn't the words to frame itself, and she managed to silence it. Even if she couldn't silence the unsettling memory of a tall, lean, bronze-skinned, hard-muscled man beneath her hands, a flat- planed almost chiseled face, high cheek bones, oddly tilted, sorrow- darkened silver eyes to her seeing.

That much couldn't possibly be true. That much had to be a hallucination brought on by hunger, weariness, and mental strain. It had to be—the brief moment of recognition, of destiny on the verge of fulfillment, couldn't have actually happened. Could it?

For the briefest of evanescent seconds, Jane the reasonable and logical was replaced by a vulnerable, dreaming woman who knew love, first love, only love. Then the feeling was gone, replaced by the real Jane, the Jane who, knowing Will was lurking somewhere nearby, snapped, "Well, are you going to answer me or not?"

THE WIZARD Wagon, its gaudy splendor not yet beginning to fade, had been his home for the past several months. It held his books, his medicines, his everything, and it should have felt like the home it had been before he had gone world-traveling. But it didn't.

It was, partly at least, because of the off-world woman, even in her borrowed garb she still knew who and what she was, and that who and what didn't fit, didn't belong—and perhaps it never would. Perhaps Sojourner's seeing had gone awry, perhaps this woman wasn't...

Will sighed, sifted a little on the stool he had pulled out of one of the bottom cupboards, and looked toward the sleeping cat. The spell still held there, but the woman was moving about, asking questions in a voice that could barely be heard over the rumble of the wagon wheels, the jingle of harness, and the creak and groan of the wagon body.

He was weary beyond belief; not even the Restoration Potion he had swallowed earlier had added much to his alertness. In the ordinary course of events, working magic came close to draining him dry, but the events of the past day or so had been far from ordinary—and he was way beyond dry; he was empty. He knew he should get up, go check on Jane—she was, despite her contrariness, the victim in all this and it was his responsibility to get her back to that world of hers. And he would tend to it just as soon as he found Maggie and the rest of...Maggie! Even her name gave him...No, he couldn't allow his own feelings to intrude, couldn't...

"Damn it, Will, I know you're here, so stop playing games

and answer me!"

It was the tremble in Jane's voice, not the stridency, that roused his sense of duty, made him get up, as slowly as an old man, and make his way to her bunk. "I'm sorry," he said, "I must have dozed off. Do you need..."

"I need lots of things."

She tried to sit up. Will eased his hip down onto the front edge of the bunk and put his hands on her shoulders, leaning a little harder than was necessary, but at the same time feeling oddly disconnected, not only from his surroundings, but also from his own body. "Don't. The sleep spell isn't gone entirely. Just tell me what you need, and I'll get it for you."

"Get off!"

"Sorry, I...Jane, I don't..." Will managed to sit upright, to scoot down to the foot of the bunk, and to let his body relax against the wall that separated the sleeping compartment from his closet.

"What's the matter with you?"

"Just tired."

Perhaps he fell asleep, or spaced out, or some other not too unlikely thing, but whatever it was, he was gone into some blankness until he felt was Jane's boot kicking his thigh, not gently. The next thing he heard was her voice saying, "Will! Will!" with what sounded like honest concern for his well-being.

But he was fairly sure it wasn't. He knew what he was to her, knew why it was to her best interest to keep him hale and well, that she needed him if she was going to get back to her own world. But that need didn't explain the question she was asking, "The cat. Who is he?"

Guile wormed its way into what was left of his brain. Jane Murdock didn't believe anything he had tried to tell her, and she wasn't going to believe...He gave himself a mental shake and said, "Sojourner is a cat. A big black cat...he's...he's..." Will tried to think of the proper word, one that she would understand and felt a moment of triumph when it came to him. "Sojourner is my familiar."

"Bull shit!"

"He..."

"Damn it, Will, stop being an ass. Tell me. I have to know."

His eyes were closed, so he couldn't see her, but she sounded as if she were very near to tears, and that surprised him. If anyone had asked him, he would have said Jane was as hard a stone, with a heart to match, and, as far as he could tell, she had never shed a tear in her life. She was one unemotional lady, but something had happened out there when she...

Chapter 9

"Why did you faint?" The question asked itself, showing Will that his brain might possibly still be functioning on some minor level, making connections that he should have seen, but didn't. "Out there in the meadow, when you touched Sojourner, why did you keel over?"

The skinny woman didn't answer, instead she repeated her own question. "The cat, who is he?"

Who was Sojourner? Will wasn't sure he could answer that, or even that he should. Jane wasn't going to believe a word of it, and he certainly didn't have the energy to try and convince her. He relaxed a little more, drifted a little nearer to unconsciousness.

She kicked him again. "Tell me."

"You won't like..."

"Stop jerking me around and tell me. I have a right to know to know who or what he is."

He didn't know why she thought that, but Will surrendered, gave her what she wanted. It seemed to be the only way to get her off his back so he could rest his eyes, if only for a few minutes.

"Once," he mumbled, seemingly unable to force the words through his numb lips. Will swallowed, tried again. "Once, in another time and in another place, there was a man who did something terrible, no one is exactly sure what it was, but for doing it, the man was stripped of all his possessions, cursed, and cast out."

"Turned to a cat?" There was no disbelief apparent in her voice, but there was something else, something he couldn't read or understand.

Will sighed. "Yes, a black cat. Sojourner. And, or so the legend goes, he will be a cat until he can find That Which Was Lost and makes atonement for his misdeeds, or..." He hesitated, then went on, "Some say if his One True Love comes, the one that was foretold, that he will..."

Will shook his head, wouldn't allow himself to continue that telling, the one that said Sojourner would die if she came too soon. Instead, he said, "The curse makes him an eternal wanderer. He can't stay very long in one place or..."

"Or what?"

Her voice was stronger, and now there was no mistaking her lack of belief—not that she said so. But, then again, she didn't have to. "Or he will gradually weaken, grow more feverish until he dies," Will said, letting a little of his fear for the cat and his irritation at Jane add unplumbed depths to his voice.

She stirred. Will opened his eyes, learned that even more of his night vision had been eaten up by his weariness. He was still able to see, if only vague outlines, as she turned to her side, drew up her knees, gave him more room. It was symbolic gesture that withdrew her from the source of contamination, from him the madman who believed in legends.

Jane's voice sounded distant, but not entirely cold, when she said, "I suppose Sojourner told you all this junk about himself."

"No," Will said softly, remembering the night the raiders came, burned his home, killed his family, and tossed him into a snowdrift, left him there to die of cold and hunger. And he would have, if the Sojourner hadn't come, hadn't wrapped his warmth around a shivering child. "He has told me nothing, but he's Sojourner, I know that much."

"How?"

It made hard telling, but Will dredged every hurting piece out of his memory, gave them to her one by one, complete with blood, smoke, and grief, finishing with, "My parents were dead and everything else was destroyed. I was just a child. There was nothing for me there, nothing but death and tears. He knew that and somehow he made me know it also.

"The next morning we began walking and three days later I was standing outside the walls of a wizard's castle. Sojourner had friends within. They tested me for Magic Potential and kept me, teaching me what they could, and when it was time, they sent me on, as is right and proper."

"To that wizard college?"

Taking a deep breath, Will nodded. "And when I had learned my trade at Wizardholm, this wagon, newly made, freshly pained, fully stocked, was waiting outside the gates, along with the team. It was my graduation gift."

Her words were ladened with scorn. "From a cat?"

"I do not know the giver, but the wagon was there and the Master Wizards insisted it was mine. Perhaps it was of his giving, I don't know. All I do know is Sojourner joined me when I was scarce a month on the road and has been traveling with me since."

"Why were you coming here?"

"We weren't. We were just going to some place or another. It's a big country and we were just traveling, with no set destination in mind. Young wizards do that until they can afford their own castle, travel around and do odd jobs of magic along the way. It was good until we came to The Great Northwest."

"And then?" Her voice sounded absent, uncaring, as if she were thinking of something else, or something far away.

But he answered her anyway. "Then the men hired me to bring in some brides for them. They said they would pay me in gold, but I wasn't going to do it until...Sojourner wanted me to...I think you're the one he saw in his vision, the one who can..."

Her question was almost too quick, too eager. "Can what?"

"He didn't say. He just asked me to do as the men wanted and go to your world and bring back the brides. He said it was somehow important to his quest for That Which Was Lost."

"Is that why you came to New York even though you knew Cordelia was going to lose her cool and give you to the lynch mob?"

Damn the woman, didn't she ever listen? He pushed the fingers of one hand through his tangled hair, dug his fingertips into his skull. "I told you," he said.

"No, you didn't. You started in some nonsense about love and wizards but then your cat got sabered and we had to go out and rescue him." After a minute or so of silence, Jane said, "We have to find Maggie, and I want to go home, either with or without her, but...Does Cordelia have her?"

"I don't know," he answered slowly. "Maybe, but, well, it's really complicated and you aren't going to..." His tongue was dry and words were loath to leap from it, but Will mumbled on, told her about Cordelia's mad passion for Max Farrel and the man's lack of same for the wizard. "She wanted to marry him, but he told her he wasn't interested."

"He scorned her advances?"

"Yes. Then she said if he wouldn't have her, then no man in The Great Northwest would have any female companionship. All the women were gone in a thrice, or in the snap of her fingers, or in the incantation of her spell. Anyway, she got rid of the women and girls and set up an interdict, sort of a magical fence, that kept other women from coming into The Great Northwest."

"So, I suppose you're trying to tell me that's where you came in?" Her voice was sharp-edged with what had to be anger, anger and disbelief.

"I didn't know about the interdict and..."

"Why don't you put that imagination to good use instead of stealing women and selling them into white slavery or prostitution, or whatever the hell you've done with them? Why do you have to go around hurting innocent people like Maggie? All she wanted was to be loved and to have a husband, a home, and babies—and look what you've done."

Jane might think she was intelligent, but she wasn't. Nothing he'd said had even penetrated her wall of disbelief. Will felt a moment of aching sadness, not for her, but for Sojourner. Jane Murdock certainly wasn't Will's idea of a One True Love, or any other kind of love. Before he could explore that thought, sleep grabbed him and slung him into nothingness.

NOT NORMALLY a patient person, Jane chose the cautious way and let the young wizard sleep as long as she was able to contain herself, which wasn't very long, possibly an hour, but probably much less. And it was the restless movements of the great cat that made her act, made her kick at Will again and say, rather urgently, "Will, wake up. Sojourner's sick or something."

Oddly, beyond comprehension, she wanted to tend the cat herself, but the terrible yearning spurred its own fear, caused it to swell and expand. She couldn't touch the cat; she didn't dare. She jabbed the heel of her boot into Will's leg again.

With all the shutters and doors closed tight, locking out light and air, it was sweltering hot inside the wagon. The light was still too murky for much actual seeing, but Jane knew Will's face was gray, his eyes sunken, and his movements slow. But, he came awake between one breath and the next, sat up, and asked, "What is it? What's..."

"Your cat."

"I told you he isn't..." None the less, Will was at the cat's side, touching the beast's shoulder, and sounding worried when he changed conversational directions. "He's hot, fevered. I gave him willow bark tea and used a healing spell. I don't know what to do next. Cats don't always respond to human medicines and..."

"Give him what you would a man." The words were out of

her mouth before she could censor them, turn them into something other than the betrayers they were. And then, hoping to save the situation, she added, "You said he was a man, didn't you?"

Will wasn't so easily fooled. "What did you see out there, in the meadow, when you touched him?"

Some part of Jane knew what she had seen, but it wasn't the reasoning part, and it wasn't the part that said, flatly, "I saw a big black cat. A leopard or something dangerous like that."

"Sojourner isn't..."

"Forget that, and get busy with your doctoring."

"Did you...did he talk to..." Jane heard the hesitation in the young wizard's voice, even if he did start digging through one of the drawers under Sojourner's bunk. Something prompted her to say, in her most scornful tones, "I suppose voice projection is some more of your great and wonderful magic?"

"Well, no, but he does talk to me and I thought..."

"Don't try to feed my any more of that crap. He's a cat, and that's all..." The rumbling of the wagon died, the swaying motion ceased, keeping Jane from uttering her own lie, a lie that said the silver-eyed cat was only that, nothing more. She knew he was more—or else she was losing her own sanity; and that wasn't a thought she cared to actually entertain.

"Grub time, wizard," a man shouted as he opened the wagon door, allowing a shaft of bright sunlight to stream into the tiny room.

Jane held her hand over her eyes, shielding them from the sudden onslaught of light, as she sat up, her empty stomach having no trouble understanding the waddie's vocabulary. Dizziness swam in her head, but she sat on the edge of the bunk for a moment before she, refusing to allow herself even that small weakness, stood up. Ignoring all of Will's admonitions to wait, she walked to the open doorway, and looked out.

Jane had never been fishing. She never seen a hooked fish lying on the shore, gasping for breath. But she knew, exactly, down to the sharp pain in her chest, how those poor creatures of another world felt when they were exposed to something beyond their learning.

Air didn't want her go into her lungs. Her mouth refused to close. She stood there, frozen in place, not by fear but by knowledge, terrible, mind-wringing knowledge that was trying to storm the citadel of her reason, her logic, overwhelm her.

She stared. Tried to lift her arms, to rub her eyes, to turn the sunny day into...into...She didn't know what. A traffic jam maybe, with cops blowing whistles and waving their arms and swearing at idiots. Or a busy airport, complete with 747's and thundering jets.

Nothing quiet, nothing filled with grazing beasts. Nothing like... "Dear God," she whispered, sort of whistling the words out through her suddenly trembling lips. "They're unicorns! Black-and-white spotted unicorns!"

"And a right pretty sight they be, too, ain't you thinking. Boss raises 'em and these pintos do be his pride." The waddie standing at the bottom of the wagon step, probably standing guard so they didn't try to escape, grinned up at her. "Them little black-and-white babies, with their nubbin horns, be making a man know the real why of this good green earth. They do be fine."

"Unicorns," Jane said again, awe and wonder stealing into her voice, giving it a little more power. And there were hundreds of them, thousands maybe, anyway, a large herd of mythical...No, they were real, ivory-horned, silky-maned, powerful-muscled real—and they couldn't be. Could they?

The watching waddie touched the brim of his battered hat with his forefinger and thumb in what was obviously a gesture of respect for her. "Iffen this be your first seeing of the likes of them, do you be a city wizard, ma'am?"

"City?" The single word brought her back to herself, mostly, enough so that she could semi-function, almost think. "Yes, I live in New York and..."

Suddenly, she was unsure what she had been intending to say, or why she even wanted to say it. None of it made any sense—maybe New York didn't even exist. Maybe it never had.

Jane swallowed hard, gripped the side of the door. She said, because it was, purely and simply, the truth but somewhat of an understatement, she was, at that moment, sicker than any dog, on any world, had a right to be, "I feel like hell. I have to..." Jane released her hold on the door, turned, staggered back to the bunk she had so recently vacated, and dropped down.

"Jane?"

Will's voice seemed to come from a great distance. It sounded tinny, unreal, and so did her own when she said, "It's true, isn't it? All of it, everything you told me, is true?"

And she didn't need his answer to know it was so. The herd of pinto unicorns had given her all the proof she needed.

"Ma'am?"

She knew it was the guard waddie, but saw no reason to respond.

As far as that went, she probably couldn't have if she had wanted to. When your world is up-ended, given a good shake, and returned to you in a different shape, a different form, it doesn't leave any room for small talk. What was there to say when reason and logic and everything that had governed her life had become superstition, odd beliefs, legends. Reason was dead; only the impossible remained.

Jane shuddered.

"I be bringing you some grub, ma'am, and then be leaving you to your rest," the waddie said, his voice nothing but kind. "Eating and sleeping do be making things look better."

Hysteria was nipping at her, at all that was left of her logic, her gibbering mind, perhaps even at her very soul, making her want to howl, to start screaming and never stop, to...Stop it, she told herself. Just stop it and try to think.

Thinking was all she could do, thinking a host of wild thoughts that chased each other round and round inside her head, beginning and ending in the same place, a place that couldn't exist. But it did.

She ate some of the food, it looked, and tasted like mushy, overcooked, red beans and some sort of salty, hard-to-chew meat. It brought Jane a small measure of comfort. Either it or the fizzy potion Will insisted she drink when she had pushed the tin plate away. A potion that would, or so he assured her, calm her nerves, relax her, help her mind accept what was totally unacceptable.

But, regardless of what he promised, neither food nor potion could still the torment of her thoughts, her growing sureness that she was actually insane, that none of the past day or so had even happened, that she was still safely in New York, in the phycho ward of a major hospital.

She was bonkers.

It was, indeed, a pleasant thought, so pleasant that it coaxed her into sitting up, removing her hot, smelly boots, lying down as if she were home in bed, closing her weary eyes, and then it waltzed her into sleep.

Whatever else it might be, the sleep was far from being dreamless.

Chapter 10

SOMEHOW JANE knew it was a dream, possibly even a nightmare, but it was totally different from any dream and/or nightmare that she had ever had before. This one was compelling, almost as if it had a desperate need of its own, a mission to fulfill—both of which involved her in some inexplicable way.

Whatever its obscured purpose, she didn't like it, didn't like being in that place, in that time. And some part of her did not want to know, did not want to see, did not want to feel as the drama unfolded, revealed secrets and events that were not of her doing, not of her world. And decidedly not some sort of twisted fears out of her own past.

But, try as she might, she couldn't fight the dream. She was powerless against its terrible urgency. She had to go where it sent her, had to feel all it imposed upon her. Jane had to know, in her bones and blood and heart, if not in her mind, that it was a true seeing, a dream of real happenings, real pain. And it was important, terribly important, but not how that was so, or why she should endure the seeing.

Resistance was useless. She surrendered, went to that place, and in the doing became less than a participant in the true dream, but more than just a casual observer. Much more.

It was cold, bone-aching cold, black cold that froze the spirit, killed hope beyond all dreams of renewal, or redemption. Even the light was cold, murky, bluish, glacial where it fell on the horde of too silent watchers. Faces pinched, eyes empty, they stood, rank on silent rank, and they neither shivered nor stove for warmth or life.

Ragged, dirty, somehow beaten, they, men, mostly old, all infirm, women with babes in their arms, wee ones clinging to their threadbare skirts, other children huddled close, waited in total, absolute silence— but there was no sense of expectancy, anticipation.

Or even dread.

There was nothing to break the terrible quiet, no wind, no bird, no beast—even the dark border of evergreen trees stood without a murmur or tremble. Even the low-hanging blue-black clouds were without form or movement; all of their rain-tears frozen, silent and unshed.

Drifting out of the sheltering trees, to the edge of the crowd, Jane still knew, or almost so, that it was all a dream. It was a dream of cold and silence that had to be a painting, a picture drawn from some horror hidden deep in her own mind. She wasn't afraid, not of the silence and the cold, her fear didn't come until the movement began.

The man, cowled and cloaked in deadly, unforgiving night, hooded, faceless within its icy shadow, walked, soundless but with a fearsome grace. He stode through the bluish-gray, low-lying ground fog that spread across the village square, making it writhe and roil, like agitated wraiths, at his every step.

And he wasn't alone.

It had to be a dream, or so Jane tried to convince her sleeping self. But there was a strong sense of reality about it, a terrible reality so overwhelming, so strong that Jane stood as still and silent as the other watchers and, scarcely daring to breathe, waited for what-would-be.

The man, his black-gloved hand a steel-hard prison around the woman's fragile wrist, led her toward the small, black stone, windowless building that cowered, alone and forsaken, in a barren space at the bottom end of the squalid village square.

Her richly embroidered, gold-on-green gown ragged and thin as any beggar's, the dream woman, her sun-bright hair tangled and fallen, her eyes too full of grief and pain, stumbled along beside the man on bare and bleeding feet. The Black Opal Crown of Seeting, her badge of royal office, still rested on the queen's bowed head, but now it mattered not.

Its gold was blood-tarnished, its opal heart-fire banked, nearly extinguished, leaving only a hint of sullen smolder at the center of each of the nine, black, polished stones, nothing more. The power was gone, gone like her throne, gone like her country. Gone.

All around Jane, the air grew colder. The ice-blue light shifted, hid the hooded man in even deeper shadow, outlined the captive queen, called attention to who and what she was. Barely able to draw the frozen air into her lungs, feeling the band of winter tighten around her, take her warmth and life, Jane looked at the woman she knew was a queen.

She felt sorrow rise within her, fill her soul until she wanted to weep. And the need was even greater when she looked upon the bright-haired woman, realized she was great with child and that her time was fast upon her, squeezing her swollen belly in an iron-hard grip of pain.

"No," Jane tried to whisper, the feeble word of protest unuttered, frozen fast to her tongue.

Nonetheless, the shadow man, suddenly aware of her existence, turned toward her, stared at her with unseen eyes. Unable to do otherwise, she stared back and wanted to wail, to whimper, to cringe before the faceless void, the black nothing, that lurked inside the hood.

He assessed her with his gaze, and she knew he smiled, a strange cold smile of recognition and disdain, and knew, too, his tongue, like an adder's forked tongue, flicked across his thin lips in some sort of dreadful anticipation.

But he said nothing. Jane wanted to move, to run away, to wake up, but the dream held her fast, froze her with its icy agony, as the man led the silent, unprotesting woman into the house of dark stone. Jane, because she could do nothing else, waited with the other watchers for what might have been hours or only minutes.

Tears froze on Jane's face when the black-clad, faceless man came out alone, the Opal Crown of Seeting dangling from the fingertips of his left hand. It was just the spoils of war, a bauble without meaning. Seeting was no more.

His voice deep, tolling like a great iron bell, a death bell, he pulled a naked babe from beneath his dark cloak, held it high in his right hand, and said, "Your land is destroyed. Your queen is dead. Her babe yet lives!"

The watchers, all except Jane, went down on their knees, moaning out their grief and fear.

The man lifted the child higher, his black-glove hand a horrible blemish on the small, white body. "It is demon get," he said, knelling doom in both the tone and the cadence of his incredibly beautiful voice. His grip slid to the babe's heels and he swung it in an arc, up, up, and then down, hard, against the stones of its mother's crypt.

The terrible frozen silence returned and one by one the mute watchers lay down in the blue-gray fog, let it cover them like grave soil, until only Jane remained standing.

Jane and the dark, foreboding figure of the man.

The dead babe discarded, lost in the sheltering veils of vaporous cold, his black cloak swaying with each gliding step, the man came toward Jane. She couldn't move, not even when he stopped in front of her, and held up the crown before her. It came to life, the stones of polished black blazed with cold, inner fire, dazzled her with explosions of reds, greens, and blues. She wanted to blink, but couldn't.

Lowering the Opal Crown of Seeting, he reached out with the gloved forefinger of his other hand, his killing hand, gently touched the frozen tear on Jane's cheek. Then he walked on, vanishing before he had gone more than a step or two.

It was a dream of horror and despair, the great-grandfather of all nightmares. Jane wanted to believe that, wanted to know that none of it was real, but that knowledge wouldn't come to her, wouldn't ease her trembling, soothe away her mind-numbing fear. So, all she really knew was that the dream, if that's what it was, was important, terribly important, but she didn't know why.

And, more than all else, she wanted to wake up, but, in the way of dreams, she didn't, or couldn't.

The frozen dreamscape blurred, ran like melting ice, and faded into a different dream. It was a common, ordinary dream of grazing unicorns, black-and-white unicorns on a meadow of green, a dream that reminded her of where she was and what had happened to her. But it was a dream that didn't have any urgent need to be remembered. Unlike its predecessor, the icy dream of death and despair, it didn't have to be remembered in her heart as well as in her brain.

AND WHEN SHE woke, the cold dream still lived in her mind, but it was far removed. And Jane did her level best to be sure it stayed that way. That summer heat and the jolting of the wagon were all that added to her discomfort.

"The only thing I can see to do is challenge her to a duel."

Hot, sticky, itchy, both in mind and body, she was tired of riding in the shadowy confines of the jouncing wagon. She hungered for some strawberry yogurt and a green salad, wanted to brush her teeth, take a warm, rose-scented soapy shower, and exchange her smelly clothes for something soft and clean. Carefully keeping her mind away from icy dreams and outer reality, Jane stopped her mental bitching, sat up on the bunk, and stared at Will. What he had said, about fighting a duel, didn't really make sense, or given the waddies' sabers, maybe it did.

Still, dueling with swords was nearly as uncivilized as a lynch mob, wasn't it. And why? What had he said while she was making a mental list of her grievances. Jane knew he had been talking and had tuned him out—he was verging too closely to the real. A real she wasn't yet ready to accept—and couldn't deny.

"A duel? With whom?" She didn't want to know, but wanting had nothing to do with it. If Will was planning on getting himself killed before he sent her home, he could just come up with a different plan. Jane Murdock wasn't about to stay in a world where magic and unicorns lived and airlines didn't. She was going home—and one way or another, she was going to take Maggie with her.

"Cordelia," Will said, leaning over Sojourner to dribble some foul smelling brew onto the cat's bandaged shoulder, all but falling sideways when the wagon wheel rolled over a rock and thudded down with tooth-jarring force.

"With swords?"

Regaining his balance, Will finished his doctoring and returned the corked vial to its appointed place in the cupboard above Sojourner's bunk. All before he answered, sounding rather huffy and irritated, as if he had repeated his plan once too often. And perhaps he had; Jane didn't know. She had been too intent on her own internal conflicts, which didn't exclude not even looking toward the great cat, to spend much time listening to Will.

"Jane," he said softly. "Please, pay attention. If I send you back now, which I can't because I need to set up the traveling spell and there isn't enough room in here, then I won't be strong enough to do the seeking spells. I just said that but, depending on what the seeking spell reveals, that is, if Cordelia has Maggie and the rest of the brides magically prisoned, I might have to fight a magic duel with her to get them back."

Magic and unicorns, they were real! The stomach-sinking, mind-swooping feeling came back in a heart-pounding, breath-stealing rush. And Jane wasn't ready to deal with her current reality; to her thinking, it still couldn't be true. She looked down, saw her clenched fists, the black opal rings on either hand, and felt the tremor begin, start to spread.

"Jane, are you sick or..." Will reached out, attempted to put his hand on her face.

Jerking away before he could come close, Jane said, her voice shrill with panic and, if the truth be known, with fear, "Don't touch me!" A small portion of her mind, that part that still clung, stubbornly, to the power of reason, knew it wasn't Will she feared but the dream.

The nightmare had left an icy spot on her cheekbone where

a gloved finger had so briefly caressed it.

It wasn't something she cared to remember, so Jane, calling on old habits, old drives, old discipline, disposed of it, tossed it into the discard pile. It was a dream, nothing more, and dreams couldn't come close to harming you, could they?

"Jane, are you all right?" His voice was tentative, young-sounding, and for a brief moment, Jane thought he might actually care if she were ill or something. That, too, was nonsense. She was his burden, his guilt, but he certainly didn't have any fondness for her.

The gloom was too deep inside the moving wagon for her to see the expression on his face, but she suspected it would reveal distaste, disappointment, and a certain amount of dislike.

Well, it couldn't be helped. She had been brought here against her will, and it was as much his fault as it was the lovelorn Cordelia's. There was no reason why she should be a happy camper, and she wasn't. She was pissed, at him, at the delectable Cordelia, and at her own namby-pamby actions.

What kind of a wimp was she to be afraid of some horned horses and some slight of hand? It was stupid, and it was going to stop. Right here and right now. She was a grown woman, and she was going to take charge of her own life again.

But, she wasn't going to touch that cat. He was dangerous, and she knew it. Will might believe that garbage about Sojourner being cursed and cast out, but she knew better. Curses were given by wicked witches and they only happened in children's tales. And she damned sure wasn't child; in fact, she didn't remember ever being one.

Besides that Will had lied to her. She knew he had and she could prove it. She had seen the evidence with her own eyes and had forgotten until just that moment. "They were horses all the time, weren't they?"

Will took a step back, gave her a wary look. "Jane, some people get travel sickness when they move between worlds. It's not exactly like your seasickness or even jet lag, but it can cause some mental and physical upsets, maybe that's why you...I think I have a some willow bark tea left, maybe if you..."

Fairly sure he had been lying about his night-sight too, that he couldn't see any better than she could, but on the off chance it was true, Jane scowled at him. She did, however, manage to fight back the temptation to stick out her tongue at him as she snapped, "Don't change the subject!"

"I wasn't. I just don't...are you sure you feel all right?"

"Clyde and Cleo, the horses we brought out of the livery stable, you lied to me about them, didn't you?"

"Lied about Clyde and Cleo? About what?"

It was her moment of triumph, and she hadn't had many in the last day or so, so she savored it. "I saw them yesterday morning when the waddies took them from us and led them away. No matter what you try to say, they're horses, just great big gray horses."

"No, Jane, they aren't. They're unicorns. Draft unicorns, not riding ones like Farrel raises."

She had him, and she wanted to crow, to chortle with glee as she delivered the final blow. "If they're unicorns, like you say, why don't they have horns?"

"Why should they? They've been dehorned."

It wasn't what she wanted to hear, but she was primed for combat and she was about to give up without a fight. "That's barbaric! Why on earth would you do something like that?"

"Clyde and Cleo are fairly tame now, but...Jane, the unicorns here, on this earth, are real, and most of them are working animals. They can be willful, stubborn beasts, especially when they're frightened, and their horns are a very dangerous weapon. And, they don't mind using them either."

The wagon rumbled to a halt. Male voices, engaged in some sort of information exchange came from outside the wizard wagon. But no actual words could be distinguished, so Jane didn't know what was going on.

And Will didn't seem to be at all curious as to how their fate was being decided. While they waited for whatever was going to happen, Will said, sounding more like a teacher than a wizard, "Jane, unicorns are our beasts of burden and are very common on this world. But, they aren't mythical beasts, as they are in your literature, and they have no special powers. Besides that, cattle are dehorned on your earth, do you think that's terrible?"

"Oh, shut up," she muttered, keeping her voice too low for him to hear.

Not that hearing her obvious poor-loser retort would have mattered at all. Will was already turning away from her, heading toward the opening back door and the man who was inviting Will out, welcoming him to Farrel Ranch with a really pathetic smile and an all too obvious need.

Chapter 11

THE BACK DOOR of the wizard wagon swung wide, allowing entrance to a broad slant of brilliant sunlight. Jane squinted her eyes against the sudden almost painful glare and, based on what she could see, jumped to some fairly obvious conclusions.

Their prison warders, the unicorn waddies, were finally releasing them from the sweltering dark inside the wagon. But, beyond that simple fact, there was a much more complex one: the unicorn rancher, Max Farrel, Jane presumed, was waiting for Will, like anxious father waits for his first-born son.

So, given the givens, they had, plainly, arrived at their destination, were maybe going to be tried for trespassing and sentenced to the gallows—and Jane wasn't about to let that happen without having her say in the matter. She had been jerked around, undervalued, mistreated, and magicked enough; more than enough. It was going to stop right here and right now.

She was Jane Murdock, not some commodity from another world, and she was going to make sure both the wizard and the rancher knew it. And knew it from the onset—or from the get go as some of her more colorful clients were apt to express it.

Her blistered feet were still too sore for wearing the stolen boots, but Jane had her feet, encased in both pairs of the smelly socks, on the wagon floor in a flash. It was far from being a flash of lightning, but something much slower. A something that had sore muscles and a large curiosity and a determination to see her own brand of justice done this once, and done just a quickly as humanly possible.

Taking just enough time to grab her big purse and hang it on her shoulder, Jane was right behind Will when he stepped out of the wagon and into the cloud-speckled sunlight of Farrel's front yard. It really was just an open space with hitching rails and weedy grass. And bare patches of sandy dirt like the one she landed in after gingerly stepping off the folded down step at the rear of the bright red Wizard Wagon.

The dirt cool and damp under her feet, she was looking at the large rancher when he introduced himself to Will, or maybe staring describes her act better.

Well over six-feet-tall with shoulders broad enough to give

Atlas world-holding lessons, Max Farrel was too handsome to be believed. He had dark blonde, shining clean, shoulder-length hair, a cleft chin, piercing blue eyes, snowy-white teeth, and a body, judging from the way his tight pants and open-throated blue shirt displayed it, to incite envy from 99% of the men in the known universe. And instant, unadulterated lust from the same percentage of women, give or take a couple of percentage points.

If the story Will had told her about Cordelia's insane love for the man was true, Jane could certainly see why the blonde wizard had gotten palpitations and a panting urge to indulge in the act of procreation. He was what was commonly referred to, on Jane's world and by the younger members of her gender, as a hunk, but he certainly was not common. No indeed. Max Farrel was probably close to being unique.

Physically at least, the man was the answer to every maiden's prayer. Jane wasn't above a shortened breath or two herself. But all she wanted to do was look; and maybe not do too much of that. He was trouble, and she already had an over abundance of that, far more than she could actually handle. However, that was one bit of weakness she wasn't about to admit to anyone; not even to herself.

Straightening her thin shoulders, lifting her chin high, she reminded herself that she was Jane Murdock, and she could handle anything.

Anything except being ignored by all and sundry.

Will didn't even have the courtesy to introduce her to Farrel. Farrel wasn't too eager to introduce himself to her either, as far as that went. He was too intent on his own problems to even see, except perhaps vaguely, Jane.

His tanned hand on Will's shoulder, the rancher said, sounding too damned piteous for words, "Wizard, you have to help me. That...that love-crazed female is driving me out of my mind. You have to get rid of her. I don't want her hurt or anything like that. I'll do anything you want, pay whatever you ask, if you'll just feed her a potion or zap her or do something to her that will make her quit loving me. I can't stand it."

For just an instant, Jane thought he was going to begin weeping, but, of course, he didn't. He just stood there, looking drawn and haggard and wan and all the rest of the words that describe a man driven to the edge. The edge of what Jane didn't know, or even care. She had a different agenda, and the rancher's love problems didn't come close to being included. He wasn't even on her top ten list.

But, as far as she could tell, her list didn't seem to be of any importance to anyone except herself. Will and Farrel ignored her presence. Will just stood there, like he wasn't sure what to say, looking off into the distance, toward one of the multitude of flat-topped table mountains that surrounded the lush green of a very large, irregularly shaped valley.

And Jane, after her own quick survey of the surroundings, decided the ranch was far tidier that she would have expected to see on this backward world. Neat fences—board not barbed wire—divided corrals from pasture. Several barns were dotted about, intermingled with several other outbuildings of various types. One of which, a long, low building with a porch running the entire length of one side, Jane thought had to be the bunkhouse for the waddies.

And Farrel's house was a sprawling one-story log structure with rock chimneys, a shake roof, and all the rest of the rustic doodads. It looked like it had been imported straight out of the best of western movies; even if it did have that rather seedy, unkempt, neglected look, the one that begged for a woman's touch.

Not that Jane knew anything about that; she didn't do windows, arrange flowers, or any other of the woman-touchy things; nor did she have any leanings in that direction. She was just making a mental observation, not applying for a position.

The sun bright and warm on her shoulders, Jane took a deep breath of incredibly fresh air, and started to say something. She wanted to demand that Will attend to her problem first and then brew up an anti-love potion or whatever it was Farrel wanted him to do.

Almost as if he could read her mind, the wizard forestalled any protest on her part by saying, "I'm sorry, Mr. Farrel. I know the Wizard's Oath requires that I help those in need, and you certainly are that, but there are those in even greater need that I have an obligation to aid first. Especially since it was my bungling that placed them in their current danger."

There might not be any telephones or TV or radios, but news certainly seemed to get around fast. Farrel knew more about what was going on than Jane would have thought possible—and she didn't know, or really care, how he had found out.

"The off-world brides? Has that she-devil got her witchy claws on them, too?" The fury in Farrel's voice was real, real enough to flush his tanned face, narrow his pale blue eyes, and thin his mobile lips into a narrow slash.

"I'm afraid so," Will said softly. "Cordelia is...She tripped the transport spell before it was quite ready and the brides vanished. They didn't arrive with me and...

"Mr. Farrel, I don't even know if Maggie and the others are still alive. But, I do know those women trusted me to keep them safe, and I failed that trust. So now, I have to find out what has happened to them—and save them if they are still alive—but what with everything that's happened, there hasn't been time to..." Will shook his head.

"Maggie?" Farrel picked out the one word, looked at Will with what could only be compassion, and asked, "Wizard, your voice tells me much. This Maggie, is she your intended, the bride you would claim..."

Will's answer came too quickly to be entirely believable. "I guess I just know her better than the others, but Maggie is just one of the brides."

Always a little slow to recognize relationships, Jane came to the rather belated realization that Will had more than a casual interest in her secretary. And, she suspected, remembering Maggie's attitude and words before they had gone to the brownstone, the feeling was probably mutual. That complicated things, but not much. As soon as they found Maggie, Jane would ask her. If the young woman wanted to stay with Will, Jane wasn't going to try and talk her out of it. But why would anyone want to stay in a world where microwaves and probably flush toilets and showers weren't...

"Jane?"

Will's voice penetrated her thoughts, brought her back to the present, made her say, "What?" a little sharper than she intended.

"Mr. Farrel has invited us to stay here, in the main house with him, while I seek out the exact location of the brides. He has promised to go with me to free them if I find them whole and unharmed—even if we have to go to Cordelia's castle and do battle. Do you have any objections to staying here until I am free to send you back to your proper place?"

Still caught in the throes of her fit of pique, Jane wasn't about to give in easily, so she took a final swipe at the wizard. "Did you tell him about the rope-toting posse that wants to measure your neck?"

Will looked pained, slightly embarrassed, and maybe even a little miffed.

Max Farrel looked at her, seemed to actually see *her* for the first time. What she was came as an obvious shock. His eyes widened, and he said, "You're a...a woman? How in the name of...Does Cordelia know you've evaded the interdict? She'll hurt..."

THE MEMORIES pummeled him, beat him with whips of fire, and Sojourner fought them, tried to force them away, but he was too weak; and they were too many. And it was the night-eyed woman who had called them out of hiding, made him face what could never be.

She was the one, the One Love, the True Love, the one foretold that would bring him all happiness, ease the torment of his soul, make him whole—but it couldn't be. It was too late; he had destroyed what should have been, torn the very fabric of destiny, and now he had to pay. But she didn't.

Jane. Even her name was a caress, a soft hand on his heart, and he loved her with a passion that took all strength from his muscles, left him bereft. He loved her, had always loved her, since the beginning, since Old Derna had conjured Jane's face in the fire, since Jane had looked at him with those beautiful midnight eyes and smiled.

But that was before. Before a kingdom had fallen. Before a people had been ripped from their homeland and set adrift in an unkind world. Before a crown had been stolen and a wee babe shattered in death.

Before. When Sojourner had a name and a future. Before. When Sojourner was still a man.

Despite the pain in his wounded shoulder, the fever that burned fire-bright in his body, the great cat's every thought was of Jane, the need to send her away, to know that she was safe. He crawled off the bunk inside Will's wagon. He stood for a moment or two, trying to drive the memories out of his head, to do, just once, what was honorable and right, to save his love before she could be a part of his destruction.

But it was so hard. Jane saw him in all truth. He knew that, knew she saw a man, felt a man, and it had been ages since anyone had seen him thus. Not even Will, whom he loved as a son, knew him beyond his cat seeming.

But Jane was his love and love saw true.

Staggering, fighting a battle with his physical weakness and own terrible need, Sojourner padded to the door and out into the sunshine. He was determined to win, to save his love from his own terrible fate. And, he didn't care much if he died in the trying.

BEFORE JANE COULD answer Farrel's astonished questions regarding her gender, he asked another, "Is she one of the brides?"

Will shrugged and started to give a simplified version of what was a very long, very complicated tale. One that Jane preferred he not tell, especially the part about her short stint as the town's two-bit whore, so she said, "No, damn it, I'm an interfering idiot. I just came along for the ride."

Sojourner chose that moment to stagger through the back door of the wagon and down the step, halting at Will's side. Tail lashing ominously, rumbling deep in his throat, he looked like the original cat from hell. His eyes were glazed and burning, feral, his fangs were exposed, and his fur was rumpled, dead looking.

Jane looked at him, and for just an unbearable instant, she thought her heart was breaking, literally. Her chest hurt so damned much that it had to be that; or a heart attack that was going to kill her within seconds.

Drawn by a force that was beyond time, beyond space, beyond understanding, she took a step toward the snarling cat.

Farrel, ever the gentleman, leaped in front of her, prepared, obviously, to defend her with his bare hands. Jane wasn't used to being defended, and she discovered, rather rapidly, that she didn't like it one little bit.

"Damn it, get out of my way," she said, her snarl equaling the cat's.

"Ma'am, he'll tear you to..."

"Move!" Reason had no part in her reaction, nor did logic, or any of the other intellectual functions that had ruled her life for years. This was a primitive need, one she couldn't have fought, even if she had wanted to; which she didn't. All she wanted to was to get to Sojourner, to put her hands on...

"Better be listening to her, boss. She be the wizard I be telling you about," the sage advice came from the mustached ranch foreman as he stepped close, but not too close, to warn his boss of all the possible dangers Jane, Will, and Sojourner posed.

Max Farrel wasn't eager to accept the warning, but he moved, albeit reluctantly, when Jane put out her hands, shoved him, and practically shouted, "Stop acting like an damned fool and get out of my way." He didn't move far, just far enough to grab a saber from one of the waddies, and head toward the cat.

Both Will and Jane beat him there, stood in front of Sojourner like a shield. Jane's fingers scrabbled in her bag for her spare canister of pepper spray. Will got some small magic up and running. It provided a wall of shimmering light, prismatic light of green, blue, red, pink, and all hues and combinations in between, that circled and swooped, but was shockingly hot to anyone who dared to enter its field of protection.

Any other time, the pulsing light, appearing as it did out of nowhere, would have frightened Jane into a fit. But now she had other things to worry about and didn't really notice—except to hope that it gave the big cat some measure of protection.

Jane wanted to keep him from all harm, but was scared to death to touch Sojourner. It wasn't because she thought he would hurt her, she knew he wouldn't, but because her mental state couldn't process what her fingers would feel, her eyes would see.

But careful as she was, Jane's free hand inadvertently brushed Sojourner's ear and, once again she heard his deep voice, a very human, very male voice inside her head. "Love of my heart, keeper of my dreams, you have to go back to your home world before it's too late. There is nothing for us now. Make the young wizard send you back—cannot...I want..."

And then the great cat's strength seemed to melt away. He wavered, swayed, crumpled to the damp earth—and only the rapid rise and fall of his chest told her he was still alive, if only barely.

Jane Murdock, vice president of a Fortune 500 company, a woman well aware of who and what she was, didn't agree with the great cat, didn't demand to be instantly repatriated.

No indeed. She sank to her knees, reached out, her hands hovering over Sojourner, and whimpered, deep in her throat, holding back what wanted to be a keening wail of loss, a loss beyond mortal bearing.

Chapter 12

THE PROTECTIVE shield, hastily erected, built, in the main, of scant magic and ample despair, was fizzing and snapping and sputtering, sparking across from strand to strand, glowing faintly red, sickly orange, and fading far too fast. Will, to use a cliché from Jane's home world, was clutching at straws, trying to keep himself afloat in a whirlpool, or some such nonsense.

Above all else, he had to keep Sojourner safe from swung sabers and other life-threatening objects until the great cat could look to his own safety. It wasn't easy. Weariness, hunger, and worry and all the rest of Will's troubles had taken too much out of him, leaving a very little more than an empty husk.

One final straw tickled his brain, hoping it would work, would save the cat when the shield fell, he put it into action. "Don't let them touch him, Farrel," Will shouted, or, to be more accurate, croaked like a terminally ill raven. "He's my familiar. If you kill him, I'm finished and, sooner or later, Cordelia will have her way with you."

"Don't touch the cat," Farrel shouted, evidently taking Will's lie as nothing more than total truth, a truth depicting a future that he didn't want to anticipate, couldn't tolerate.

Still fingering their drawn sabers with decidedly nervous fingers, the pack of advancing waddies halted instantly, started to back away from their intended victim at the most fortuitous moment.

The same moment the weak shield fell in a small shower of yellowish sparks. The wind freshened, picked up the fragments, sent them toward a pair of saddled unicorns tied to the southern-most hitching rail, just beyond the parked wagon and its hitch of draft beasts. Will's animals were used to Sojourner, accepted him without question, but the riding unicorns were made of less stern stuff.

The fiery bits of fallen shield, coupled with the cat's spicy odor, rushed at them on the wind, spooked them soundly, drove them into a fear frenzy. Screeing loudly, sounding like an enormous hawk, one reared up, pawed the air, tried to break its leather tether. Nostrils flaring, ears back, the other unicorn followed the first's lead, succeeded where the other failed, turned tail, and galloped away. The first unicorn, not to be outdone, made his own bid for freedom, found it in a wild, bucking instant, and ran, iron-shod cloven hoofs thundering against the sandy earth, ears back, teeth bared.

Large mustache fairly quivering, the enraged foreman shouted words unfit for a lady's delicate ears, sending a trio of waddies hustling after the totally frightened, and rapidly disappearing, riding beasts.

The fleeing unicorns weren't Will's worry, and he didn't accept that particular guilt. Instead, he said, giving orders with far more confidence that he was feeling, but knowing he didn't dare show any weakness, "Thanks, Farrel. Now, have some of your men carry Sojourner into the house so I can tend him."

Farrel wasn't entirely convinced, or perhaps he wasn't used to accepting orders, "I said I'd do whatever you asked, even to storming Cordelia's castle, but he's an animal and doesn't belong indoors with...He might be dangerous, and I would prefer that you...There are several outbuildings that would be more suitable cages for..."

Jane was kneeling at Sojourner's side, her hands fluttering helplessly, not quite touching the cat, and she was breathing in air in a manner that might have suggested suppressed sobs. Staggering slightly, putting his hand on Jane's shoulder to keep his balance, Will was adamant. "In your house. Now. Unless, of course, you'd prefer to have Cordelia continue to plague..."

The threat worked. Within seconds, waddies had converged from several directions and were, with great care and silent diligence, sliding a thickly woven blanket under the cat. They lifted him with a gentleness and care that gave lie to the narrow-eyed, clench-jawed looks they gave both Will and the cat.

Moving along beside them, Will had scarcely a thought to waste, but he did remember, at last, that Jane...He frowned, paused, looked over his shoulder, and saw Max Farrel helping her to her feet before he dismissed her from his mind and concentrated on Sojourner.

SO MUCH HAD been lost at the changing. So very much. Sojourner wasn't sure what was real, or what were just wishes and hopes of his own making. Perhaps none of the tellings were true, perhaps he had always been a cat, a cat who loved like a man, with his entire being. It went beyond the need to mate, far beyond, into a area of emotions where cats should never venture, an area where love, caring, and enduring devotion were the order of the day.

Jane, his Jane, had come at last, but there was nothing for her now, nothing for either of them. And the longer she stayed, the greater the danger became. He knew, from what few bits and pieces he had managed to unearth, that she was in danger, that the curse that held him could reach out, destroy her...

That couldn't be. He already had too much guilt on his soul, he couldn't allow Jane, his One True Love, the one destined from the beginning of time, to fall prey to his demons. He had to protect her, keep her safe, even if it meant all else was lost. That much he knew. But knowing and doing are vastly different. And the difference mocked him, sapped his strength, felled him, leaving him only words, words that begged her to leave.

The love-words, the fear-words gave way to darkness, fire-shot darkness that spoke in other tongues, phantom tongues he couldn't decipher. And then they were lost to the movement, the lifting and carrying of his wounded body, the harsh stab of pain that pushed him deeper and deeper into the nothing.

SHAKEN, FAR MORE than she cared to admit even to herself, Jane watched the waddies carry Sojourner toward the sprawling ranch house. She shrugged Max Farrel's solicitous hand off her arm and barely heard his soft-voiced, "Ma'am, are you all right? May I assist you into the house?"

"I don't need any assistance," she said, as decisively as possible, knowing it was a flat-out, bald-faced lie. She was trembling, scared silly of Sojourner, her own emotional response to him, the sense...She didn't know what it was and wasn't real sure that she wanted any part of it. But what really scared the bejeebers out of her was the growing knowledge that just maybe she wasn't going to have any say in the matter. She wasn't going to allow that. No indeed, she was...Dear merciful God, she was what?

The wind, hot enough to dry the sweat that suddenly beaded on her forehead, switched directions, whirled on itself, picked up dried twigs, from the tall rows of what looked like poplar trees that bordered the log house. It pitched them up, carried them in a spiral that rose higher and higher. She watched the miniature tornado blankly, heard Farrel say, "Please, ma'am, let me help you up. I..." He sounded bemused.

It wasn't a word in her usual vocabulary, but it seemed to fit his state only too well. Besides that, his use of ma'am didn't seem nearly as put-down-ish or humor the old-lady-ish as Will's did. For one giddy moment, Jane wanted to smile, to giggle madly, or maybe even bat her eyes and simper up at him. It wasn't a pleasant sort of giddy; she was more than a little ticked.

She probably could have given him cowboy points for courtesy and consideration, but she damned sure wasn't going to. The handsomest man in nine universes was treating her like a very desirable woman, and she knew damned well it wasn't because of her girlish charms; of which, she had few or none. Oh, no, it was because she was the only woman still alive and breathing in The Great Northwest.

Instead of telling him just what she thought, Jane, who was used to using any weapon to achieve her goals, extended her hand, allowed him to pull her to her feet. When he didn't release her hand, Jane didn't jerk free. She lifted her chin, looked him square in the eye, and said, as arrogantly as possible, "My name is Jane Murdock. I was brought here against my will by your ladylove and until Will finds the brides and can return me to my own world, I shall require a private room, bathing facilities, and some decent clothing.

"Until that time, I would appreciate it if you would pass the word that I am not one of the brides, nor am I available for courting, hanky-panky, or any other male-conceived sexual games. Do you understand what I'm saying?"

Farrel's blush did nothing to detract from his incredible looks, neither did his stammered, "Yes, ma'am, I understand perfectly. I'll make sure that none of the waddies bothers you in..."

"Include yourself in the hands-off group and we'll have a deal."

The red that burned on his face would have suited bricks better than a man, and Max Farrel's stutter was nearly incomprehensible, but Jane decided he was probably agreeing to her terms. Nevertheless, she thought it was prudent to add, as he led her, without touching so much as her shirt sleeve, up the front steps. As they crossed a broad, very littered verandah, and into the large, dimly lit, very neglected-looking living room of the ranch house, "I don't clean, cook, or sew, so don't get any stupid ideas in that direction either."

"Yes, ma'am. I mean, no, ma'am. I won't. I didn't mean to offend..."

She almost snapped, "Cut the crap," but exercised a modicum of prudence and asked, rather nicely, she thought, "My room?"

"Uh, since Cordelia took...Maudie, the foreman's mother kept house for me and...There's clean bedding; we take the dirty clothes into town and...Ma'am, I don't know much about..."

"If you're trying to ask me if I can make my own bed, the answer is yes," Jane said, trying to keep down a crazy impulse to laugh. The whole situation was ludicrous, idiotic; so much so that it wouldn't even make a really bad sitcom for Friday night TV. She knew her bad manners were only making things worse. But, she couldn't find enough energy to care.

But she did summon up enough energy to feel a small amount of surprise when he led her down a long hall, showed her into the large, square bedroom at the very end. It came complete with a huge bed, several dressers, and a walk-in closet. The turkey red carpet was dusty-looking. The cabbage-rosed wallpaper, with its big, blood-red roses and nasty green leaves, was a long way from being a sight for sore eyes. The small window panes were made of some thick, wavy greenish-tinged glass. And the whole room smelled of disuse, mice, and wallpaper paste.

But whatever misgivings she had, the striped mattress resting on a wooden bedframe laced across with rope, looked clean. So did the linen sheets and handmade, pieced quilts in a multitude of jewel-like hues, he pulled from the cedar chest at the foot of the bed.

"The bathroom is through there. And it's real private. I keep this room special for buyers, who sometimes bring their ladies, when they come to inspect my herds," Farrel said, pointing toward a closed door on the left wall of the room. "The water's hot, from the underground springs, not from magic spells, and there's plenty of soap, but..."

He shook his head and hesitated, obviously choosing his words carefully. "Ma'am, I don't know about clothes for you. Maudie was a large woman—and I think all her clothes went with her when Cordelia did her spell setting and..."

He gnawed on his lower lip, tried not to look at Jane. Finally, he said, "I don't know if it's true or not, but the word is your young wizard was supposed to have enough garments to outfit a large number of women. The brides needed to dress right for here and..."

Practically drooling at the thought of a bath, of washing her hair, of feeling clean again, and not wanting to wait, Jane stood, shoeless and weary, on the dust-dulled carpet. She put her hands on her narrow hips, and said, still being reasonably civil, "Thank you, Mr. Farrel. I vaguely remember Maggie mentioning something to that effect, so I would appreciate it very much if you would ask Will..."

"Excuse me, ma'am," the foreman said, halting in the open doorway, "when we be carrying the cat into the wizard's room, the wizard bethought himself to say as how you do be a-wanting these here duds."

He stepped aside to allow a wizened little man, his arms piled with garments and other female fripperies, entrance into Jane's bedroom. "This do be Coodie."

"The cook, ma'am," the man said without a single glance in her direction. He edged into the room, dumped his burden on the mattress, and scampered out far more nimbly than Jane would have thought possible. When he was safely outside her room, Coodie turned, gave her a shy grin, ducked his head, and said, "Supper do be on the table in an hour, best get for getting."

Jane got rid of Farrel and the foreman with little more than a meaningful look. It was one that she had long practiced and had used on numerous occasions to rid herself of any number of petty annoyances. The foreman touched two fingers to the brim of his black-felt hat and vanished without a word, but Farrel wasn't content with such simple expediences.

"If there's anything more you need, just..." he started, but Jane interrupted with, "Right now, all I need is a bath and some clean clothes and I can handle both of those rather nicely by myself. And I would like to do so."

She increased the intensity of the *look*, and he almost scurried out of the large bedroom, closing the door behind him with a decisive click, leaving Jane to her avowed pursuits. And she pursued them in typical Jane fashion, full-bore and with single-minded intent.

The old-fashioned, unfamiliar array of lace-trimmed, knee-length drawers and similarly bedecked camisoles and petticoats, long, full skirts, high-necked ruffled blouses, and fringed shawl were a semi-surprise and a source of irritation.

On the other hand, after Jane had culled a few suitable bits from the pile of clothing, headed toward the designated bathroom, and opened the door, she received a surprise of mega-proportions; and felt no irritation whatsoever.

It wasn't a grotto, it was more like a spa, a small paradise of thick, opaque skylights, gray stone floors, brilliant green ferns, chuckling waterfalls, and sand-floored pools of both pungent, steaming water and cool, totally clear water. Water, she found to her delight, that had a high-mineral content, which accounted for the sulphur odor in the damp air. It soothed her aches, eased her pains, and gave her a new outlook on life.

But, if the water was marvelous, the soap left much to be desired. Harsh and evil-smelling, it did its job with great dispatch, but it was far from gentle in the doing. But, given the choice between it and sweaty grime, Jane opted for the soap. She ignored her strong suspicion it was made of lye and other unsavory items like rendered fat and would probably take off some of her hide with the dirt.

However, when she finally rinsed her body and hair in the constantly changing water of the coolest pool, she felt better than she had in days. There was only one towel, rather small, dingy enough to have come from Jake's upstairs rooms, and stiff enough to scratch her skin, but Jane wasn't to be deterred. Not even by the strange garments that knew nothing of such modern gadgets as zippers, elastic, and Velcro, but used hooks and eyes and a series of ties for fastening.

By dint of great perseverance and not a little smoky language, Jane managed to tie the drawers and one petticoat around her waist. She couldn't figure out how to keep the stockings up, so she pitched them into the same discard heap that held corsets and other unnamed items. The camisole's pale-blue ribbons tied easily enough and the dark skirt and white, terribly frilly blouse, even if they weren't to her liking, were on in a thrice, as were a pair of soft kidskin slippers.

After she had found a comb in her purse and paid some scant attention to her unconditioned, unmoussed, and prone-to-curl locks, Jane wanted to find a mirror. She needed to know just how silly she looked, but there wasn't one. So, hearing the faint clang of what had to be a dinner bell, Jane lifted her chin, took a deep breath, and set out to face the world.

A world that contained a cat, a large black cat who spoke and loved like a man. A cat who called her love and begged her to leave, all in what seemed the same breath.

A cat she couldn't have known before coming here, but did. And it was that knowing that shivered in her soul, ached in her heart, hid in the darkest corners of mind, and refused to surrender to reason or logic.

"Hurry, Will," she whispered before she opened the door. "I don't know how much more of this I can..." She couldn't finish, Will, looking drawn and old, was waiting outside the door, and the news he gave her was both good and bad.

The good was: Will had found the remedy for Sojourner's wounds. The bad was: the great cat's healing and Will's magical seeking for the brides were going to take time, lots of time.

Jane stepped close to the young wizard, said as softly as possible, "Will, I can't stay, I just can't."

"I know," Will said, just as quietly, "but there's no other course I can take. The brides are..." He took a deep breath and his voice was anguished when he said, "Sojourner is my family, but, Jane, I gave Maggie and the others my sacred word honor as a wizard that they would be safe. I cannot break that word, even for him."

Jane patted his shoulder, an act of kindness and comfort she wasn't known for performing, and said, "Do what you have to do. Everything will be all right."

But she knew she was lying. Everything wasn't all right, and it never would be again.

Chapter 13

"RIDERS BE coming in, boss! There be a mort of 'em!"

The shouted warning, from an unseen sentry, was loud enough to penetrate the confines of the gloomy, not overly clean, dining room and bring Max Farrel to his feet with a stifled exclamation.

The unicorn rancher was heading toward the living room before Will, fearing the worst, could get his pounding heart to slow. That accomplished, he followed after Farrel, but only after he said, sternly and with hastily assumed authority, "Stay in the house and make sure you keep out of sight, Jane, it might be the posse."

"What about you? Why are you going out?"

Will sighed. "The wagon's still parked out in front. If it's really them, they know by now that I'm here. But, Jane, that doesn't have to mean that I brought you with me, does it? Please, just stay out of sight and maybe I can keep them from finding you."

He knew she wasn't about to take his orders, but that didn't keep him from trying. Contrary and opinionated as she was, she was still his responsibility, and, posse or no, he wasn't about to let her go back to Jake's. But after the way she had saved Sojourner, he was more than willing to admit she was right about one thing.

Inside that skinny shell, Jane Murdock was some sort of woman, a woman with brains and guts, and she was worth a hell of a lot more than two-bits; not that he intended to tell her so. He wasn't anywhere near brave enough for that. She'd have his head; that's presuming the posse didn't get it first and hang it from the nearest tree for all and sundry to see.

"'Evening, marshal."

Farrel's greeting, delivered from the open front door, took all vague hopes that it was just casual visitors from Will's mind and brought back all of his fears. It was the posse from town, and Will's red wizard wagon was still parked in front of the ranch house for all to see. There wasn't any way he could hide, so without Farrel's help the new arrivals were going to...

Will stopped, looked back at Jane, who, of course, wasn't

more than three steps behind him, and said, quietly and trying not to sound too self-pitying, "They know I'm here. If I can't talk them out of hanging me, someone has to take care of Sojourner until he's well enough to go on by himself. I...Please, will you..."

She nodded, but she looked pretty fierce in the doing. Still, it was enough—it had to be. Taking a deep breath, he walked across the dusty, shadow-filled living room and stepped out into the late afternoon sunshine slanting into the west facing verandah. Some part of his mind breathed a small sigh of relief when he heard Jane's following footsteps stop inside the house. She was safe, for that moment at least, from whomever or whatever awaited without.

WIPING HER sweaty palms on the hindering folds of the full skirt, trying to keep from gasping in air, Jane crept close to the open doorway. She was close enough to listen but not be seen, close enough to hear the mutters and growls of angry men, men who were intent on their deadly mission. It was a mission that, evidently, met with the full sanction of the law; or what passed for the law on Will's wild and primitive earth.

Lifting the skirt and underlying petticoat up to her knees, Jane edged a little nearer to one of the small windows, striving to see as well as hear what was transpiring in Farrel's yard. It wasn't a terribly pleasant sight, just a bunch of sweaty, dusty men mounted on unicorns of various shades and sizes. What she heard brought new prickles of fear to dance up her spine, lodge in her throat; fear for Will as well as herself.

"Thanks for catching him, Farrel," a man with a shiny badge pinned to his black vest said, saddle leather creaking as he dismounted from his big, roan unicorn. "We'll be taking care of him from here on in. This be one lying wizard what ain't gonna be doing no more thieving and cheating, unless he be doing it from the limb of an oak."

Farrel stepped off the porch, and with Will only a step or two behind him. They walked out to the hitching rail to confront what had to be thirty or so scowling, tired-looking men who ranged in age from very young to really old.

One of whom, a medium-aged, squint-eyed runt, seemed to be amusing himself by swinging a hangman's noose back and forth. Most of the other unicorn riders dismounted, stretched the kinks from their muscles, and fingered the hilts of the sabers, some fairly rusty, that hung from their belts.

The marshal wrapped his mount's reins around the rail, ducked under it, and grinned at Will. "You be ready, boy?" he asked, moving closer to Will, "cause if you ain't, we is. Ready and willing to..."

"Whatever it is you think he's done, I can say with some certainty that you are wrong in your construction of events. To my personal knowledge, Will has been busy trying to locate the brides Cordelia has spirited away and hid. Knowing of my own distrust of the woman, Will has enlisted my aid in insuring the off-world brides' safe return. Which, of course, I was most happy to give," Max interrupted smoothly. "If you want the ladies, you'd better leave him to the search. Remember, Will's a wizard and he gave his word—all of you have to know what that means."

Farrel was smiling, friendly, even affable as he added, "A wizard's honor is bound to his word. He took the oath, and now he has to keep his word. I'm not sure exactly how it works, but we all know it's true. Right, marshal?"

The marshal rubbed his finger against the side of his rather small nose, looked at Will's red wagon, at Will himself, and then back at Farrel before he nodded, but, in Jane's opinion, without much vigor or enthusiasm.

If the marshal agreed, he wasn't exactly in the majority. The low-voice murmur got louder, men looked at one another, frowned, asked questions Jane couldn't hear.

Their rather hostile reaction didn't seem to be bothering Farrel in the slightest. He said, just as smoothly as before, "So, now that that's settled, why don't the lot of you just light and wash up while I get Coodie to rustle up some grub. After you eat, you're welcome to spend the night in the bunkhouse and then ride out in the morning. It's going to take a while, but rest assured, the wizard and I, with my waddies' help, are going to undo the wrong Cordelia has...."

There was no instant agreement, just a few nodded heads and what looked like relief on several faces. But, they weren't in the majority. And, evidently they didn't have much to say. There was an even larger huddle of sweat-stained men, more surging protests, louder counter arguments. Finally one, slightly querulous voice that said, "That be okay for the wizard, Farrel, and them what be wanting brides and babies and such, but what about that ugly whore what Cordelia be giving the rest of us. He be stealing her and we be wanting her back."

Without hesitating more than a moment or two, Will

cleared his throat, swallowed twice, and said, sounding so sincere that Jane almost believed him herself, "I'm terribly sorry, but...Well, Cordelia didn't do you any favors with that one. She died from the whore-pox just about three hours after we got out of town. It was a terrible thing. I didn't want to touch her because..."

He shrugged and looked incredibly honest, boy-next-door-ish as he said, "I couldn't bury her, so I used magic to...You know. I hope none of you went up to her room because..."

There was instant silence. It lasted what seemed an eternity before Jane heard one of the posse members say, "Farrel, I do be thinking that you be right. Grub and a bunk sounds mighty fine, I do be taking your offer."

He wasn't alone in his thinking. Within seconds the rest of the posse, with only a handful giving the still dangling noose a regretful look, were leading their unicorns to the barn and readying themselves to be company rather than lawmen/executioners. One of them untied the marshal's mount and led it away with his own, leaving the marshal free to come back into the house with Farrel and Will.

Driven by a sudden thought, needing to avert still new danger, Jane, although it wasn't her usual form of locomotion, held her skirts high and scampered to the dining room.

Given the fact of her recent demise, there were three plates on the table where only two should be. She wanted to remedy the situation and hide out in her room before new complications arose; complications that could send her places she had no intention of going.

Coodie, the cook, was there before her. Her plate, still holding a fair amount of food, her napkin, and silverware, was in his hands. He gave it to her, winked, and said, very softly, "Don't you be a-worrying none, they no be a-finding you here. We be taking good care of you."

Oddly relieved, Jane smiled at him before she, with great haste, sought the sanctuary her room, with the door shut fast and the key turned in the lock, offered. Late the next morning, after the posse had departed, it was Coodie who knocked on the door and told her it was safe to come out.

"They be coming back though," he said slowly, worry adding new wrinkles to his face. "They no be trusting the wizard. He be telling them it takes time to do the finding." He shook his head. "I don't know how much time they be giving him."

STEPPING OVER discarded saddles, unicorn blankets, bridles, ignoring the pots of dead plants and dried-up flowers that someone, probably the departed Maudie, had loved and tended, Jane stood on the verandah and watched the sunset with blank unseeing eyes. It remained the same, always, except that the advancing year had yellowed the grass, chilled the night air, and told her nothing more than summer was rapidly disappearing.

But it wasn't gone yet. The wind, what there was of it, was hot and dusty-smelling, but it was a relief just to be out of the house—a house that had aspirations of being a ghost house, or maybe already was one.

Not that the verandah was much better, but it gave her a different perspective on the world and, she hoped, on her own particular dilemma. She worried the problem, but could see no real solution.

The sky turned deeper red, purple, dark blue with astounding rapidity, but Jane didn't care. She turned, with a flare of skirts and continued to pace, her thoughts running faster than her feet.

Will wasn't wrong about needing time. Neither was he available for complaint when she thought he was taking an inordinate amount of that commodity to achieve his magical seeing. And it was time, long day piled on top of long day, building week after week, that Jane had no way of filling. It was the wasted time that set her to pacing, muttering, and glaring at all and sundry; not that anyone lingered very long in her vicinity.

There were no books to read, no files to write, no TV, no radio, hardly any sounds of life. The unicorns, except when fear made them scree, were remarkably silent beasts; not that Jane got that close to them. The eternal wind kicked up dust and rustled in the leaves of the trees, but the thick log walls of the house kept most of that sound outside. She had been discouraged, rather strongly, to attempt any walking or wandering in the outdoors.

She was so bored that she was tempted to clean the living room and dining room, but didn't succumb to that idiotic temptation. However, she did clean her own room, did her own laundry, and had the bathroom glowing with elbow grease. It wasn't enough to fill days that seemed to stretch beyond possible.

Will, when he wasn't locked inside the wizard wagon, was

locked inside his room. What's more he was daily growing thinner and more haggard-looking.

Farrel had his own work to do. From the quick peek Jane had given his office, he wasn't very good at it. Her brain itched to tackle the clutter in that room, to reduce the chaos to some form of order. She intended to do just that, whether he liked it or not, just as soon as the rancher went out on the range to do whatever it was that ranchers did.

It was almost too dark to see, but still Jane walked, kicking aside the jumble of stuff that tried to block her way. The verandah was a mess, one that would have made a good housekeeper cringe. Jane didn't care; in fact, she needed it. The inanimate objects gave her a place to vent her ire—and she needed lots of venting to keep from going nuts, or to keep from kicking more than old saddles and other oddments of ranch life.

Scowling, gritting her teeth, Jane stomped on, trying to keep her anger at bay and her clouded thoughts from stomping on her. Not that she was having any luck in that direction; or, as far as that goes, in any other direction. She was trapped, pure and simple, and there was no way out of the trap until Will did his magic junk and got Maggie back.

But, until that happened, she still had to endure the stifling boredom of the ranch. Coodie was the only one who actually talked to her and he didn't have much to say. After one brief visit, Jane was very careful to stay out of the kitchen. It's magical gadgets gave her the shuddering creeps. They were too different to be believed. The kitchen, more than anything else except the herds of unicorns, made her know she was far from home; and not, seemingly, making any progress toward getting back there any time soon.

A sound behind her halted her frenzied pacing, but Jane didn't turn. She didn't have to. She was sure she knew who was there, who was watching from the shadows.

On his feet now, but still weak, Sojourner tried to avoid her. Jane knew that. She also knew that when he thought she wasn't looking, he watched her with sorrow-tarnished eyes, loved her, but didn't dare come too close.

That was fine with her; she had her own wants and needs to battle. And each day was proving to be a new skirmish in a never-ending war. A war, she was beginning to suspect, although she had never had occasion to wage that particular fight before, against that terrible aggressor, love, a love that couldn't be.

But, no matter how hard she argued, how many cold baths

she took, she couldn't banish her yearning. Her hands ached to touch him, her eyes begged for another glimpse of the lean, bronze-skinned man who lived inside Sojourner, and her wayward heart was unruly indeed.

But Jane still had enough sense, enough reason left to know she wouldn't allow it; she couldn't allow it. If she gave in to her heart's demands, she knew she would be doomed, would never be able to leave this place; and she had to. She had to go back to her own world where reason and sanity were her daily companions, where love couldn't and didn't exist. Her own nice, safe, sterile world.

The slight sound came again.

Against her will, Jane turned looked toward the doorway, saw a man, not a cat, and her quickly repressed sigh was not a sigh of relief. Taking a deep breath, she said, before she could come close to stopping herself, "Will, please, send me home. I have to go home."

Even to Jane's own ears, it was a cry of total despair—and she couldn't call it back, couldn't make it unuttered.

Chapter 14

HER DESPAIRING wail seemed to echo, to bounce off walls, magnify in the empty spaces, then grow too large and too loud for the narrow confines of her own mind. Jane wanted to call it back, to hide the poor, pitiful, whimpering thing in the dark recesses of her brain, but it was too late. She had already shown her weakness to the world; or, at least, to the young wizard.

A shadow among shadows, Will took two steps toward her, reached out as if to touch her, to pat her shoulder, to bring the silly, overwrought, weak woman some modicum of male comfort and reassurance. "Jane, I'm sorry but..."

Her mood changed, whipped about. Fury assaulted her, battered what little control she had left, shook her like an aspen leaf in a hurricane. Jane backed away from him, backed until her heel caught on something and she stumbled, would have fallen if she hadn't caught hold of the peeled pole that was the rather primitive verandah railing, held herself erect.

Breathing hard, trying to quell the emotions that were ravaging her, Jane finally managed to say, apropos of nothing, asking a question she hadn't even known was bothering her until that very moment, "Where's the moon?"

"What?" Will stopped his forward advance.

It wasn't truly important. She honestly didn't care. But talking nonsense was better than blurting out her real fears, fear that had more to do with an irrational love and silver-eyed cats than they did with absent moons. *That* she was not going to do.

No matter what had happened, no matter what world she was on, she was still Jane Murdock, and Jane Murdock always took care of herself. So, Jane Murdock, swallowing tears and fears, said, "The moon. Where is it? I haven't seen it since I got here and..."

"There isn't one."

Will sounded more weary than anything else, but there was worry in his voice too—but whatever else he sounded, he didn't sound young any more. He sounded old and defeated, like a man who had gambled everything and lost and was looking for a bridge to leap off...Fear came rushing back, attacked her anger with needle-sharp teeth.

The fear-quiver, the shaking started somewhere in her middle, threatened to spread out engulf her completely, but she quelled it, beat it down to a small tremble. That done, Jane ignored Will's weariness and said, or rather demanded, "What happened to it?"

"It fell. A long time ago, thousands of years. I don't know why." He took another short step in her direction. "Jane, why don't you go lie down and get some rest. You..."

"Don't be an ass!" Jane snapped, snarling out the words from a bubbling pot of pure fury. "I am a perfectly competent human being, not some fragile doll that needs coddling. I want something to do, to have something to read, that is if I can read what's written here."

"Yes, you can read the language as well as speak it. It's all embedded in the traveling spell and..."

Jane ignored him and went on with her list. "I want someone to talk to about real things. I do not want to be left out, ignored, treated like an idiot incapable of thought. Can you understand that?"

"Jane, I...I don't have any time to...Maggie, and the others, of course, might be in danger. I can't take time to..."

"Worry about my boredom?" she asked, far too sweetly. When he didn't answer, she asked, just as sweetly, "Has it ever occurred to you that I'm worried about Maggie also? That I am educated, logical, and organized? That I just might, and that's a fairly strong might, be able to help you?"

"No," he said, anger taking some of the weariness from his voice, "it didn't. How can you possibly help? You don't even believe in magic, and that's all I've got to work with."

"So, what it boils down to is that I'm nothing more than a pest?" She asked the question so calmly that she surprised herself.

"Not exactly that, but..."

"But nothing!" Jane pushed herself away from the verandah railing and stormed passed him into the house, saying as she went by, "If magic exists, I'm sure I could learn how to do it. After all, you did, didn't you?"

FLABBERGASTED, furious, and somehow deflated, Will stood there for a moment before he turned to follow her, to try to explain that magic took practice and study and that there wasn't time for her to learn. A soft, indulgent chuckle sounded inside his head and he heard Sojourner say, "She has fire in her soul, my lady of the midnight eyes. She is made of steel, that one. The finest steel and tempered true."

Will peered into the darkened living room, hoping to catch a glimpse of the cat, but Sojourner was lost in the shadows. "Part of her is steel and honed to a sharp edge," he said, "and I'll bet she could flay you with it and walk away without a backward glance."

"She is lonely and afraid."

"Sojourner, that woman isn't afraid of anything in this world or her own. She's what they call there, hell on wheels, a real bitch."

"I would not have you speak so, young wizard." The deep voice held more sorrow than warning, but Will understood, or thought he did, what was implied. It was the implication that kept him from saying more about Jane, instead he said, "I have looked in all the books, tried every formula I can find, and still there is no trace of Maggie and the others. And I cannot do as you ask and send Jane back until I find the others."

After a few seconds, Will summoned enough courage to say, "Sojourner, I don't think I can do it. I'm afraid Maggie is doomed."

There was no answer. Will snapped a magelight into being, set it adrift in the living room. It revealed dead plants, dusty tables, empty cups, leather chairs, a long couch, and other detritus of daily life, but no living thing; Sojourner, if in truth he had been there, was gone.

Will pushed his fingers through his tangled hair and wanted to swear—and would have if he hadn't been so damned tired, and so damned worried about Maggie. And the rest of the brides, he reminded himself, with far more haste than honesty. He went back out onto the verandah, heading for the wizard wagon, hoping to dig more text books out of the cupboards to bring into the house. Books that just might hold the answer to his arcane search.

And as he walked, he felt the faintest tinge of guilt. Jane really could read, which wasn't at all common in this world, especially for women. She was bright, bright enough, perhaps, to find what he was missing, to find the formula that would break the concealing wards Cordelia had set around the brides.

For just an instant, Will considered the idea, and then he shook his head. Bright as she was, Jane Murdock was too damned bull-headed to even try. He knew that for sure—even if Sojourner didn't.

And he also knew that nothing good was going to come of the whole affair, that Jane was going to hurt Sojourner, hurt him bad. Will wasn't sure he could do anything to prevent it—but he did know he had to try.

Sojourner was his family, was first in his heart. First after Maggie, his heart told him, and Will acknowledged that fact with another sigh, one that was heartfelt and hurting.

Something he had heard once, from Sojourner perhaps, wound its way into his knowing: Love isn't always kind; it is selfish, demanding, and jealous, wanting nothing more that total possession of both the lover and the object of that love. That description certainly fit Cordelia, but did it fit him too. It was a disturbing thought, one that made him itch in an unscratchable place until he fought it down, subdued it.

Love had already caused too many problems, Will wasn't going to allow it to cause more—and somewhere in his mind, Sojourner's voice seemed to say, quietly and sadly, "Ah, you are young, wizard, so terribly young."

"STUPID SKIRTS," Jane muttered as she stalked down the short hall that opened off the dining room rather than the living room, going to Farrel's office not her own bedroom, going there with one purpose in mind. And it was a purpose that had nothing to do with love. Or so she would have told anyone who would have dared to ask

But love, or some derivation of it, like lust or something, might have been a motivation factor for others, such as Max Farrel. He looked up from the papers spread out on his desk. Startled by her abrupt entrance, he was a bit tardy with his manners, a trifle slow jumping to his feet, smiling a very warm welcome, and saying, "Jane, my dear, what a pleasant surprise. Is there something I can do for you?"

"Yes," Jane said, trying not to sound testy and irritable, but not being in the least successful. She was in a full-blown snit, and she knew it. She looked around his office, saw little that would differentiate it from an office on her own world; an office straight out of the 1880's.

An office in the 1880's that had just undergone a severe windstorm, probably of hurricane proportions. It was truly a mess. There were wooden file cabinets, five of them, each with their drawers gaping open, papers peeking coyly out, their tops buried under papers and other unnamed things. His desk was likewise buried, so were two chairs, a side table, and several square feet of floor.

There was no phone, no fax, no computer, no typewriter. There was nothing to make bookkeeping and filing easier except some bound books that looked to be ledgers and journals and file folders still boxed and hiding under one end of the side table. But none of that bothered Jane too much. It was the sorry state of the thick, creamy paper. It was obviously expensive and probably handmade and just as obviously orders, bills, receipts, unanswered correspondence. Those nagged at her.

It was Jane's own business training and experience that made her say, probably nastier than she needed to, "You ought to be ashamed of yourself. This is an absolute disgrace. How on earth can you run a business like this?"

Red burned his face, as it was wont to do in Jane's presence, and Farrel, without quite looking at her, stammered out what could be called either an excuse or an explanation. "After Cordelia's interdict took... The man who did the books...His wife was one of the women who was spirited away and—He didn't want to stay here without her, so he left and...Jane, I don't know how to..."

Trying not to be too judgmental, but practically rubbing her hands with glee, Jane asked, "How long has it been?"

"Months." Farrel took a deep breath, expelled it slowly, and added, "It's getting on into fall and that's when we have our roundup, cull out the herds, and do a lot of selling. It's...I really don't know what to do now, but I'm afraid this is going to ruin me. I...I've been trying to figure out what..." He gestured helplessly. "It didn't look like this when he left, but now..."

Her hand dove into her omnipresent shoulder bag, searching for the solar calculator and her black-rimmed reading glasses. Jane smiled and did a little gesturing of her own, which including pointing toward the door as she asked, "Why don't you just go do whatever it is that you do and let me take care of this?"

Horror was thick in his voice when he said, "I can't do that, you're a *woman*."

She had known that for any number of years and hadn't found it too hard to accept. "Yes, I am. So?"

"Women can't..."

As reasonable as humanly possible, at least under those rather peculiar circumstances, Jane asked, keeping her voice even, "Why? Is there a law or something that forbids it? Or is that just one of the more asinine rules of a male-dominated, frightfully ignorant society?"

Farrel flushed again, came out from behind the desk, and said, sounding too polite by half, "Jane, I'm sure that your world is perfectly fine place. And I certainly don't want to seem discourteous, but on this world things are different."

"How?" Jane asked, more tempted by the smell and feel of paper and the lure of numbers than by his nationalistic, or would that be worldistic, views of what was right and proper. It didn't really matter; she wasn't going to be involved in his world any longer than it took Will to do his deed and get her gone.

Max looked at her, took a step closer, reached out as if to brush back her short hair. It had managed to go completely wild, with the aid of the minerals in the water and the lack of conditioners.

Jane stiffened, lifted her chin, looked him in the eye, and said, "Well, are you going to tell me or not? If you're not, why don't you get out and let me get to work. If you are, just get on with it. But, whatever you do, make it quick. I don't intend to hang around doing nothing while you..."

She almost said, "While you blow smoke," but changed it to, "While you dither around about what's right and proper. There's nothing proper about me being here, or your Cordelia's hand in it, so what's your beef?"

His hand drew back, rather rapidly, fell to his side, and Farrel stepped back. "It's just that...On this world, no one except wizards, scribes, number-keepers, and a few eccentrics, can read or write beyond what's needed to sign their names and other small chores."

Jane felt a moment of pity, one that made her ask, rather softly, "Can you?"

Shaking his head, Farrel said, "I really can't. That's why the office..."

"Then, Mr. Farrel," Jane said, "that's why you should go brand unicorns or something and let me do what I do best, which is read, write, and crunch numbers."

"If that's what you want," he said, what could only be admiration brightening his incredible eyes, making him smile down at her.

Jane thanked him. She was too busy sorting papers to even know when he left the room, closing the door behind him, but not before he paused, looked back at her, and smiled again. It was a very bemused smile, but far from enigmatic, almost lustful.

CONCEALED IN shadow, some of which were of his own making, Sojourner saw the rancher and read the smile a-right. Max Farrel was falling in love with Jane—and that should have been good. But it wasn't! By all the forgotten gods, it wasn't!

His lip drew back in a silent snarl and he slipped, as silent as the shadows that hid him, down the hall, following the man. Jane Murdock, the woman with the midnight eyes and fiery soul, was his, was born to be his One True Love, coming from beyond time and space to fulfill a destiny long delayed.

Knowledge took his fury, old knowledge, knowledge of deeds done and lives destroyed, terrible knowledge of change and transformation, of loss, unending loss. Jane was no longer his; she was all woman, all night and fire. He was a cat. Only that, nothing more. A cursed cat who was doomed to wander or die. He could not gift her with that.

He turned, padded back down the way he had come, took up his silent vigil outside the closed office door. Turmoil churned within him, turmoil that could never be resolved—and within that turmoil was love, enduring love, eternal love. He couldn't have her as wife, but he could, and would, watch and protect his love until Will could send her safely home. Or until his own weakness and the unabating fever took his life.

THE BEGUILING odor of spice, exotic spice, drifted under the door, wafted its way across the office and, as immersed as she was in the flood of paper, touched Jane's nose. She recognized it instantly, and that recognition drove all thoughts of business from her mind.

The opals on her fingers burned, reminded her of the icy dream, but the memory fled in the face of a greater need. Jane clenched her long fingers into fists, dug her blunt nails into the palms of her hands. It was crazy, beyond crazy, but she desperately wanted to jerk the door open, to fling her arms around the great cat, to know the man who dwelt inside. To know him in all ways.

Heat coursing through her, burning hot and hotter with its own need to be quenched, she sat down behind the desk, in Farrel's leather chair, and stared at the door until tears came to run unchecked down her face.

"Will," she finally whispered, knowing no one would hear her plea, "please find Maggie and the rest of the brides. I have to go home. I can't stand much more of this."

Chapter 15

CRYING WAS FOR fools, namby-pamby, whining women with nothing to occupy their so-called minds but silliness about love and all the rest of that stupid junk. The sighs, the quivers, the shortness of breath, and the warm, ignorant dreams that went with it.

Jane had never been such a woman, and she didn't intend to become one now. No indeed! Both crying and loving were snares for fools, and she knew she wasn't one.

Wiping away her tears with the sleeve of her blouse, a frilly, pink, overly-feminine blouse that she detested, Jane sat behind Farrel's big desk without moving. She let her disordered thoughts wander where they would as she tried to regain control of herself. She fought to regain the practical, logical, reasonable Jane that had ruled her life with an iron hand; not even bothering to hide it in a velvet glove.

It was a loveless life and if she ever managed to return to it, she would breath a big sigh of relief. But still she wondered what would have happened if...What the if was, Jane didn't know. Nor would she ever know, but she did know, if only dimly that somehow destiny had been thwarted, twisted into something ugly and painful.

Telling herself the current emotional aberration, the fixation on Sojourner, the burning need to touch him, to know him had to be some sort of illness. It was the probable result of the traveling spell. Will had said that some people got travel sickness, hadn't he? Well, that's probably what was wrong with her. No well person would go all silly over a silver-eyed cat, would they?

It wasn't a question that she could answer truthfully, so she avoided it, sent her thoughts down a new, and less emotionally charged, path.

If love ever came into her life, which she really doubted, she'd rather take matters into her own hands and...And what? Act like the fair Cordelia? Disrupt other people's lives? Throw temper tantrums if she couldn't have exactly what she wanted? No, not like Cordelia.

Like Maggie then? Fall in love with a man from another

world, a wizard at that, and go... *Whither thou goest, I will go.* That quotation from the Bible leaped unbidden into her mind, and Jane knew, where love was concerned, there were no safe paths. All roads led to disaster.

Jumping up, calling all her old habits of work and concentration into being, Jane set about the task she had appointed herself. She *would* get Max Farrel's affairs in order before she went home, and she wasn't going to loll around like some hormone-driven adolescent while she did it. That was for damned sure.

It took her several days, but the office was tidy and Farrel's books were in order when Coodie tapped on the door and said, "Jane, there be riders coming. The boss be thinking it be the posse a-coming back after the wizard. Best be getting out a-sight."

Wasting no time, Jane did exactly that. She stayed out of sight for the full three days of the posse's visit. On the second morning, she heard a slight sound outside her door, a thump like something falling and what might have been a very self-satisfied giggle—a feminine giggle where one couldn't possibly have existed.

When Jane took a cautious peek, all she found was a small, red book, what was, evidently, a child's first book of magic, but nothing else. She assumed either Will or Farrel, or maybe even Coodie, had left the book to help her pass the time while she was incarcerated.

She read through the primer rather quickly and then read it again—at a far slower pace. It gave her several matters to contemplate; none of which added much to her attitude, which was, by that time, surely in sore need of a fairly radical adjustment. To put it mildly, Jane Murdock was in a snit, was irritated, and was even feeling bitchy as hell. And the way she saw it, she had ample reason.

Despite all Will's high-minded, holier-than-thou statements regarding magic and the wielders of same, he was just a scholar. Wizardry was a scholarly pursuit, and he was just doing research, looking through books to find a spell, actually directions, like a recipe, that would enable him to find Maggie and the rest of the brides.

That really made Jane furious. She could read, damn it. She could have, probably, cut his job in half, or, at the very least, made it a lot more efficient. And she could have gone home long before she got into her present state, which was probably brought on by boredom, not by love or any of the rest of that silly claptrap.

And she certainly intended to inform Will of that fact, carefully edited, of course, just as soon as the noose-happy posse departed and she was free again. Damn Will anyway, this was all his fault. His and that...that...Not even in her irritation could Jane bring herself to damn the cat. Sojourner was...

She didn't know what he was and didn't dare think about him long enough to figure out the truth; if such a thing were actually possible. She shook her head, drew back her arm, and threw the small book across the bedroom with a fury that gave lie to reason and logic.

Anger, distrust, and a love she didn't want and wasn't about to take churned inside her, producing heartburn and not much more except pure frustration. She wanted to break something, smash glass, bust furniture, but she didn't. Jane Murdock just sat there, legs dangling down from the edge of the bed, and glared at the door.

WILL LOOKED AT Sojourner out of the corner of his eye, shoved his fingers through his messy hair for the fifteenth time, and said, weariness and defeat in every tone, "There's no hope for it otherwise."

His once smooth coat roughened by the unremitting fever, his silver eyes tarnished, dull, the great cat didn't move. He just stood, staring out the window, watching as the marshal and the posse mounted dancing, fidgeting unicorns and rode off, their expelled breaths clouding the air with vaporous white, into the first really frosty morning of autumn. By not so much as a muscle twitch did he indicate he had heard, much less understood, what the young wizard was asking of him.

Torn between loyalty to Sojourner, new love and old, and his own oath of honor as a wizard, Will tried again. "Cordelia has Maggie and the others, I know that for sure now. And that means I have to... Sojourner, please, try to understand. I saw the brides and they...She has them penned, like animals, and they were hungry and dirty and crying like...Maggie wasn't crying. She was..." His voice broke.

Will swallowed hard before he could say, "She told them that I would come. That I would save them. Don't you see? I have to go. She...Sojourner, I would give you my soul if I could, but I..."

"You love her then? This Maggie? She has your heart?"

The words came, soft and caring, to his mind, and Will could give the great cat nothing less than the full truth—he owed him that, and more. So much more. "I love her, yes, but I can't tell her so. She's promised to someone else. I made the promise and I can't have..."

"Young wizard, the young woman will make up her own mind. That, I know, was written into the bride contract that both brides and bridegrooms signed. Perhaps she is wise enough to know your worth."

As if he were confessing a terrible secret, Will walked over to where the cat stood and said, "I cannot ask her. She came here, to this world, because she wanted a husband, a house, and babies. I cannot give all those things to her, at least not soon, and possibly never. I can't ask her to settle for less."

Sojourner changed the subject. "The curse pulls at me. I cannot deny it much longer, the wanderlust fills me and soon I must..." He turned stiffly, walked across the room with no remnant of his previous grace. "But, young wizard, I cannot go as long as..."

"Jane?"

His cough sounding like bitter laughter, the cat said, beginning to pace the bedroom, detouring around stacks of books, a table and chair, and several other traps for unwary feet, "Jane? A common name for an uncommon woman. She owns my heart, young wizard, and I cannot leave this place for as long as you let her linger on this world; not even if staying takes my strength, makes me a puling babe, and I..."

Sick at heart, but knowing he had to ask his question one more time, Will followed him. "Max Farrel and his men are going with me to raid Cordelia's castle and free the brides. Jane can't ride and Farrel says you frighten the riding unicorns, so neither of you can go with us."

Sojourner stopped pacing, eased down to the floor, and laid his massive head on his forelegs, but he said nothing.

"Please, try to understand. Jane isn't safe here. The posse is coming back; for her safety, they can't be allowed to find she's still alive." His voice dropped lower. "And even if she could ride one of the unicorns, she can't go with us. Cordelia isn't to be trusted—I'm afraid she would harm..."

Sighing heavily, Sojourner finally broke his silence. "Ask her, ask the woman with midnight eyes if she will be my companion for the time of your going. But, be warned, she fears me greatly, and rightly so. The love that was so long destined pulls at her, and if let free from all restraint, will surely destroy us. But, young wizard, if that be her choice, I will abide by her wishes. I can do no less."

THE BOOK WAS clutched, far too tightly and with far too much anger, in Jane's hand when Coodie tapped on her door and told her she was free, for the moment anyway. Black eyes blazing, long skirts flurrying, she stormed out of the room with a bare thank-you to the cook and went in search of Will. She fully intending to find the wizard and enlighten him as to the proper way to deal with a woman of her ilk.

The cover of the magic primer felt warm beneath her fingers and Jane thought, or imagined, she heard laughter, malicious laughter. But she didn't pause in her self-appointed stalk of Will and her quest for justification. Not even when the hair on the back of her neck, curly hair that now revealed too many inches of its black roots, tried to stand on end, to warn her of some unknown, but very potent, danger.

She was too damned mad to worry about some piddling danger. What could hurt her anyway? The posse was gone. And Sojourner would never...

"Where did you get that?" Will's shout jerked her around to face the dining room, where the wizard stood, whey-faced and twitching.

Jane took two long strides toward him before he broke free from whatever was holding him. He raced toward her, muttering spells, twisting his hands into what had to be arcane gestures, trying, and just as obviously failing, to birth some magic.

Why she neither knew nor cared. Maybe he was just trying to keep her from waving the magic book in his face and demanding to be allowed to participate in the search. Whatever he was trying, it wasn't working, so the wizard resorted to other, more physical means to get the chore accomplished.

He tackled her, knocked her back against the wall, and shouted with pain as he wrested the book from her gripping fingers and threw it toward the front door. Landing without a sound, it burst into instant flame, blazed high, burned hot, and smelled like feathers, oily, over-ripe feathers from a scavenger bird burning in a plague fire.

"Where in the hell did you get..."

Will's question was aborted by the sudden appearance of Cordelia, or rather of Cordelia's beautiful face, hanging suspended in empty air, and Cordelia's laughter, a sound no movie villain would have been shamed to claim as his own.

The female wizard tossed her head, flipping back a tendril of her lovely hair, and said, looking directly at Jane, "So, whore, you want to be a wizard, do you? I'll be happy to help you to that end. All you have to do, whore, is learn how to read. Catch."

Another book, not much larger than the primer but bound in leather, and having ornate brass corners and a heavy brass lock, tumbled through the air toward her. Will tried to bat it away, but it evaded his waving arm and drew a bead on Jane's head, flew like a missile, seemed intent on Jane's destruction.

Without time for thought or plan, Jane raised both hands, caught the flying book, and held it for a long moment before Cordelia said, "Good catch, whore. When you learn how, read it from beginning to end. I'm sure it will give you something to contemplate until I come for you and send you back to your proper place: Jake's."

Her snicker had an ugly, almost evil sound and she added, "Two-bits is actually a bit over-priced for your sort of merchandise. I don't actually need the money, so maybe this time, you'll be on the house."

Cordelia began to fade and was almost transparent when Max Farrel, his handsome face bleak, came in from outside, saw the female wizard, and asked, his voice cold with dislike, distaste, and disgust, "What do you want?"

She smiled, pouted, and licked her full lips before she said, in a throaty voice, "You."

His skin got grayer and he seemed to age before he straightened, drew himself up to his full height, and thundered, "That's never going to happen. Get out! And stay out!"

She laughed again, said, "Don't get too cozy with the whore, Maxie love, you belong to me and I always claim what's mine." Cordelia puckered her lips, made a kissing sound, and faded to nothing visible.

But not before Jane had caught a quick glimpse of the corral behind the lovelorn wizard. It was an uncovered, open to the elements corral that held a filthy, terribly tired-looking Maggie and a multitude of other women. And there were far too many women to be just the twenty or so brides that Will had signed up in New York.

Jane swallowed hard, trying to rid her throat of a lump of very real empathy for the abused women in Cordelia's grasp. Then she snarled, directing the words at both Will and Farrel, "Why in the hell are you just hanging around here? Those poor women will die if...Damn it, Will, why aren't you doing something?"

Both men looked at her rather strangely, but only Will had enough courage to ask, "Jane, what are you talking about? Did Cordelia spell you with..." He muttered something, made a few passes with his hands, and then shook his head.

"Stop being an idiot. Those women are right out in the sun and the rain without any shelter whatsoever. And from the looks of them, dear Cordelia hasn't been feeding them with anything near a lavish hand."

Will's hands were on her shoulders, shaking her, his demanding voice was loud in her ears, shouting questions, almost before she saw him leap toward her. "You saw them? Where? How?"

Farrel was asking the same questions in the background, but he seemed to think Jane had been so frightened by the sudden appearance of the female wizard that she wasn't able to think straight, was imagining things.

Will thought otherwise.

Jane knew otherwise. Not even looking at Farrel, she told Will exactly what she had seen, and even included the deduction she had drawn from the number of prisoners in Cordelia's corral.

The foreman, who had joined the group without Jane's knowledge, probably coming in from the kitchen with Coodie, who was also an avid listener, was the first to speak. His voice was icy with anger when he said, "My mother be with those women, boss. I be going after her and ain't no be-damned stinking she-male wizard gonna stop me."

He was half-way to the front door before Will said, "We're all going, but we're going prepared. Cordelia is acting like a spoiled child, but she is far from a child and she has power that..."

"My mother be a good woman. I'll no be having her hurt or treated wrong. So, you'd best be getting prepared, wizard, 'cause I be going with you or without you. And, I be going right soon."

"Wait." Max Farrel's voice held the ring of command, and the foreman obeyed, if somewhat grudgingly. "Do you know where her castle is?"

The shake of the foreman's head set his mustaches to wagging, but the stubborn purpose never faded from his eyes. "I be finding it."

"Do you know, wizard?"

"Yes, but..."

"No, buts," Farrel said. "We'll saddle up and be out of here in an hour."

"No, not like that." Will's mouth and eyes held their own form of stubbornness, and he obviously wasn't going to be dissuaded. "She has them spelled and warded against everything known to man. If we go in like that, Cordelia will win. Besides, it's a full day's ride, we'll need bedding and food—and food for the women if we can free them."

"Take care of it," Max said to Coodie and the foreman. They weren't slow in their departures, one back to the kitchen, the other out the front door.

"There's more," Will said, giving Jane the barest of looks before he dug at his scalp with his fingers. "Sojourner can't go, and we can't leave Jane here. Cordelia knows where she is, and the posse might come back before we finish what we have to do. I can't go until I know both of them are in someplace safe."

"I'm not going to stay with Sojourner!" Jane fought to bring her panic-shrilled voice down to a more acceptable level before she added, "I'm going with you."

"We're going to be riding, Jane, and you would only slow us down," Farrel said. "Besides, the waddies would..."

"If we lose," Will said slowly, "Cordelia would have you in her power. She would delight in sending you back to..." He stopped, took a deep breath, and said, very softly, "Please, Jane, Sojourner is so weak I'm afraid he...Stay with him, please, and just as soon as the brides are freed, I'll send you back to your own world. I swear it on my honor as a wizard."

Every instinct, every ounce of her self-preservation, every ounce gut reaction, told her to scream, "No," at the top of her voice and run for her life. But Jane's own honor made her say, not very graciously, "Okay, but you'd better be damned quick in your saving."

Chapter 16

THERE WERE NO stars out. The wind had died with the setting sun; the bird sounds, few as they were, had dwindled into nothing shortly thereafter. Darkness was cold and heavy all around her, strangely odorless, oddly soundless, awfully close to being, if not quite totally, intimidating. She wanted to get up slowly and creep back into the wizard wagon, but still Jane lingered, hugging the woolen shawl around her narrow shoulders, tucking the long skirts more firmly about her long legs.

Huddling on the back step of the wagon, she felt forlorn, like a lost child, the child she had truly never been. She hoped that weariness was all that was causing the feeling of strange oppression, the sense that something was brewing beyond her limited vision. Something that meant her no good, no good at all.

Fighting off her skin-prickling, but unfocused fear, her melancholy memories of a sparse, joyless childhood and of an aunt, now long dead, who had raised Jane, taught her, but never loved her, Jane clutched her large purse with both hands. She held it, with Cordelia's brass-bound book of locked magic carefully concealed inside, against her chest as if it was a lifeline, the only connection between her and the world she had been torn away from without her leave or permission.

And, as far as that went, the heavy black purse and its jumbled contents were exactly that. Her familiar clothes were gone, so was Maggie, her secretary, and now even the wizard was elsewhere. Jane was alone in the wilderness with a huge black cat, a bright-red wagon, and a gift-book from a deranged lovesick female wizard. A book Will had seemingly forgotten almost as soon as Cordelia had thrown it at Jane's head. And Jane was, to put it mildly, not exactly enjoying any part of the whole unadulterated mess.

The back step of Will's gaudy wizard wagon wasn't, by any stretch of the imagination, a comfortable seat, especially with the maw of the steep-walled canyon just beyond the cumbersome vehicle's present resting site. It was parked near the banks of a small, and what should have been noisy, mountain stream, and within the thicket of young evergreens, that should have been pungent but weren't. All they did, supposedly, was surround and hide the wagon's overwhelming redness from too interested eyes. Or so she sincerely hoped; and just as sincerely doubted.

Still, it was the safest place she could be, or so Will had said, several times, as he rushed around the camping place, talking rapidly, setting the concealing spells and the wards against danger. So Jane would be protected and Will could put her and Sojourner out of his mind and go galloping off to rescue his ladylove and the rest of the fair maids. And others not nearly as fair, all caught in Cordelia's foul clutches.

"Cordelia'll not find you here and neither will the posse," he told Jane as he mounted a crow-hopping, long-horned, black-and-white unicorn, "and we'll be back in less than a week to get you. By then, the brides and the rest of the women Cordelia is holding captive will be saved and you'll be free to go back to your world."

She had been tempted to wail, "I'll never be free," but old habits, and hard won, refused to allow such a display of unseemly emotion in front of anyone. Instead she had nodded in what he probably thought was agreement. She stood beside the wagon, and watched Will, Farrel, and a horde of saber-armed waddies ride off to do battle with, as the foreman had so aptly put it, a be-damned she-male wizard. She would have worried about the men and the wizard's prisoners both if she'd had any worry to spare, but she didn't.

Her worry was all for herself, and for the great cat that lay sprawled on a bunk inside the wagon. He was still fevered, and growing weaker by the day, and she was still scared livid of being cooped up in the wagon with him; and that fear wasn't of Sojourner.

So, in the hours since Will's hurried departure, she had stayed outside, trying to reduce the chaotic feel of the past two days into something with a distant kinship to sense.

It wasn't an easy task; as a matter of fact, the recent past wasn't much more than a blur, a foggy haze with a few moments of momentary brightness. She knew she had scoured her room and the adjoining bathroom, seeking out and removing every trace of her occupancy, packing not only her own new garments but the stolen hat, boots, socks, and pants—the shirt had been returned, with suitable thanks, to its owner, the villainous-looking ranch foreman.

The wizard wagon had been loaded, not only with her

meager belongings, but also with food supplies and some extra bedding. Either then or later, Will had taken her aside and given her instructions in the care and preparation of the food packets. Not that she understood one word in ten of what he was saying about magefires and setspells and triggerwords and all the rest of the gobbledegook he was giving her. But she did remember, with great care, the medicine dosages he was prescribing for the cat.

The wagon ride itself had taken most of a day—a day of bouncing and jouncing over non-roads, out of Farrel's valley and high into a maze of canyons, table mountains, and severely untamed wilderness of brush, stunted juniper trees, oaks, aspen, and what smelled like sage. And then, after the wagon had be situated, the team unharnessed and led away to a place of better forage, Will and Max Farrel, looking too damned eager and excited to suit her, rode off with a full force of waddies to tilt with magic and interdicts, and she was alone, sitting in the dark, scarcely daring to breathe.

Emotions she didn't want to feel, clamored at her, tried to make her enter the wagon, put her hands on the cat, and see and feel him as he really was. See the man, the tall, lean, bronze-skinned man, not the silver-eyed beast. But she couldn't. She didn't dare—that single touch would be her downfall. And Jane Murdock wasn't ready to fall.

"Or maybe," a tiny mocking voice whispered, a voice that might or might not have been her own, "you have already fallen, are already doomed. Baited with excitement and need, love is a trap, a snare; you can't escape."

Something rustled in the outer darkness, a branch snapped, something far bigger than a mouse crept through the small trees, some sinister something with nothing but evil intent. Or Jane told herself as she jumped to her feet and retreated, with mouth-dry, heart-pounding alacrity, into the relative safety of the wagon, pulling the door closed behind her.

It was dark, too dark to see the great cat, but she knew he was there, too close, on the other bunk. Despite her better judgment, that's assuming she still had any at all, she blurted out, "There's something sneaking around outside! Something big!"

He moved. Jane knew that much, could hear his body shift on the blankets, could smell his spicy odor, but she didn't have time to do much more than that. Because, at that moment, all hell broke loose.

That is if hell can be described as thunder cracking, directly overhead and deafening in its intensity, lightning flashing, blue-white and blinding, and rain. A rain of biblical proportions, a water balloon as large as the moon bursting directly over the wizard wagon, pouring in streams rather than drops, and gaining in intensity by the minute.

The rain beat against the wagon. Shook it. Pounded it. And roared over it, around it, like a raging river, a river gone mad, in a world where magic lived and technology didn't, a world where a huge black cat was a silver-eyed man. A man weakened by fever, by the wanderlust of his curse, a man who held her, sheltered her in his arms, whispered softly, too softly to be heard above the crashing thunder and beating of the rain.

She didn't know how it had happened, how her own arms had gone around him, holding on as if he were that last bastion of safety in an insane world, a shelter in a storm that couldn't possibly be natural. But she didn't loosen her embrace; she couldn't have, even if she had wanted to, which she didn't.

She screamed, hoping the words would drive through the storm noise and find his ear, "It's Cordelia, isn't it? A magic storm?" And acknowledging the magic didn't even give her a qualm, a shudder, or a moment's doubt.

Feeling his nod of agreement against her hair, Jane barely managed to shout, "What now?"

Her answer came, only too quickly, but it didn't come from the man. It came from without, and it came fast and loud and with murderous intent. And there was no stopping it. The wagon was little more than a chip in a maelstrom, and in the grand nature of things, Jane and Sojourner were lesser still. Cordelia's magic ruled their world, and her magic drove the wind, the rain, and the flooding waters, drove them hard, built them high.

Louder, by far, than thunder, or a jumbo jet taking off, or even a rock band with full amplification, the answer came upon them in a wall of water. It rammed into the wagon, battered it, turned it, tumbled it, beat it, and had little regard for the fever-weakened man and the woman with the midnight eyes who clung together inside.

"Flood!"

The single word sounded inside her head, but Jane didn't need it to explain what was happening. That was fairly easy to deduce from the their rate of travel, rapid passage into the canyon and beyond, away from spells and wards and safety, into a greater unknown.

But Jane didn't have time to fear their eventual destination, she could only fear what was happening at the moment. And that was more than enough. The water was, if her soaking body could be believed, seeping and/or gushing in through every crack, gap, opening, and seam in the wagon.

A wagon that was groaning and moaning like a mortally wounded beast and thrashing about, tilting and turning, whirling, and plunging into the water like that selfsame beast undergoing some truly violent death throes.

Death throes that seemed bent on adding both Sojourner and Jane's own smaller throes to its rather watery gymnastics. And it was fairly obvious, from the way drawers and doors were banging open, things were falling and flying, that the wizard wagon was undergoing some terrible, destroying throes of its own.

"Where's Noah when you need him?" Jane muttered after being whacked on the head by something both heavy and sharp, something that left a trickle of warmth to run down her face. Jane hoped it wasn't blood, but at that point, she wouldn't have bet on the certainty of anything. Except that the wagon had suddenly tipped to one side, was rolling over and Sojourner was trying, frantically, to hold her, to keep her away from the ravening hunger embodied in the raging flood. He couldn't keep her from being bruised, scraped, cut, and otherwise maltreated by Cordelia's magical display of her power, her contempt of Jane and Will.

The wagon's slow roll picked up speed, became not one but a series of rolls, each one tossing Jane and Sojourner about like corks in a whirlpool, slammed them into walls and cupboards, banged them about. And then the wagon, or the flood that gripped it changed tactics, cracked the vehicle against something hard and unyielding, upended it so that it fell on its top, filled with water, and began to break apart.

The fall was Jane's final undoing. A heavy something slammed, and slammed hard, across her head and shoulders. Agony gripped her, twisted through her, took what little breath she had left. Fighting against the pain, she gasped water into her nose and mouth, and the last thing she was aware of was stars, bright colored stars, racing toward her. And one star, more dark than bright, had Sojourner's face.

She wanted to scream, "Get out! Save yourself!" but it was too late. Water was in her lungs, and eternal darkness was oozing into her brain, taking her senses, leaving her limp.

ONCE, IN A long ago, almost forgotten time, he had been a warrior, a fierce mage-warrior and full brother to a king. Sojourner knew that, if dimly and in odd bursts of seeing, but that time was gone. It had vanished into the mists of memory lost in the horror attendant to the changing, the cursing that took the proud man he had been and left only the mourning beast. Now, he was a beast with a memory of being a man, a beast with its own sense of doom.

His world was reduced to a single moment, a dark moment filled too full of sound and fury, vile fury holding the smell of cruel magic, evil magic, magic meant solely for destruction. But Sojourner made no move to do battle, to scream his own challenge into the night, to fling bolt after bolt of his own magical fury, to defeat the magician at her own game.

He had the magic still, it breathed inside of him, but it had fallen victim to the storm and flood. She lay limp and lifeless in his arms, but Sojourner knew she wasn't dead. At least not yet. But she would be, and so would he if he didn't do something, didn't get her out of the water and into the night. He struggled against the awesome force of the flood inside the wagon. He half-swam, half-staggered, fell more times than was truly possible, added bruise after bruise, and somehow managed to gulp in small breaths of the air trapped in pockets here and there in the wagon. Working on will along, Sojourner, holding Jane close to his pounding heart, made his way to the back of the wagon— or what he hoped was the back.

But he didn't get a chance to open the door. Rearing up like one of the old dragons, coming down hard on a rock, the red wizard wagon split from end to end. It shattered open like a child-dropped melon, spilled out flotsam and jetsam and a tall, bronze-skinned man with a woman held tight in his arms. The angry flood waters rushed at him, tried to wrest the woman from him, but Sojourner, strengthened by love and manhood, held fast. He didn't release her even when the flood lifted him high, smashed him against a wall of stone. Although he could see nothing of its nature, he knew it had to be the broken and deeply fissured sandstone that made up the steep sides of the deep canyon. A canyon that had once yawned beyond the back of a parked wagon, a spelled and warded wagon that a young wizard had done his best to protect.

But the wagon was gone and the sandstone was their salvation. Using the last of his strength, Sojourner pushed Jane up onto the uneven rock face. He clambered up after her, and worked over her, pushing the water out of her lungs, setting one small healing spell in place to guard against lung fever. And then, guided by pure instinct or the trickster known as fate, he managed to drag her still, all-but-lifeless form up a slope and into the rock-rimmed, narrow mouth of a dark cave. Once there, he collapsed beside her on the sandy floor.

Sojourner knew he should strip off her wet clothes, warm her chilled body, but he hadn't the strength. His arms were around her, holding her close against his nakedness, trying to warm her shivering form even as he followed her into the dark pit of unconsciousness.

Breath rasped in and out of his burning lungs. His whole body was on fire with fever and the rocks and debris in the water had torn new gashes in his skin, letting his lifeblood seep out and be swallowed by the sand. He knew he wasn't in his right mind, that he might even be fever-dreaming that he was a man. It seemed to him that the raging waters, deprived of their prey, fell instantly quiet when he had hidden Jane away in the cave.

Sojourner didn't know that for the truth. All he knew was Jane was beside him and he was a man, a weak and fevered man already diving into the vast sea of nothing where his One True Love already swam. Perhaps they would escape its clutches and return to life. Perhaps.

But he didn't know that for sure either—and it was outside his ken, beyond his seeing, in the hands of fate and the old gods, all of whom were capricious and absolutely untrustworthy.

Chapter 17

SHAKING WITH COLD, with weakness, and quite possibly an all-devouring fear, Jane coughed, coughed hard, brought up nothing from her irritated lungs. She coughed again and again until the frenzied spasms brought her to the very verge of waking, made her semi-aware of herself and her immediate surroundings.

Her chest was on fire. Her throat felt raw and painful, but it didn't hurt nearly as much as her body, which was achingly aware of each and every one of its screaming, protesting parts. And, hanging in that shadowy space between sleep and waking, Jane couldn't quite figure out why she felt so battered or what it was she so desperately feared.

She knew only that the snarling, snapping pain and muscle stiffness was there, right along side of and mingled with the heat that toasted one side of her body, leaving the other side deathly cold and aching like a tooth gone bad.

Her clothing was dripping wet, a heavy, icy swaddle of clammy irritation, and she was lying on something hard, but shifting, uneven, like sand, fine dry sand. It wasn't truly uncomfortable, but it was strange, unfamiliar, a small puzzle in the middle of a much larger, far more pressing mystery.

In addition to the not-quite-all-there feeling, the free-floating fear, a vague wooziness, her head supported a mammoth ache, possibly the worst ache her head had ever had the displeasure to undergo. But it didn't end there, as Jane discovered when she attempted to open her eyes. It was not a terribly effective attempt.

One of her hands, the fingers cold, almost numb, explored her more obvious injuries. Her face was sore, swollen, especially down the left side, and that eye would only open to a narrow, puffy slit. What little she could see with her right eye did nothing to soothe her growing fear that she was lost, possibly being held captive in some foreign place, a place outside of time. Or maybe she had just been mugged, knocked in the head, given a concussion or something, and was hallucinating. She almost hoped that was true, that some evil person had done his deed and left her for dead in Central Park.

She knew, at some level, that she was falling prey to utter impossibilities, but knowing it logically did nothing to counteract her irrational response to what had to be greenish, phosphorescent light glowing softly on a ceiling of rock. It should have scared her silly, made her whimper and cower to discover she wasn't in Central Park, but it only made her mildly curious.

A ceiling of rock? Where on earth was she? Not on earth, she reminded herself somewhat sternly. Pay attention. You're wherever Cordelia...The female wizard's name struck a chord of memory, brought back, in flashes and shards, the night and the killer flood, and the terrors of the magestorm. It rightly pinpointed the source of her fear.

The chord also brought back full memory of Sojourner, and with the memory of the man, not the cat, Jane jerked into full waking. Or as full as her headache, and its underlying cause would allow; which was about half functioning power at best. And all things considered, Jane was far from her best.

It was a waking that did nothing to lessen her fears—it only changed them. And not for the better. Her water-wrinkled, icy cold hand, moving of its own need, reached out, touched the searing warmth next to her. And it didn't jerk back when it encountered smooth skin, skin that had to be bronze. Skin that covered a face that was burning hot, being consumed by a raging fever, the face of the man who had to have saved her life. She knew she could not have escaped from the flood on her own.

Her fear jumped out, embraced him. "Sojourner," she whispered, pushing the words out through swollen lips. "Sojourner? Please, answer me."

The arm encircling her shoulders tightened momentarily and he moaned softly, seemed to be trying to come out of what might be a healing, life-giving sleep, but, judging from the heat under her hand, probably wasn't. He moved again, ever so slightly, but he said nothing in answer to her heartfelt plea.

Moving down, her hand found his shoulder, his chest, settled over his pounding heart as she tried to count his pulse, tried to reassure herself that he was just sleeping, nothing more. That he wasn't terribly ill.

She wasn't convinced. Jane Murdock, the self-confident, self-assured, take-care-of-herself-and-no-one-else was shaken to the very depth of her being, twisted a hundred degrees off-center, and tossed, unarmed and terrified, squarely into the midst of her own wild emotions. Betrayed by reason and logic, trembling with the force of her feelings, Jane could do no less than admit the truth; at least to herself. For good or ill, she was, more than likely and against her will, in love with Sojourner, in love with a cursed man, in love with a stranger not of her world.

Then other knowledge hit her hard, far harder than her own admission of an emotional entanglement that was doomed from the start. Sojourner was sick, really sick, possibly dying, and there wasn't a doctor, a hospital, or an EMT in sight. She couldn't call 911, had never had a first aid course, and flat out didn't know what to do to make him better.

But she had to try; being who and what she was, Jane Murdock couldn't just stand by and let him die. She had to do something, even if what she did was wrong. But what? That was the big question.

Throat aching, and not just from the coughing she had done, Jane reached up, let her palm rest on his face, for just an instant, making a small, shy, unpracticed gesture of caring. It was a gesture she had never, not once, made in her entire life.

That done, she started, provoking an individual protest from each of her many cuts, abrasions, and bruises, to wiggle out of his arms and go in pursuit of some method of healing his illness. Some part of her mourned the fact that she had to leave him for even a moment, that small, trembling part, newly acknowledged, shy and innocent, wanted him ever close.

"Love," the voice came, faint and weak but somehow urgent, inside her head and Sojourner's embrace became tighter still—if only for a fraction of an instant.

Jane paused, waited for him to continue. It wasn't a long wait.

"Have care. The storm was magic-wrought. She hates you, fears you, and will not rest until...Stay. There's no danger for you here. The cave is warded." His message delivered, barely heard in the confines of her aching head, Sojourner's arms went limp. He released her as his illness regained full control, forced him back into the storm-tossed sea of fevered nothing without allowing him consciousness long enough to know whether Jane was going to obey his wishes or not.

Which, of course, she wasn't. She wanted to, but Jane knew she wouldn't be able to hide in the cave, if that's where they were, and allow Sojourner to die. Sighing, she raised herself to one elbow and fought the pain and dizziness that seemed intent on felling her.

His face was hidden in darkness, but that didn't stop her

from wanting to lean forward, touch him again, but she didn't—mostly because she was afraid she'd topple over on him and never be able to get up. And he needed her help far more than he needed any maudlin display of female emotion.

Jane said, knowing she was talking to herself and not to him, but needing to hear the sound of a human voice, "Rest now. I can't do anything until it gets light, right now I'm going to take off some of these wet clothes and..."

"And what?" she asked herself, not even aware that she was still speaking aloud. Shivering, her headache a bomb ready to explode, she managed to roll over, get to her knees, and sort of hunker there, breathing hard, fighting against pain in every misused part of her body.

"Build a fire?" she asked the silent cave, her mind sort of swooping and chattering, tossing up bits and pieces of old memories, most of them useless.

But one small chunk stayed, mocked her, or maybe taunted her best explains its impact on her current situation. She vaguely remembered a high school English class, a short story that was, maybe, by Jack London, something about a man, who was freezing, trying to build a fire. But he had matches—even if they weren't enough.

She had nothing. She didn't smoke, had no need for the book matches they gave away in restaurants. Besides, her purse was...Was where? Her brain wasn't tracking, kept jumping from this to that without any real connection between the various, and not germane, subjects.

But mostly, when it wasn't complaining about her various aches, pains, and general malaise, or jumping about like a hyper-active flea on a trampoline, her mind kept telling her to lie down, that she couldn't do anything for either of them. But Jane wasn't about to quit, or, at least, she hoped she wasn't.

If she could just concentrate, there was something nagging at the edge of her memory, something about a former client and gift, but... Maybe if she could just get warm, she would quit shaking and...Warm? She had to take off her wet clothes and build a fire.

She had to, that was all there was to it. Her cold fingers fumbled at the fasteners of her blouse, but the hooks and eyes were too tiny, her hands too clumsy to undo them and the wet fabric was too strong to tear.

Muttering an expletive, and then repeating it, and several of its more earthy Angle-Saxon cousins, a whole lot louder, Jane went down on her hands and knees and started to crawl toward some unknown destination. Her wet skirts bunched up under her knees, halting her forward progress. She reached down to jerk at the offending garments and felt something else. Something dear and familiar.

Jane was very near to tears when she picked up her heavy, water-logged purse and cradled it against her chest. And, as if utilizing some magic of its own, her pain-fuzzed mind retrieved a memory, the one that might, just possibly, be the answer to her hopes and dreams.

Knowing she was getting carried away, maybe even a tad euphoric, or possibly was a little mad, Jane opened the purse. Scarcely daring to hope, she, delved inside, searching through the soggy mess for the lighter, the gold-plated, monogrammed cigarette lighter one of her more grateful clients had given her as a token of his appreciation for her revitalization of his manufacturing plant; a plant that made, among other things, cigarette lighters.

She remembered thanking him and dropping it in her purse, but that had been...She didn't know how long ago, a week or two before she had been wizard-napped, but it might still be there. She didn't remember taking it out. Probably she hadn't. Her purse was a catch-all, the one area of her life that was disorganized.

Closing around the oblong of smooth metal, her hand was trembling when it brought its treasure out of the bag—which she dropped beside Sojourner as she focused all of her rather spotty attention on her new find. And her hand was trembling even more when she tried to flip the lighter wheel, or whatever it was, to make it light. Which it did, but not until her fifth or sixth panicked try.

The tiny flame, magnified by the glowing ceiling and a more subdued reaction from the sandy floor, cast an eerie light, more light than should have been possible from such a feeble, flickering source, but Jane didn't complain. Especially after she staggered to her feet, lifted the lighter high, and discovered a huge pile of leaves, twigs, small branches, and other unknown substances lying near the mouth of the cave.

Without giving the matter a moment's thought, Jane stumbled over to the pile and held the flame to the tinder dry, crumbly leaves. It was an instant conflagration, an inferno of less than Dante proportions but far more than adequate.

Jerking back her scorched hand, Jane retreated from the

towering fire, but not far enough to escape its welcomed heat. And the heat built almost as rapidly as the flame which crackled and danced, sent spikes of light to the furthermost recesses of the nearly round cave. It practically blazed off the ceiling, reflecting green and gold instead of red-orange. The light enabled Jane to survey all of their stony shelter, even the small trickle of water that dripped from the back wall into a tiny basin before disappearing in the glitter of diamond-bright crystalline sand that floored the cavern.

Almost round, with a short, narrow tunnel leading out into darkness, the cave wasn't much more than ten or twelve feet across and not more than a foot taller than her head. Within minutes the heat from her over enthusiastic fire had spread to the furthest corner. It happened so quickly that Jane suspected the wards Sojourner had set had something to do with magnifying the heat. But whatever the cause, the heat was more than welcome as it thawed Jane's icy fingers. It made them nimble enough, with stubborn persistence, to finally unfasten her blouse and skirt, untie her petticoat, and emerge in nothing more than kid slippers, knee-length drawers, and a lacy camisole. They were wet, too, but thin enough to dry rather quickly, besides that they didn't tangle and twine around her bruised legs like over affectionate animals, tripping up her still unsteady movements.

Dry as they were, the leaves, twigs, and whatever else had been in the pile didn't burn entirely smokeless. After the initial whoosh of flame, the fire had settled down to a snapping blaze that sent up a steady column of whitish smoke, smoke that had no chimney or other means of escaping the confines of the cave. The top of the entry tunnel was a foot or so lower than the cave proper and there were no other cracks, crevices, or other means of exit. The smoke drifted up, filled the uneven ceiling and layered itself downward until Jane's one good eye started to water, informing her that her fire building, as warm as it had made her surroundings, had created other problems.

With some barely formed plan of bathing Sojourner's fevered body with her wet petticoat, she coughed, swore, and crouched down beneath the choking blanket smoke and glanced toward the man. The light was chancy at best, flickering bright and dim. It wasn't the light that slapped at her senses, told her she had given her heart to a being beyond her understanding, that there was nothing logical or reasonable about love. Or so she had been told by the various people in her former life who had been unlucky enough to fall into its sticky clutches.

Oddly, Jane still saw a man, a tall, lean man with silver-eyes and night-dark hair, but the man had a shimmer around him—and the shimmer was a cat, a great black cat. She blinked, wanted to rub her smarting eyes, to tell herself she was seeing things; but she didn't. She just stumbled toward him, dropped down at his side, and watched as her tiniest touch drove away all traces of the cat, left only the man. He opened his silver eyes and tried to smile at her as she bathed his burning face and body with her storm-soaked petticoat.

"You must go back," he said softly, the words soft, tender, an almost caress within her muddled brain. "Find Will. Make him send you to your own world."

"No."

"My love, if you die here, I...Please. I have to know that you are safe."

Her mouth set, probably to keep her lips from quivering, Jane swiped the wet petticoat across his naked back, turned the material so he would benefit from a cooler spot, and swabbed at him again. She said, sounding just as stubborn as she was feeling, "Forget it. I'm not going anywhere without you, so if you want me out of here, wherever here is, you'd better concentrate on getting well."

"Love," now his voice was sorrowing, "I love you and I have since first I saw your midnight eyes staring at me out of the Old Derna's fire. Alas, that was long ago when my seeing was true and dreams were real."

Perhaps what he said was nothing more than the absolute truth, but Jane's love was too new, too freshly flowered to listen to his nay saying. She had to believe in dreams, if only for a little while, if only until Sojourner was back on his feet and she was ready to returned to her own earth. For now, all she could do was say, "We'll talk about it later."

His eyes closed. Jane wouldn't let him rest until she had found a bottle of aspirin in her purse and succeeded in getting two of the small tablets down his throat, with the aid of some water she dipped up with her petticoat and wrung out in his dry mouth.

"Do not love me," he said, the tardy order a tiny whisper in her mind.

"I won't," she answered, fully aware that she was lying in her teeth, that, in some unknown and unknowable way, she had loved him all of her life and couldn't stop even if it meant her total destruction.

And when he finally slept, Jane sat beside him, her hand on his arm, until pale sunlight glowed beyond the mouth of the cave and the fire had burned itself down to a heap of ash and ember. And then she got stiffly to her feet, moved away from him, despite the deep voice inside her mind, a male voice that said, "No, love, don't go."

Chapter 18

"LOVE, DON'T GO. Wait until my strength returns enough so that I can ward and protect you."

It sounded exactly like a command, and Jane was far more used to giving commands than obeying them. Besides, if they were going to ever get out of wherever Cordelia's fury had sent them, there might not be any time to be wasted in waiting around like some frail female. Too timid and weak to take care of herself. That wasn't Jane Murdock. They both knew it; even if he was, in male fashion, loath to admit it.

She hoped the aspirin she had just insisted on poking down his unwilling throat would again do their job and lower his fever to a more tolerable level. Ignoring his order and the stiffness in her own body, Jane Murdock bent her head, to keep from banging it on the low ceiling, and crept through the short, rocky tunnel that connected their shelter with the outer world. Heart beating a little too fast, breath coming a little quick, she paused at the far end to peer, with considerable caution, at what lay beyond the mouth to the cave.

Anticipating danger, magic, and heaven alone knows what other kinds of weirdness, ugly things that go bump in the night, or leap out at you in the day, Jane's expectations weren't even close to being met. Except for a large number of stunted trees, bare of leaves, and clinging to the wall of the canyon, there really wasn't much to see from her particular vantage point. Not that that bit of the non-threatening even came close to stilling the labor of her over-achieving heart and lungs.

"Don't worry," she called softly, directing the words back over her shoulder, "I won't go far." She stepped out of the tunnel and straightened up, rather slowly and with a goodly amount of muscle reluctance. Frost glittered coldly in the first light, but the sun was barely risen. Deep blue shadows still hovered in the crevices and crannies of the morning earth, hiding far more than the growing light revealed.

The deep, narrow canyon, whose wall housed their sanctuary, looked pretty much like any other canyon as far as Jane was concerned. It had high, steep, rocky walls, a rock strewn bottom, and was rather attractive in a reddish-brown, weathered kind of way. Not that it would even come close to matching the Grand Canyon, but for a small canyon it wasn't totally repulsive.

Or so Jane tried to convince herself; without much luck. It was a long, practically barren hole in the wilderness, pure and simple, and wilderness wasn't even on her A-list of good time places to be. She wasn't a pioneer, didn't want to be one. Jane Murdock had never even been to summer camp, let alone being a Girl Scout or any other of the woodsy, outdoorsy things. As far as it went, she had never even had a window box or a house plant.

In fact, she had never been interested in the wild, untamed growing aspect of the world. She much preferred city streets, tall buildings, and electric lights; not that she had much choice at the moment.

About thirty feet or so below the rocky ledge where Jane stood, a narrow stream of water, looped and meandering down the floor of the canyon, circling boulders and clumps of small trees. Even as Jane watched, tried to find danger hidden in every bush and stone, the yellowish sun rose higher, brightened the inside of the ravine. It reflected off the water, subdued the shadows, cast vague light into every possible hiding place; or, at the very least, a large share of them.

There was no apparent need for any sort of caution, no evidence of any thing untoward or evil. Gray-and-white birds, long legs dangling, yellows bills snatching fuzzy looking bugs from the air, flew up from a patch of small trees near the water, wheeled wide, and then settled again. A small brown, bushy-tailed squirrel or some other kind of wee beastie scurried across flat topped rocks to an old earth slide, setting new pebbles and sand adrift in a tiny squirrel-made avalanche. And down below the stream was tranquil, gurgling, frothed with white water at every rill, but essentially harmless—at least in its present form.

And, except for the wagon wreckage and other debris scattered about, Jane wouldn't have believed the stream had been Cordelia's weapon of choice to commit mayhem and murder the previous night. But it had to be.

Except for a few small, darkish-looking clouds hovering near the western horizon, what she could see of the sky was clear and sort of a deep gray-blue. It too looked harmless now, incapable of shooting lances of killing light—not that that did much to soothe away her uneasiness.

Wearing only a camisole and drawers and kid slippers that were too thin to offer much protection to her sore feet, Jane was shivery cold, stomach-growling hungry, and still far more fearful than she cared to admit. What she really wanted to do was sit down and bawl like a baby, but she was Jane Murdock and she didn't cave-in to vague fears and womanish vapors. No, by damn, she didn't and she wouldn't. Other people had survived in worse situations, and so would she. Survive and go back home to the world where she really belonged.

And the canyon certainly didn't look like the white carpeted, glass-walled home she was longing for. In fact, the whole scene spread out at her feet looked like it had been transported straight out of an Ansel Adams nature print, innocent, unspoiled, and quite beautiful. If you were into nature and such things, which Jane wasn't.

She sniffed, trying to unblock the passages in her swollen nose, and stood there, trying to convince herself it was just what it seemed and not a magical illusion waiting to gobble her up like she was a chocolate bon-bon.

The air was cold and still, the birds cheeping and making other bird noise. There wasn't a hint of danger, a trace of Cordelia, and magic seemed nonexistent. Nonetheless, she stood on the ledge for a moment longer, pressing her fist again the site of the nervous chills that had started in her stomach and were threatening to engulf her completely.

"Stop it," she told herself, whispering the words so the injured man waiting in the cave behind her couldn't hear a word, "stop acting like a ninny and go down and see what you can find. You both need food unless you would prefer starving to death. Cordelia would certainly approve of that."

She forced her unwilling feet to take a small, tentative step away from the cave, but she couldn't stop the flow of encouraging words that came from her lips. "If you intend to have a fire tonight, you need more wood, lots of wood. Sojourner needs a decent bed, and...Just get with it and forget Cordelia for now. Do what has to be done first and than take care of her when the time comes."

It was the best plan she could come up with at the moment. Still Jane muttered and grumbled and planned her way down the uneven slope and to the high-water mark where most of the wagon contents had been left by the receding flood. The rapacious water hadn't been exactly tidy, more like a world champion litterer, with its handiwork spread out for some distance. It had left a tangle of trees, limbs, stones, clothes, boxes, bundles, and other unknown items that might or might not be of value to an unlikely pair of castaways.

And, given their present situation, Jane didn't dare ignore a single thing, not even the very large, very dead green snake that was draped over a gilt-edged scrap of carving from Will's gaudy wagon.

THE OFF-WORLD medicine Jane had practically shoved down his throat had done its work far better than he had ever expected. While not gone, his fever was down, and Sojourner had enough strength left to stagger to his feet. Swaying, but determined, he looked around the cave. Jane's fire was all but out, giving no off no light, but to the great cat's eyes that was no real deterrent to seeing. He lifted his head, breathed deep, caught a faint animal scent, knew they weren't the cave's original occupants and strengthened the protective wards at the entrance tunnel before he walked, slowly and with great difficulty to the outer ledge.

That small effort sapped what remaining strength he had, left him weak, dizzy, but he had to be where he could see her. He had to know, if it cost him his last breath, that she was safe. Easing his body down onto the uneven surface of the rocks, the great cat stretched out in the sunshine, rested his massive head on his forepaws and watched Jane go about the tasks she had set for herself.

Will might see her as ugly and ill-tempered, but the wizard was young and sorely lacking in wisdom, judgment, and the true-sight. He would only see with worldly eyes, and Sojourner knew what the absent wizard would see.

Filthy and matted now, her gold-tipped ebony hair wasn't curling around her head. Bruised and scratched everywhere, one eye swollen and greenish-purple, her other eye large in her thin face, she looked weary, beaten, but that wasn't the truth either.

With her long, delicate bones, creamy skin, now abraded and dirty, and the stubborn jut of her chin, Jane Murdock, his forbidden love, was fire, honor, beauty, and fierce pride to Sojourner's seeing. And, beyond all else, she was love, an overpowering, bright-burning love that he couldn't take. It was a love that could only destroy her, take all she was and, in the end, leave her bereft and alone.

He could give her nothing. No home. No family. No stability. None of the things a woman's loving heart craved. All he had to offer was a cursed man and driving need to be always on the go, to seek in vain, to always wander. Even at the thought, the wanderlust tore had him, but his love for the woman with midnight eyes was too strong. It held him. He knew he should go at once, that it would be better for both of them, but he couldn't. Not yet.

Not until she was on her way back to her own world—an industrialized, reason-seeking world that had no place for such as he. It was the only future open to them, their destined love had come too late, but still Sojourner sighed and looked at her with a yearning heart and wanting eyes.

Needing, terribly, to fill his mind with memories of this woman, memories of the woman and a destiny he dared not claim. He had to have that much: memories he would store away, heart-tearing treasures that would make him want to weep when she was gone and he wandered alone. Like a hungry man at a farmers market, he watched her pick through boxes and bundles, piles of storm drift, pieces of the red wizard wagon. She brought her bits of salvage to the bottom of the trail, spread wet garments and quilts and other things out to dry, and threw broken items away as useless.

Gathering the memories carefully, he stored them away. Treasured the small shining moments, the tilt of her head, the lift of her arm, the smears of dirt that marred the whiteness of her garments, the impatient gesture as she wiped away the sweat that beaded on her brow. Sojourner relaxed his eternal vigilance. He lived only for that moment, that small space of time when they were together, set apart from the world, and she was truly his. If only in the foolish dreams he allowed himself to build, cherishing dreams that held both desire and nurture.

Love aching in his throat, he watched until the growing warmth of the sunshine eased some of his pain and weariness, took him into a restful place, a place where healing sleep beckoned. Even then he didn't retreat but stayed in front of the cave, napping and waking, until she, her arms full of wood for their fire, found him there.

She was a dirty-faced, scratched urchin, a tall, thin woman with weariness painting shadows under her eyes, but somehow a goddess straight from the thrones of the old gods. He ached with love for her when she stood over him, glaring down.

"What are you thinking of lying out here in the sun for so long?" she demanded. "Your back is red as a lobster. A sunburn is all you need..."

Her words made no sense. Sojourner raised his head, stared

at her. "Cats," he said slowly, and with what he hoped was great dignity, "do not sunburn."

"Men do," she snapped. "Especially men who lie around in the sun with no clothes on."

Sojourner couldn't believe what he was hearing. "I'm a man to your seeing?"

"Yes, and a naked one at that."

"But, how can..." He levered himself to his feet and knew she was telling nothing more than the truth when Jane, her face flushed with more than exertion, looked away from his revealed body, looked no lower that his shoulders, and said, rather softly and with a tinge of embarrassment, "Go in please. As soon as I dump this wood, I'll find you something...ah...something to wear."

"I beg your pardon, love," he said, shame rushing up to burn on his high cheekbones. "It has been so very long since anyone saw me as anything more than beast that I have forgotten the proper..." Despite his vows, his knowledge that nothing could be between them, Sojourner reached out, gently brushed his hand along the line of her jaw, felt her pulse leap under his fingers, and knew, with that single touch, he had brought his doom upon them, had destroyed them both.

Her eyes widened, at least one did, the other was too swollen to do much of anything. She just stood there, looking at him.

The breathless, fragile moment stretched beyond time, beyond dreams, stretched until it was severed by his tiny grasp on the last remnants of sanity. Rose-gold and sweet, love beckoned, promised eternal summers and delight exceeding hope, but it could not be. He would not be the instrument of her destruction.

Barely able to suppress a groan, letting his hand fall away from her beautiful face, Sojourner stepped away from Jane; but not before he had seen her terrible hurt, the sheen of unshed tears that burnished the blackness of her single visible eye.

SHAKEN BY BOTH his acts, tenderness and rejection, Jane had no gauge to measure her feelings against. She had never loved before, never experienced its joys and terrors, and was shy and vulnerable and hungry—and the chaos she was feeling scared her silly.

He had gone into the cave alone. She was still standing on the ledge, holding the wood, fighting her own battle with a body that was rebelling against discipline and reason, a body that had warmed at his touch, swore it loved him. Jane's mind quashed desires and needs and rampant fantasies with a heavy hand. The man was ill, weak with fever, and she wasn't entirely a fool or a lust-driven female. Jane Murdock was a woman and too much in command of her own life to fall apart at his merest touch; or so she tried to convince herself.

"Even fools can fall in love," one tiny part of her brain whispered. But Jane wasn't ready to listen. She had work to do, lots of work, before it was night again. And, by then, if she worked hard enough and long enough she wouldn't have the urge to close her eyes and run into the maze love had set before her. It was a maze of caring, desire, and dreams from which there was no real escaping. But, at that moment, escape, or any of its synonyms, wasn't even in her vocabulary. Neither were the two words that had always ruled her life: reason and logic.

But they, along with utter, mind-numbing weariness and an overwhelming sense of foreboding, a sense of events traveling too fast, had returned to their proper place by the time evening jumped into night. Jane's outside chores for the day were called because of darkness.

And now she had to face the night, a warm, fire-lit night, in a snug, dry cave, sleeping along side a long, lean, bronze-skinned man. Perhaps it was fear that made her ask, as she tripped a spell and set some of Will's magic food to heating, "Will and Max will look for us, won't they?"

His silvery eyes darkened and his answer was anything but comforting. "If Cordelia doesn't savage them with her magic, they will come." His voice grew infinitely more weary and he rubbed his hand across his face, took a deep breath before he added, "And, for both our sakes, I pray to all the old, forgotten gods that it is soon."

Jane knew he spoke nothing but the truth, and she wanted to join him in his fervent prayer, but she said nothing. They were both trapped; or perhaps cursed was nearer the truth.

Chapter 19

WEARINESS WEIGHED on her, demanded she get some rest, but Jane was a very long time going to sleep. She tensed at every sound Sojourner made, every rasping breath he drew, every fevered murmur that passed his sleeping lips. And all of her fear was for him, not of him.

The cave was crowded and untidy, but she didn't do cave work. Sojourner couldn't. Not only was he beset by fever weakness, he was a cat until her actual touch made him otherwise. Jane didn't understand that either. Mostly she could see the man and discount the shimmer of cat that surrounded him, but he couldn't. Jane squirmed into a more comfortable position on the hard bed and tried to think of something else.

The spoils of her day of hard labor, mostly magically preserved food and some still damp garments, were piled, helter-skelter, around the outer edge of the cave. With the dried branches and all pieces she could find of Will's storm-wracked wagon, firewood she had gathered, damning the labor intensive work with every drop of sweat on her brow, taking up the largest amount of the space. She had found both bunk mattresses, which evidently had been waterproofed and had suffered no great harm, and enough semi-dry quilts to make two separate beds. They were too close together to add anything to her peace of mind.

But his closeness, while it might add to her awareness of him, wasn't what was keeping her awake, fear for the silver-eyed man was doing that. His fever was back and her supply of aspirin was limited. And, nestled beside that worry was another demanding her attention. One that wouldn't give her any rest either.

She hadn't a clue as to their present whereabouts, but wherever they were, it had to be high in the mountains, high enough so that fall was nearing its end and winter was coming close. If it snowed, which she was sure it would, then they would be trapped. And their supply of food, while ample for their present needs, wouldn't last a winter, or even a month. Jane knew of no way to get any more.

She had to quit worrying about all that destiny and

mind-mushing love stuff and concentrate on getting him well. And, if Will and Max Farrel failed in their attack on Cordelia's castle and were blasted by the woman's rather vicious magic, then it would be up to Jane to get Sojourner back to someplace with a little more civilization. Maybe even to Wizardholm, where they could cure him and send her back to where she belonged, back to her job and her orderly life, back to where she really wanted to be.

And just before she finally dozed off her mocking, unbelieving inner voice said, "Yeah, sure." But the mockery stopped short when sleep pulled her deep and the unquiet dream began. It was a dream of a boy with wind-tangled ebony hair and silver eyes, a dream of that laughing, carefree boy and his brother. Both were handsome and wild, both sons of a mighty king and a powerful wizard, a foreign wizard who had bespelled the king, enchanted him, and married him; much to his subjects' utter consternation and displeasure. Or so it was said, never aloud, throughout the kingdom. It was a tale, perhaps untrue, that grew with the telling.

Jane knew that, and she knew also that the people feared Lizan, the black-haired wizard, as much as they loved Anthor, their king. She knew she was dreaming. She knew, too, that she had to dream, even if it wasn't a particularly riveting rendition of what could have been a minstrel's song or a bardic recitation of dark and evil deeds and love gone awry.

But it was neither of those. It was just an odd dream, more like a soundless docudrama with still shots and bits of moving pictures, all in sepia tones, spliced together and narrated by an anonymous actor, in an impartial, unemotional voice-over. Except, in Jane's dream, the voice-over came as knowledge, dry, impersonal as a history book written by a pompous scholar, inside her sleeping mind.

Jane knew she either had to be dreaming, or else she had fallen into some sort of half-baked teaching spell set loose by Cordelia. Her rational mind favored the dream theory because the subject matter seemed to be far removed from Cordelia's ken. Whatever it was, she knew she still lay on her pallet, practically touching Sojourner, as she watched his young life, and that of his just older brother, unfold.

At first, it was neither frightening nor unsettling, in fact, it was, if anything, just a bit boring. The young princes roamed the walled castle—an overgrown pile of stone that gave new meaning to the word sprawl. When they were older, they ventured further afield, going into the rather messy, narrow streets of the obviously unplanned town, also walled, that had grown up around the far from stately castle.

As they matured, the two boys were taught the princely graces: riding prancing unicorns with élan and grace, sword play with their Master at Arms, dancing with beautifully gowned maidens, hand-kissing of the same maidens and their older female relatives, and the dead-serious and sometimes deadly art of ruling. Even though only one, the older one, Damian, would grow up to marry the princess of the neighboring Kingdom of Seeting. They would govern those two kingdoms as one, under the joint rule of a king and a queen, as was set forth in the marriage contract signed by their two kingly fathers when Damian and his bride-to-be, the small, bright-haired Annette, were practically still in swaddling cloths; making it a marriage of state rather than one of love.

And only one prince—the younger one, the betrayer whose true name was no more, had even been erased from dreams—had been a wizard born, his mother's true son, if not the one first in her heart. Both facts, known far and wide, weren't facts that were lost on the fomenters of discord, the purveyors of lies, and the hungry for power; of which there were many, perhaps too many for so small a kingdom. All hiding behind smiling faces, hanging blood-suckers on the dark underbelly of a very rich kingdom.

Evil of intent, carefully placed by those who would see another on her throne, the whispers about Lizan grew ever darker, and it was not long before they found their devious way to King Anthor's ear. He loved his wizard queen and at first was loath to listen to any tales of her wrong-doing. Too soon, the whispers of blood sacrifice, demon conjuring, and other dread deeds came too thick to be dismissed as the nattering of envious fools.

They weighed on Anthor, invaded his rest, and in the end he, with his elder son at his side, visited his queen's chamber and told her what was being said and demanded to know the truth of it.

Queen Lizan didn't, by so much as a blink of her silvery eyes, acknowledge the fact that he had accused her of unholy acts. She just looked at him and said, "I would not have you think this of me, but demons exist in us all. And it takes only the smallest of things, not wizardry, to call them out, to make them our masters. I have loved you truly and well, Anthor, and that love has not yet soured into a bitter vintage. But, love alone is not enough, I can not live where..."

Not bothering to finish what she intended to say, she turned to her eldest son, who was now almost a man grown, and she said, "And you, Damian, is this also your belief?"

His mother's favorite, the chosen child, the only child of her heart, looked at her for a long, considering moment before he smiled, a truly beautiful smile, and said, "Yes, Mother, it is my belief."

With his smile still warming his face, if not the black cold that lived deep in his eyes, Damian added, "And if mine was the sentencing, I would send you to the block. Headless wizards conjure no demons."

BETWEEN ONE breath and the next, Jane came, instantly and heart-thumpingly, awake. The dream was still in her mind demanding attention, but that wasn't what made her grip her quilt in trembling fingers, sit up, and stare around the cave. It wasn't the dream that left her dry-mouthed with fear, it was the cacophony of snarling yips and deafening moon-howls coming from just outside the mouth of the cave.

The fire she had intended to wake and replenish, to keep burning throughout the night, was almost dead. It gave off only an ember glow and an occasional flicker of bluish flame, barely enough light to bring a reflective glow to the ceiling. It wasn't nearly bright enough for Jane to see if the howlers had actually invaded the caves.

As a city dweller, one who hadn't the time to even visit the zoo, she didn't know enough about wild animals to be sure, but she thought they were wolves. And, she was pretty sure it was a whole bunch of wolves, a huge pack of starving wolves who had a large craving for human flesh. She wasn't enjoying the thought of being their dinner one little bit.

Terrified, not knowing what to do, she leaned forward, reached out to touch Sojourner, to draw some small measure of comfort from his nearness if nothing more. Her questing fingers touched rumpled quilts, the still warm mattress, nothing more. Sojourner was gone.

"Where are you?" Jane's despairing wail was answered by the mind-chilling, goose-bump-making scream of a great cat, a fever-weakened great cat prepared to fight to the death to defend his love.

"And get his fool self killed in the process," Jane muttered as she jumped, rather slowly and with a smoking epithet or two at her own body stiffness, out of bed. She crept to the smoldering fire. And if her swearing was offensive, it certainly wasn't loud enough to be heard over howls of the attacking wolves and the defiant squall of the cat. Both of whom sent chills in a wild foot race up and down her spine, chills wearing spurs, using them to jab her into further action.

With fear for Sojourner first, and then for herself, as her motivation, Jane wasn't slow in working at the task she had chosen. Grabbing up several storm-splintered branches of what she hoped was dry wood, she poked them into the embers, stirred until the coals were hot and glowing, poked again, held the ends of the wood against the smolder.

She was almost in tears before the end of one of the branches started to crackle with a smidgen and then a slow spread of orange flame. She wasted no time dropping the rest of the branches across the coals and fanning the fiery tip of the brand into a real blaze. It might or might not be a formidable weapon, but was, for damned sure, going to light up the battlefield enough so she would know who the bad guys were.

Although vague memories of old movies spoke of methods and means of fighting beasts with fire, what she could actually do about them remained to be seen. On one thing her heart and mind were united: if Sojourner fell before the wolfish onslaught, he wasn't going to go alone. Not if she had anything to say about it.

And she certainly did, or so she thought; even if it was the last reasonably civilized thought she had. Adrenaline rushed through her, her old brain took charge, and she was in her fight or flight mode. Jane had never run away in her life, and she didn't now.

Like a tidal wave, an earthquake, or some other natural force, primitive emotion displaced all her reason, all her logic. Holding her fiery torch out before her, screaming like a berserker, Jane leaped into the tunnel, ran out to the ledge to take her rightful place at Sojourner's side.

Blazing high, the torch only served to enhance the blackness that pressed close to the ledge. If there were stars shining in the night sky, the canyon was too deep to allow their light to enter. There was only thick dark and the stark scene revealed by Jane's smoking beacon of feeble illumination.

Fangs bared, rumbling a deep-voiced warning, the great cat, and he was totally a cat to her seeing, faced three of their would-be attackers. A fourth, its throat torn and bleeding gouts of bright red, whimpered as it tried to crawl away from where it had been dealt what was surely a death wound. The great cat ignored it and its futile attempts at escape and screamed a wild challenge at the remaining trio of fell beasts.

Jane lifted the torch, pushed the light to new limits, and choked back a gasp of disbelief. Whatever they were, the blue-white animals certainly weren't any of the wolves she had ever seen pictures of. They were too big, their teeth were too long, too ice-bright, and their eyes were too white, dead white. And the electric blue, spectral nimbus surrounding them wasn't natural. It was...Jane didn't know what, but whatever kind of creature it was, it made her shudder with stomach-grabbing fear, reach out toward the battle-ready cat.

His "Don't touch me," came too late, came after her comfort-questing hand had brushed his lashing tail, came after he was once again a man, a fevered man crouching on a rocky ledge, a naked, weaponless man facing fierce enemies.

Knowing her thoughtless act had almost doomed him, Jane jumped to one side, away from all contact. But her hasty retreat was not in time, not before the foremost of the attackers had leaped, slavering mouth wide, white eyes burning with blood lust. Lust for Sojourner's blood.

"Nooooooooooooooooooooo!" Her howl of protest slammed into high canyon walls, echoed again and again, but Jane didn't pause to listen. Not even feeling the sting of the black frost on her bare feet, she took two strides forward, gripped the blazing torch in both hands, and rammed it into the beast's gaping maw.

Black night grabbed them all, Jane, Sojourner, and the injured beast. Only the beast, with a rattle and crash of falling stones and a whine of pain, moved. Jane guessed, from direction of the diminishing nature of the sounds, that it was going away.

She had no idea what the other two beasts were doing, their nimbus had vanished with her light, and it was too dark to make even the mildest surmise. She was scared silly, but she stayed, totally vulnerable, out on the ledge until the cat said, his voice soft and reassuring within what was left of her mind, "They're gone. We're safe for now. Come back inside."

Not needing a second invitation, Jane, guided by the dim glow of the embers from the kindling fire, made her way back into the cave. Breathing hard, staggering with weakness, once again a man to her seeing, Sojourner made his way to his bed, pulling the quilts up around him like he was freezing. And knowing a few chills of her own, some from the cold, others from left over fear, Jane knelt beside the fire. The branches she had dropped earlier were beginning to flame and she added more wood, carefully placing each hunk and stick, waiting for it to ignite into a full grown blaze. It kept her busy until she found enough breath to ask, "They weren't wolves, I know that much, but what were they?"

She wanted to hear his human voice, but his answer came directly into her mind. "Dires."

Her second question was harder to ask. "They'll come back, won't they?"

His laughter was harsh, but, even if it held the raspy undertone of angry cat, it was man laughter, and it was a man voice that said, "Not those four, love."

The fire took off with a roar of reaching flame and a shower of sparks, grew hot against her face, and she leaned back and away from its increasing heat. But Jane Murdock was still shivering as she tossed on more fuel, blood-red chunks of wagon wreckage. She didn't even glance in Sojourner's direction and she waited until she was sure her voice was steady before she asked, drawing a totally unpleasant conclusion from his words, "There'll be others coming to visit us then?"

His weary answer left much to be desired. "Dires are creatures of black night and winter ice who run before the storms. The men of this world call them storm-runners. They fear the fire greatly. Build the watch fire, the night fire, athwart the tunnel. They will not dare come near us."

He was silent for so long that Jane thought he had fallen asleep. Not wanting to think about their encounter with the dires, but unable to make her thoughts quit rerunning the horror, Jane started when Sojourner said, his man voice soft, almost gentle, "I saw you first in the fire. Old Derna, my nurse, said she would show me my true love. She threw something into the fireplace. The flames leaped high and you were there. Your midnight eyes looked at me and your lips started to smile."

Touched by the gentleness, wanting to hear more, Jane waited for him to go on with his tale, but after a long time, Sojourner said, "Derna had stolen the magic powder. My wizard mother was sorely displeased."

Sojourner's sigh was almost lost in the snap and crackle of the fire as Jane moved a portion of burning wood to the center of the tunnel mouth. But Jane couldn't mistake the sadness she heard in his every word when he added, "She was a silly, credulous old woman, but Derna loved me, and what she did, she did for love. I hope it was worth the price she had to pay."

"What happened?"

"Ah, love, it does no good to pick at old wounds.

"That's no answer."

"I do not know the answer. I never saw Derna again after that night."

Jane ached to go to him, to embrace him, to do something to ease his pain, but she didn't dare. And long after he had fallen into a fitful sleep, she sat by the watch fire, keeping it alive, and wondered about the man and about that far away kingdom where he had been born a prince.

There were questions she wanted to ask, but there was something about the dream that held her mute. But if she couldn't question him about his past, she could, at least, question him about the dires and what he had said about them and winter ice.

But, first she had to do her best to keep him alive until Will and Max Farrel came to rescue them; From the sound of his fevered muttering, it might be a task beyond her doing.

Unshed tears almost choked her, but she had neither the time nor the energy to waste on futile weeping. But she wanted to, dear God, how she wanted to.

Chapter 20

FEVER MOLTEN IN his veins, the need to wander tearing at his vitals, Sojourner lay on his narrow bed and watched her through slitted eyes. Once again he stored up memories against the time of their parting. It had to be soon, for her sake, never his own. The dires ran before mountain storms and were, always the first, and possibly the deadliest, harbingers of winter cold and ice. Already the frosts had killed leaves and grass, and soon the howling, snow-ladened blizzards would come. The depths of the canyon would protect them from the worst of the icy winds, but eventually the snow would pile deep.

Jane had been brave and strong, as he had always known she would be, but she was only mortal. There was no escaping what the coming winter had to offer, not with the slender resources she had at her command. He had faced other winters, lived off the bounty of the land, but he was a cat, a cat with a few remembered spells of magic.

Jane Murdock was a human without wizardry. She was a woman bred to city life and luxury beyond all this world had to offer. And brave as she was, try as she might, she was no match for the wilds. Nor could he leave her to find his own renewal. Love held him like fetters of adamant, while the curse that made him wander clawed at him, lured him, and, when he could not go, could not forsake this small part of his destiny, sickened him with fever and weakness.

But, that wasn't the worst of it; he would gladly die before he left her at the mercy of this land. But his magic was as weak as his body and, as much as he was shamed to admit it, even to himself, the truth was: he could not save her alone. And there was no one else. His mind-link with Will had been broken during Cordelia's malicious storm of sound and flood, but Sojourner had to keep trying to contact him, to let him know of their plight. "Young wizard, I beg you, answer my call."

But no matter how hard he listened, Sojourner could hear not the slightest mind-sound in answer. It was as if the wizard and all his companions had been banished from the earth. Knowing the love-scorned fury of the fair Cordelia, Sojourner wouldn't have doubted that as being fact either.

All he could do was lie on his hard pallet, shiver a little as the fever climbed higher, burned him with harsh, unrelenting fire, and drink in the sight of her.

The cave was crowded with shadow and light, both moving in some exotic dance of advance and retreat, but he had no trouble seeing what really mattered. No trouble at all. Her he could always see, with his eyes, with his mind, and with his aching heart.

A quilt draped around her shoulders, a long skirt covering her feet and legs, Jane sat, hunched and weary, before the fire. She nodded off from time to time, if only briefly and then jerked awake to feed the red-hued, hungry fire; a fire that was devouring far more fuel than she could afford to expend. But the fire was all that separated them from the night-prowling dires so there was no other course than the one she had taken.

And that, too, caused him new fear; Sojourner had taken the canyon's measure, and knew the full extent of its meager offerings. The wood available close-by, plus what she had already gathered would last no more than a ten-day, if that. Soon she would have to go further and further afield just to find more, growing more frantic in her search for bare survival.

And he could offer no real aid. Without her touch, he was only a cat, and limited to a cat's capabilities. Wanting to provide and protect, he cursed his weakness, his fever, and the dread deeds that had brought him to his present state, but he didn't curse the fates that had arranged their meeting. He couldn't do that, not in truth.

Jane Murdock was his love, his One True Love, and he would hurt beyond all reckoning when they had to part, but for now, he could only look at her and add to his small store of memories. And hope they would be strong enough to warm his future, to keep him from the bitterness of total despair when the wanderlust took him completely, twisted his senses, and forced him to go on alone.

Knowing it was a vain hope, the great cat stretched slowly, tried to ease his body to a place of greater comfort, and sighed. It was a small sound that should have been lost in the crackle and roar of the fire, the freshening wind's whine without, and Jane's own movements as she, once again, came instantly awake.

But it wasn't. And Sojourner knew that when she turned her head and looked at him with her midnight eyes, unreadable eyes, and asked, her voice too tired to hold any expression, "Is it time for your aspirin?"

She was weary beyond belief, he knew that. And he knew too that he had to help her. He got up, staggered over to where she was sitting beside the fire, and dropped down beside her, becoming a man, even to his own seeing, when he brushed against her tensely held body.

"You must sleep," he said, reaching over to touch her battered face.

"Dires are just beyond the tunnel mouth. I can hear them moving across the rocks. I have to keep the fire." After a second, she added, "You'd better go back to bed before you freeze."

"Your fire has brought some warmth to the cave."

"But not enough when... Please, just go back to bed. I don't want you to get sicker than you already are."

Worry, all for him, was heart-achingly plain in her husky voice, but he had other plans. "Share your quilt and I will keep the watch while you nap."

"But..."

"But, what, love?"

"You don't have any clothes on."

"I will be amply covered if you share your quilt and I will be a man as long as you are close, man enough to feed the fire and keep the dires away from our door."

Moving with a slowness that gave ample proof of her reluctance to fall prey to her own weariness, her need to care for him before addressing her own needs, she opened the warm bed-cover and silently invited him to enter. Sojourner wasn't at all slow in accepting, or in putting his arm around her thin shoulders and holding her close. "Sleep," he whispered, his mouth almost touching her disordered tangle of hair, "no harm will come to you while I'm here."

Even as he spoke the words, he knew he wasn't telling the truth, or, at least, not the whole of it. All harm wasn't prowling without; beyond doubt, his love for her would cause her the greatest harm of all—unless he could control it, keep destiny from mastering them both. And he wasn't sure he could; at that moment, with her warm and close against his side, he wasn't even sure he wanted to try.

HIS ARM AN anchor, holding her in that time, that place, offering her a sorely needed respite. Jane wanted to relax in his embrace, to let sleep massage the soreness from her muscles, lessen the weariness of her mind and body, but she didn't dare. Not when he was burning with fever. Not when terrible, unbelievable creatures slavered and hungered just beyond the blaze of fire. Not when the dreams, dreams of him that were not fragments from her disordered brain, lurked like assassins, waiting to...

Her mental capacities were on hold, she couldn't come up with an analogy, but she knew she couldn't face the dreams again, not until... She didn't know what until was either, but Jane knew she had to do something, so she asked, knowing full well that what she was saying was an impossibility, an impossibility that had to be possible, "Why were you cursed? What did you do? Will didn't know, he said no one knew for sure, but..."

It was a very long moment before Sojourner said, "I would tell you, love, if it were in my power, but it isn't. So much was lost at the changing. I know there was fury and blood and madness, but I do not know if it was all mine. Or if...Whatever I did, it destroyed a kingdom and a people."

"And you?" she asked softly. "Did it destroy you also?"

His answer was oblique, aching with old pain. "You must go back to your own world. You must not love me, Jane."

"It's too late to give me that bit of sage advice," she said, rather tartly, rather as she would have in her old life, and she wasn't sure whether she spoke the words aloud or not, but she rather fancied she had. It didn't really matter, she was far too tired to feel even a speck of embarrassment or a whisper of dismay.

But she did lean away from his burning body, even though he still kept his arm around her as she reached down, found the strap, and dragged her purse up onto her lap. Jane paused only briefly, just long enough to find a dab more strength in some hither to forgotten place, before she started to dig in its soggy interior for the bottle of aspirin. Murmuring a prayer of thanksgiving that she had been tempted by the sale price and bought the extra-large bottle. A bottle that was emptying far too rapidly for her peace of mind.

Her search was blocked by a hard something, a sort of square, thick, hard something, and for just a moment she didn't recognize it, couldn't remember why it should be in her purse. And then Cordelia's face intruded, jarred Jane's memory. Jane lifted out the scorned wizard's water-soaked gift, intending to dry it out by the fire and maybe, if there was time, and her reading glasses hadn't been smashed in the flood, try to get it unlocked and see what sort of magical spells were hidden away inside.

It was no longer a locked book. The brass lock was gone and the book fell open to her touch. And, as her touch wasn't long in discovering, it was only wet on the outside. The inner pages of thick vellum, and there weren't very many of them, were totally dry. But the same couldn't be said for the rest of the purse's motley and mostly ruined contents.

The remaining canister of pepper spray was probably still usable and the lighter had already saved her sanity; if not her life. But, as for the rest, Jane didn't know; and she didn't deem it the proper time to try and find out. And she was too far gone in fatigue and sleep deprivation to worry about it.

The aspirin bottle in her hand, she poured out two, replaced the child-proof cap, and gave Sojourner the pills and an order. "If you insist on being an idiot, at least take these. You're burning up."

After he obeyed, without question or demur, Sojourner asked, his voice too sharp for what had to be an idle question, "Where did you get that book?"

Oddly, it wasn't a question she wanted to answer. Stuffing it back inside her purse, she dropped the bag to the sandy floor and sounding almost sullen, even to her own less than discriminating ear, asked, "Why?"

"It smells of magic," he said slowly, almost absently, and for an instant his embrace became almost painfully tight. She thought he was going to reach across her, take the volume in question; she didn't want that to happen.

"Cordelia gave it...well, really she threw it at me that last day, the one when Will discovered where the brides are. It was locked and... Well, I kept it because I thought it might be important, but Will didn't seem to think it was much, he didn't even seem to notice I had it. I just stuffed it in my purse to..." Jane took a deep breath and went doggedly on, "I kept it to prove something to her. I know she did it to taunt me, to give me a gift that would show me how stupid I am and how smart she is. She doesn't seem to think I know how to read."

"This is a backward world," Sojourner said.

Jane knew he was going to say something else, ask her more about the book. It wasn't a subject she cared to discuss, so without really knowing why it was important that she do so, she changed the subject. "This is your home world, isn't it?"

His answer gave her new, and fairly unexpected, data to ponder. "Perhaps it is, I don't know. The curse has driven me hard, love, and I wandered many worlds, seeking, always seeking, but never finding That Which Was Lost."

"If you find it, what then?"

"I don't know. Once, when I was still young and had dreams, I believed the finding would make me whole again, that I would stand erect and go on a new quest, one that would have brought me to you. But, dreams are...My love, I do not know what will happen when..."

"What was lost?"

His answer was a harsh whisper, one that broke her heart and left her without speech or comfort. "I don't know. By all the old, forgotten gods, I do not know. I only know that I must seek, wander through eternity alone, always searching, never finding. Always alone."

Her throat was clogged with unshed tears. Her hand was trembling, almost without strength, but it made its way to his face, caressed his cheek. But there was nothing she could say, nothing that would take away his terrible loneliness. Not even her love, love she did not want to feel, could do that.

Unused to the ways of love, Jane was wise enough to know that her love for him could only cause him more pain. She didn't want that, would never want that, but she trembled a little when he caught her hand, held it in his own. Held it with great tenderness, but only for an instant, only until he released it and said, "Sleep, my love, and rest. I will keep the watch until dawn drives away the prowling beasts."

Perhaps he added a small spell to his words, Jane didn't know. She didn't know when her eyes closed and sleep, already saturated with unquiet dreams, seized her in jaws of unrelenting steel and carried her into a netherworld where only old deeds and best forgotten memories dwelled, a world where only nightmares thrived.

She no longer had the strength to fight and kick, but Jane Murdock did not go quietly. She tried to scream, and in her dreams she did. Unversed in magic, curses, nightmares, and eternal love, she could not know the only sound she made was a whimper as her body melted into sleep, leaving her mind to deal with the horror, the hate, and the undying taint of old madness, that awaited to embrace her with too avid eagerness.

"YOUNG WIZARD, I beg you, answer me."

Sojourner's plea wandered into Will's sleeping brain, knocked, fruitlessly, on spell-locked doors, blundered down dead ends, and tried each hidden way until at last it found entrance into the young wizard's knowing, brought him awake with a pounding heart and fear-dry mouth. Lifting his head from the unicorn saddle that served as his pillow, Will looked up at the star-bright night sky and tried to find the great cat's message in his conscious mind.

Neither it nor any awareness of Sojourner was there. Will found it difficult to even focus his sleep-dazed thoughts on the cat. Jane proved to be even more elusive. It was as if she were a figment of his imagination, a creature of smoke and mist, one that had never existed in this world or any other.

All around him men, curled in quilts, slept on the ground. He knew who they were: waddies from Max Farrel's unicorn ranch. He knew the rancher when the man raised his own head and asked, his voice a barely heard whisper, "What is it? What's wrong? Has Cordelia found us?"

Will's answer was wrung from his heart, from the fear that raced in his blood, "Sojourner is...Something has happened to him. I don't..."

Max's question came too quickly to be idle or without interest, "And Jane? Is she..."

"I don't know," Will answered. "Something is..."

Something exploded in a shower of brilliant, eye-blinding white light and mocking female laughter. The light fell to the earth and died in the next instant, but the laughter lingered until it was replaced by words.

"So, you would play at wizard games, would you?" Cordelia asked, her voice coming out of everywhere and nowhere, waking sleeping waddies, spooking unicorns, and creating her own brand of chaos.

It wasn't a question that begged an answer, but Will, all thoughts of Sojourner gone from his mind, answered anyway, "We are coming for the brides and if it is a duel you want, then that's what we'll have."

Her laughter was nothing more than a convulsion of pure mirth, mirth followed by a lightning bolt that slammed down in their midst, igniting grass and brush and sending the waddies and Farrel scurrying to save tack and mounts.

Will gathered his own magic and waited.

It wasn't a terribly long wait, only long enough for Cordelia to ask, her voice honeyed, "Max, have you changed your mind about my honorable proposal?"

Max's answer was succinct, obscene, and a definite

negative.

Cordelia didn't take his rejection with a forgiving heart. Her laughter had frozen into bits of tinkling ice, black ice that would never thaw, and her voice was ugly when she said, "So that's the way of it, is it? You are enamored with the whore. She won't have you, neither will the rest of the whining off-worlders. I'll kill them, one by one, and enjoy the doing, before you can touch a single one."

Will tried to direct his magic, tried to find her whereabouts, but he tried in vain. His magic was still gathering force when she blasted him.

He barely had time to erect a shield over Farrel and the waddies, and even then her blazing sword of arcane fire cut through, slashed the legs from under one waddie, the life from another.

Will released his own lance, but it found no target in the emptiness of the night. She returned fire, sizzled the campsite with blood-red lightning, pounded them to the ground with thunder, and then Cordelia was gone. So were their unicorns, their supplies, and well over half of their men. Gone without a trace.

Shaken, weak, drained of power and hope, Will knew he had been defeated, that he had lost, that Maggie was in grave danger, and he could give her no aid.

Max knew it too. "It's a long walk back to the ranch," he said, sounding as old and tired as Will felt, "so we'd better get started."

"Sojourner," Will said, his voice hoarse, "we have to find him. He can help." He didn't voice the thought that had wiggled into his mind and formed a canker: if he's not already dead.

Chapter 21

IN SOME DIM recess of her mind, Jane knew she was sleeping, knew she was in a cave, knew that Sojourner was beside her, keeping her from all harm. The knowledge was enough to allow her to float out of her sleeping body and into the big middle of the beckoning dream without a qualm or a quiver.

It was just something that needed doing. Although she didn't know the why of it, Jane was very sure that it was needful. And the need might have been his far more than it was hers, but that part was all tangled in her mind, twisted through the golden bonds, unbreakable bonds, that stretched between worlds, beyond time, and could only lead to pain.

"Love," she practically snorted the word as she drifted, in the strange misty dreamlight, above the vast, untidy, obviously unplanned, towerless castle that she had visited in a previous dream. Or, at least, heard about in that rather pompous dream. She had no trouble recognizing it as the castle that belonged to Sojourner's mother and father, the foreign wizard and the king.

Made of stones, some quarried, some not, some gray, some brown, some marble-looking, all stuck together with some sort of whitish goop, it wasn't any more attractive in this dream than it had been before. And, truth to tell, over and above its rather tacky appearance, the castle had a very distinctive odor. She tried to identify it. Eau de outhouse? No, what then? Overused garderobe? Overripe midden? Open sewers? Dead dragon? Demon bait? Whatever it was, it was a nearly visible miasma so chokingly strong that Jane was hard put to keep from gagging.

And then she gave herself a very strong mental shake. She was here for the dream, not to go wandering off into a some idiot fairy tale of demons and dragons and heaven alone knows what else. Come on, Jane, she told her dreaming self, act your age and quit whatever it is you're doing. You ought to be ashamed of yourself. Demon bait indeed!

Of course it was silly, demons didn't actually exist, but, even in her nebulous, floaty state, Jane couldn't resist a quick look behind her. Not for demons, she assured herself, just to see what's there. What was there was just more of the castle sprawl and what looked to be a group of...did she call them unicornmen and women? Riders on unicornback? It couldn't possibly make any difference what she called them, but in the way of dreams, Jane puzzled the words. And she drifted closer and closer to the group of well-dressed, maybe even richly dressed, riders who were, with a fanfare of trumpets and smiles and waves to the lesser beings crowding the sides of the narrow streets, rapidly approaching the castle gates.

Swooping down, Jane hovered just above the heads of the leading riders, accompanied them through the wide gates. She noticed, absently, noting there was no moat or drawbridge or one of the metal things with spikes on them that dropped down from above and behind the gates.

What were those things called? It started with a "P," she was fairly sure of that, but she could not dredge the word out of her sleeping mind. It irritated her a little, made her frown, but that didn't keep her from doing what the dream commanded and go where the riders led.

Once through the gate, Jane and the troop came into an open space. Maybe it was the keep, her knowledge of castle nomenclature was less than adequate. She didn't know for sure what to call the place where other richly dressed, smiling people waited and came close as the riders dismounted and groom took away their unicorns.

Jane saw them all, riders and waiters alike. However, her attention was riveted on the girl with sun-bright hair, the very young, very pale-skinned girl wearing a pearl-sewn cloak of white velvet, fastened at one shoulder with a golden broach, and the fire-flashed Black Opal Crown of Seeting sat firmly amidst her golden hair.

Cold rushed into Jane's dream body, shivered through it, and Jane felt icy tears burn in her eyes. The girl had to be the princess, Princess Annette, Damian's betrothed. Or so Jane judged from the richness of her white satin gown, the fear and eagerness in her eyes, and the blushing adoration that added even more beauty to her heart-shaped face, she had come to the castle as his bride, had come to her new home riding on a pure white unicorn, the perfect match to the one Damian had bestrode at her side.

Hand in hand, the bridal pair walked across the open space. Jane went with them, but only for a short way, and then she was tugged back to the cave by Sojourner's movement as he bent down and tossed more wood on the watch fire. Or perhaps that, too, was just a part of the dream, one of the odd shifts in space and time that seem to be the characteristic of dreams.

Stiffening in his embrace, whether it was dream or reality, Jane fought to come awake, to help him defend the cave from the night prowlers, but his arm tightened, his lips brushed her forehead, and he whispered, "Sleep, love. Nothing is amiss."

And she believed him totally, or at least enough to allow her to sink back into dreaming or to switch to a different dream channel. Whatever it was, it wasn't, however, the same dream, or maybe it was. The same dream, like a soap opera is the same drama a year or two down the road when characters have undergone a series of traumas, conflicts, love affairs, and maybe even a bout or two amnesia but are following a darker storyline.

The castle was the same, only this time it was night, and really cold, and she was inside the castle, in the great hall or the dining room or something like that. A big room with huge fireplaces at either end and a weird combination of tables in the middle. The tables formed a T, with Annette sitting alone at the crossbar with one of the fireplaces at her back.

The Black Opal crown was alive with power. It flashed green, blue, and red fire with every small movement of her head, but it was a direct contrast to her sun-bright hair. Its former beauty gone, her hair was dry, lifeless, and the woman herself was crying, crying deep wracking sobs, crying as if her heart was breaking, her world ending.

Both fireplaces played host to a multitude of blue-white flames that leaped high, but gave out only a wavering, uncertain light and no heat at all; or none that Jane could feel. Against her will, Jane drifted closer to the crying woman, drawn there and held in place by some force outside herself, and waited for whatever the dream had in store.

"Damian hates me," Annette said softly, pushing the words out between wrenching, completely undainty sobs. "He's going to kill me soon. He said he was. I think he must be mad."

"No," another female voice said and only then did Jane see Lizan, Sojourner's wizard mother, sitting in the chimney corner, wearing black, blending with, lost in other shadows. "My beloved son is not mad, or he would not be if you were a loving and dutiful wife. It is you that pushes him into madness. You that consorts with his brother, running to him with all your petty problems, whining and crying, begging him to help you. You that..."

"I...I...his brother is a gentle man and he...he knows of Damian's..."

"He knows nothing more than a few bits of tawdry magic. Oh, he will dry your tears, hold your hand, protect you as much as he is able, but, my dear, no matter what you think, however much you scheme, he will never love you."

Lizan rose, looked directly at Jane, or so it seemed, and laughed. "My younger son loves a woman he has seen in the fire, a woman he can never claim. A woman who does not even exist. He hungers for her, and that hunger will destroy him. I have seen that in the flames, in the scrying bowl, and in pure crystal."

She laughed again, and the sound sent chills to climb Jane's spine. But it was the cruel laughter that made her gasp in a small breath and back away, retreat from the pure malice she saw in the woman's silver eyes. Eyes so like Sojourner's own, but only in shape and color, never in expression or content.

"Damian is mad," Annette said again, only now it was a whisper, a whisper devoid of all hope. "My father is dead. I am the queen. I have to go home to Seeting, go to my people before Damian destroys..."

"Fool!" Lizan whirled, advanced on Annette, grabbed her by the shoulders and shook her. Shadows ran with the wizard queen, hid her face, her form, and crept around the younger woman, completely concealing her from Jane's view.

She could see neither woman, but she knew it was Lizan who said, "You are his wife and Damian wants you here, Annette. Here you will stay until my son says otherwise."

And then shadowy wizard was gone, leaving a white-faced, trembling Annette standing by the table, an obviously pregnant Annette who swallowed hard before she whispered, "No, no matter what you say, Lizan, I won't stay here. I have to go to my people. They need me now. He will help me, I know he will."

Without his name ever being mentioned, Jane knew the "he" both women referred to was Sojourner. The knowledge wasn't what made her shiver with a sudden terrible cold when Annette sort of crooned, "I'll be safe in Seeting and so will my baby."

Jane knew there was no safety for Annette, not in Seeting, probably not anywhere. That hard, cold knowing sent her dream self scurrying back, not to the cave and the comfort of Sojourner's arms, but out of the dining hall, out into the gray-white dream world where her own familiar office, with its white carpet and lush ferns, its computer and files, its windows overlooking the city, waited for her, begged her to return to the safe, sane world it represented, the she had worked so long and so diligently to claim as her own.

It wasn't the same. And Jane knew, even before she heard the cruel, mocking laughter, a woman's laughter, that it would never be the same again. Her safe, secure world was lost, perhaps forever, and grieving tears burned the backs of Jane's eyes. But she didn't weep, she couldn't; some sorrows are too deep for tears. Nonetheless, her throat was aching as she walked through the silent office, touching, with gentle fingers, each artifact of that dear place, not exactly bidding them farewell but close. So very close.

WILL'S RIDING BOOTS, borrowed from Max Farrel before their sortie into Cordelia's domain, and a size too large, had rubbed a painful blister on his heel. He limped along beside the rancher, backtracking their own trail, walking the many rugged miles that separated them from the canyon mouth where Sojourner should be waiting. But, if Sojourner's plea was any point to judge by, they probably weren't.

He was alone, except for Max Farrel. The waddies, those remaining after Cordelia's blast, had headed straight for the ranch where they were going to round up some more riding unicorns and do whatever else needed doing, like eating and getting some uninterrupted sleep.

Dejected, maybe even severely depressed, by his defeat at Cordelia's hands, Will wouldn't allow himself to even think of the pain in his foot. It was just punishment, and pretty mild at that, for the disaster his overconfidence had brought upon them all.

A disaster, or maybe a catastrophe, that was still happening. More than likely, it wasn't going to come close to stopping until Cordelia got Max in her bed, Jane back at Jake's, and himself swinging in the wind at the end of a rope. He sighed. Maybe then she would free the brides and the rest of the women, the ones she hadn't already killed, but Will doubted it. Doubted it very much.

And there wasn't a damned thing he could do about it, any of it, including whatever had happened to Sojourner, Jane, and the wizard wagon. Because, after hours of walking, stumbling through the dark, expecting Cordelia to launch a new attack at any moment, they had, finally, with the first light of morning guiding their weary feet, topped the last rise.. They stood there, looked down into the small, sheltered valley below, the valley that should have contained the carefully chosen camping site, the wagon, the great cat, and the off-world woman.

It didn't.

"It has to be the right place," Farrel said, thumbing back his broad-brimmed hat and rubbing at his eyes as if that might change what he was seeing. "It has to be, but..."

Will didn't rub his eyes, he just stood there, staring at the chaos that had been wrought since they had left Jane and Sojourner a bare two nights before. The thicket of evergreens that had hidden the wagon from the casual viewer were uprooted, scattered about like straw. The valley had been struck by lightning, scoured by flood, and tortured by forces wielded by a madman, or, what was more likely, a madwoman. The destruction was unnatural and complete. And it was against every law wizards imposed upon themselves, laws that forbade storm magic in all its forms.

Will took a deep breath, to still the pounding of his heart, wiped his sweaty palms on the red wool coat he was wearing, and tried not to believe what his senses were telling him. He tried not to believe that Cordelia had done all this to get rid of Jane.

Farrel had no such doubts. "Cordelia," he said, muttering several choice curses under his breath. "She did this, didn't she? Because she was jealous of Jane?"

The smell of magic was all around, not even beginning to fade. Will took another sniff before he nodded. He didn't know if she was jealous of Jane or not, but Cordelia had, seemingly, broken every bit and piece of the Wizard's Oath, ruined her own honor by what she had done, all in the name of love. And now the whole country was going to suffer for her misdeeds. If she had indeed conjured a storm, disrupted all the natural weather patterns, then it could well be a severe winter, a terrible winter with killer storms and freezing temperatures.

It was an awful thing to even think about, an act entailing consequences that could take many lives, but he had to be very sure before he condemned her. It was for the Council at Wizardholm to decided her punishment, and they wouldn't do that without real evidence of her crimes. And the Council was hundreds of miles away, following their own pursuits.

And he was here, but Sojourner was gone, vanished completely, perhaps... And the Council could do nothing about that, could not make the great cat reappear safe and sound. Could not...

"We have to find them," he said, his voice rasping and old sounding even to his own ears. "Jane and Sojourner are there somewhere, they have to be. Come on." Disregarding his weariness, the blister on his heel, all caution and wariness, Will plunged down the slope.

Max Farrel wasn't a half-step behind him as they ran into the valley, straight into the face of the north wind, the storm wind with teeth of ice and snow. The wind of winter.

It dried the sweat on their faces. It set both men to shivering long before they had clambered over fallen trees, stumbled over storm debris, bulled their way through tangles of branches and brambles to the spot where the red wizard wagon had once rested.

Will was cold, cold to the bone, colder than he had ever been, but it wasn't just the wind that froze him into numbness. Hands buried in the pockets of the wool coat, ears almost covered by its upturned collar, Will walked, slowly, his shoulders slumped, down to the bank of the small stream.

Farrel stood his ground, looked at the dark mouth of the canyon that yawned less than a hundred feet away. "You have to find her," he said through chattering teeth. "You have to find Jane. Winter's coming early and... Damn it, Will, that cat of yours can take care of itself, but Jane is..."

"Jane is..." Will didn't say, "I don't care where Jane is, Sojourner is my family, my friend, if what happened to them was survivable, then he did," but he turned from his contemplation of the water and said, his voice as frozen as he felt, "We have to go back to your ranch."

"No, we have to find..."

Perhaps love had something to do with his decision, but it was his sense of honor and duty that forced Will to say, "If Jane's seeing was true, and I'm sure it was, the brides and the rest of the women are out in the weather, unprotected. If, as you say, its going to storm, then we have to do what we can to see them safe before we can do anything else. And I have to send a message to Wizardholm and tell them what is happening. They need to be warned and maybe they can set some spells to counter what Cordelia has..."

"And leave Jane alone?"

Farrel didn't understand, Will knew that, knew the rancher had no way of knowing what Cordelia's rage had done to an entire country. He just sighed and said, "Sojourner is with her."

"A cat! What can it do! She's from the city. She'll die down in that canyon, and you know it."

It wasn't a pleasant thought, but there was no real alternative that Will could see. Counting the brides, there had to be well over two-hundred women penned up like animals somewhere near Cordelia's castle. Will, at least according to the way he saw it, was the only one who could come close to freeing them. No matter how much it hurt him personally, he had to go back to the ranch, gather up some supplies, and attempt to rescue the women after he had sent a message spell to Wizardholm.

Will turned and started to make his way back up the slope.

"You can't!"

Farrel's cry of anguish didn't come close to drowning out Will's equally anguished, "I have to." He stopped before the rancher caught up with him, went back to the campsite and left a magical note, one that both Sojourner and Jane could read. If they managed to climb out of the canyon and find their way to the site.

It was a very big *if.* One he didn't dare allow to draw a breath.

Chapter 22

"PORTCULLIS," JANE muttered, eyes closed, muscles relaxed, leaning against the warmth of Sojourner's body. The disturbing dreams behind her, she was drifting aimlessly in the narrow, undemanding shadowland between waking and sleeping and was still trying to make sense of the unimportant, the tiny details. She poked at them with mental hands, turning them this way and that, perhaps in a vain attempt to evade the important.

It could have been the last delaying action of a brain too long accustomed to a world where the only "real" magic was on the silver screen, all the rest being high-tech grand illusions; occasionally presented with David Copperfieldian *élan*. Carefully educated and culturally indoctrinated into the mores of her own realistic, industrialized world, Jane's brain absolutely did not want to believe in true dreams, hurtful dreams of love gone wrong and hate triumphant. If that's what Jane's dreams really were, and not just what they seemed. Not that even those persistent dreams with their message of doom and gloom could actually invade the borderland that held her, that gave her a moment's respite from worry and care, let her play her small mind games without interruption.

"Portcullis, that's right. That's what it was, that spiky, trellis thing that's supposed to crash down inside the gate and keep the bad guys out," she said.

Jane had no way of knowing she was speaking aloud or that Sojourner had turned his head, was looking down at her with great silver eyes.

"But it wasn't the keep where the unicorns stopped. It was something else, maybe the front yard. I don't know what it was, but the keep is the tower, a place to keep important things, and there weren't any towers, were there? When I get home to New York, I'll have Maggie go to the library and look it up for me."

Sojourner's forefinger found her lips, touched them with unbelievable gentleness. His voice was warm velvet, softer than a butterfly's caressing wing, and it held an ageless sorrow that went beyond tears, when he said, "Ah, my beautiful love, I would give you a crown of stars and a mantle of the night sky, if it were in my power. But for us, there will be no crowns, no castles, no cottages, no sweet, shared dreams of a bright tomorrow. On my head lies the blame, I am sorry, my dearest love, so terribly sorry for destroying the wonder and delight that could have been."

She heard his voice, if not exactly what he was saying, felt his finger across her lips, and Jane's sleepy ruminations were a thing of the past. Her eyes popped open and she was awake and functioning in an instant, less than an instant, and her first thought was of their safety. "What is it? Are the dires..."

Without waiting for his reply, she pulled away from his encircling arm, felt cool air rush in between them, and reached down for the purse resting against her ankle. At that moment, she needed the reassurance of the single canister of pepper spray it still held.

"Nothing is threatening our cave." He tried, unsuccessfully, to laugh. "You were talking in your sleep and I..."

Straightening up, the purse strap in her hand, Jane was almost afraid to ask, "What did I say," afraid she had talked about his mother, about Annette, and about the dream or nightmare or whatever it was. She hoped not because she wasn't ready to do that, couldn't come close to telling him what she had learned, couldn't ask any of the questions the nightmare dreams had raised. She wasn't prepared to listen to his answers yet. Perhaps she would never be.

"You were just muttering something about a castle, but...Jane, once I lived in such and I..." He shook his head, pulled her back against him, and held the quilt a little closer around her. "There's nothing to fear for the moment, but soon we are going to have to make plans to leave this place. Then you will need all your strength, so why don't you go back to sleep for awhile?"

Her body was still exhausted, but sleep wasn't something Jane even wanted to think about. It was too full of dreams, true dreams holding memories, perhaps all the terribly painful memories that were no longer his, memories that he had lost at the changing. She needed time and a hefty injection of courage before she could dare face that way again.

But, whatever she needed didn't actually enter into her actions. She couldn't tell him of her fear, couldn't even tell him about the dreams. Something, a spell maybe, or some other unknown thing, kept her from even mentioning that she had been dreaming of his family, especially of his mother and sister-in-law.

As things turned out, she didn't have to say a word—but she didn't know whether that was good news or bad. Not just to change the subject, but based on genuine concern for his well-being, she opened her mouth to tell Sojourner that just because his shoulder would was healed to a pink scar didn't mean he wasn't still sick, that he needed rest more than she did. Without looking at him she pulled the heavy purse into her lap and reached up to feel his fevered brow to reinforce her words just as nature took a hand in their decision making.

Acting on some whimsical weather thing, or maybe a hangover from Cordelia's weather interference, the wind changed directions, came directly out of the north. It howled like several lost and very unhappy souls, accelerated to gale force velocity, and came charging in through the entrance tunnel. Screaming straight through the watch fire, it scattered burning sticks, kicking up a shower of bright sparks and cloud of thick, white smoke.

The smoke blasted them first. Blinking back tears, trying not to cough, tossing the quilt aside, Jane grabbed the purse and jumped to her feet, practically in unison with Sojourner's similar leap. Her survival instinct in full charge, Jane slid the purse strap over her head. Then, working like one possessed, she pulled their most flammable possessions away from the wind-driven blaze, and began to beat out the sparks where they landed on the beds and were beginning to smolder. There weren't that many to extinguish, but those small spark fires were only the beginning of their problems.

The tunnel was the only chimney the fire had and it had done its work with admirable dispatch, allowing only a foot or so of smoke to linger near the rocky ceiling of the small, crowded cavern. But all that changed. Within seconds, or so it seemed, the smoke, pushed back and refused exit by the wind, had filled the upper reaches of the cave and, layer by layer, was coming lower and lower to envelope them in a choking haze.

The wind blew harder, colder. The smoke swirled, billowed. The orange-red flames shot high, reached across the intervening space, lapped at Jane's haphazard pile of wood, and began a slow red nibble at one edge, a nibble that grew, with unseemly rapidity, into great, gulping bites.

The wind blew the lurid smoke down in ugly billows that seemed intent on her demise. Swearing and coughing, but absolutely determined to save what had cost her so much labor to gather, Jane crouched down and made for the wood pile.

She was snatching flaming brands from the pile and flinging them onto the main fire when the wind revved up a notch, fanned the fire to new heights, and sent a white-hot lance of fire straight at her head.

Man or cat, it made no difference, all his thoughts and attention were on her. He moved almost in time with the flame that scorched her ear, her hair, and the sleeve of her too frilly blouse, or, at the very most, not more than a second or two behind the hungry fire. Sojourner's arms caught Jane around the waist just as her blouse kindled, her hair scorched, threw her down onto the sand, and rolled her about until she was fire-free; and madder than she had any right to be. But not at Sojourner.

Her fury was directed at the wind, the fire, Cordelia, and maybe at herself, at the foolishness that had made her do battle with the wind-driven fire for a few worthless chunks of wood. It didn't improve her temper one bit to smell the stench of her fire-ravaged hair or to see the fire had won both the battle and the war. Her horde of sticks and branches were deeply involved in their own funeral pyre and would be until they were little more than charcoal and ash.

The tears caught her unaware. In fact, Jane didn't realize she was crying until Sojourner lifted her up from the cave floor. He wiped away her tears with his fingers, touched her burned ear and the side of her face with healing fingers, taking the pain and heat away with a single bit of spelling. Finally, he held her close to his naked chest, rocking her back and forth like a loving parent rocks a hurt child.

"It was my fault," she said, between bouts of coughing. "I shouldn't have put that damned woodpile so close to the firepit."

"No, love, you..."

Being coddled didn't sit well with her, and male soothing only added to her general ire. Even if his healing spell had spread far enough to take the swelling from her face and probably the purple from the bruises gathered during their wild ride through the floodwaters. And if the spell gave her strength and healing, it was also taking something from him; although she didn't know what. But, he was sick and she wasn't and wasn't going to be.

She pulled away from him, if not quite completely, and snarled, "Damn it, Sojourner, don't treat me like a baby. I know whether something was my fault or not—and this bit of asinine stupidity was all my fault, and you jolly well know it."

His laughter was sweet, clean, real, and all together beautiful; even if it did end in a fit of smoke-provoked coughing. He caught his breath, and moved them both closer to the back of the cave to sit on the salvaged beds, which were still below the worst of the layered smoke. There, he asked, with mock seriousness, "And the north wind that came uninvited, is it, too, your fault?"

"No, if it was anyone's fault, I'd be willing to bet our dear Cordelia wasn't above the doing," she answered, knowing full well he was teasing her, trying to make her feel better about the whole mess. It was a good try, but it wasn't working.

For that moment, Jane wanted to wallow in guilt and despair. It kept her mind off of more serious things, things she didn't yet understand. And wasn't sure she really wanted to. Except, where Sojourner was concerned, she was afraid she didn't actually have much choice. The love and destiny business had definitely kicked into high gear. Even now, when she was dying of smoke inhalation, was furious because her wood was being consumed with gluttony and gusto by the fire, as inappropriate it was to the time and the place, she still managed to be a little too aware of him so close beside her. And that wasn't to be allowed.

Lifting her chin high, she looked at him. Which was a big mistake. Right about then, time itself conspired against her, did a magic trick of its own, it stretched and stretched until it made her fully aware of something else. Despite all her posturing to the contrary, she would give him her very soul if he even hinted he wanted it. It wasn't pleasant knowing. Jane shivered.

"Jane." His hoarse whisper was less than sound, beyond meaning. He reached for her, pulled her close, and then whispered, "Ah, love, as much as I...I am a fool, it can never be. I have destroyed..." His voice died. His arms tightened fiercely, if only for a second, and then he released her.

Jane shivered again, didn't know whether she wanted to have a temper tantrum, demand he love her, or just to sit there like some fire-sale dummy and do all her hurting inside.

She knew she wasn't hurting alone when he groaned, deep in his throat, the helpless groan of a strong man pushed beyond his limits.

Cognizant of neither love nor loss nor renunciation, uncaring that Jane was trembling with cold and hurt, that Sojourner was cursing destiny and damning his own unremembered sins, the wind snarled through the fire again. It brought up another slanting fountain of fiery sparks, more choking smoke, added a bit of gritty sand, and threw the whole foul mixture straight into the couple's faces. The wind burst sent them both into a new frenzy of coughing. It was the coughing that separated them, sent them back into the real world where smoke and flame and a new pack of howling dires had to be dealt with. And love and its many manifestation had to be postponed. Or stamped forbidden and canceled for all time. The wind carried the sparks and seeds of flame into every part of the cave, and fanned them into ready growth.

"Put out the new fires, love," he said, his voice echoing inside her head. He was all cat now and all killing fury. "If they enter the cave, love, you have my promise: the dires will not live to see the dawn."

As if to refute Sojourner's brave words, dires, many dires, howled in the darkness beyond the fire, howls that came from the tunnel proper, not from the ledge at its far end.

Sojourner's head went up, his lip drew back, showing lethal, gleaming fangs and his answering challenge was enough to give the icy wind chills of pure fear.

She saw him crouch, gather his muscles beneath him, and knew, with a hammer-blow of fear, for him alone, that almost stopped her heart, that Sojourner wasn't going to wait for the dires to come to him. He was going to leap across the blaze and take the fight to his enemy.

"No," she cried, stumbling as she got to her feet, moved toward him, "damn it, you can't go! I'll not stay in here and die alone!"

Her only answer was the snarling cry of a great cat, a cry that held her name in its heart, a heart that would cease to beat before it would allow her to come to harm.

HUDDLED CLOSE TO a tiny fire, one they had built inside the bare shelter of a ring of huge stones, Max Farrel and Will were still awake when the first snowflake came out of the cloud-covered night sky. It was followed, fairly rapidly, by several others and a severe drop in the temperature. The two facts that nothing to increase either man's mental or physical comfort.

"It probably won't stick, but..." Farrel let his words dwindle to nothing as he poked a large, resinous limb into the fire, watched it as it crackled briefly before it flared high, lighting up the house-sized boulders around them with flickering orange light. Seemingly mesmerized by the fiery torch, he lifted it once, held it up to the sky in some sort of salute, and then pitched it on the campfire.

The earth icy cold beneath him, grief for Sojourner a tight ache lodged somewhere in the general region of his heart, Will shivered inside his heavy coat and held his hands out to the warmth of the fire. Hunger growling in his stomach, weariness aching in his feet, he sat there for a long time before he said, knowing it was truth beyond disputing, "We have to go on now."

A silence broken only by the hiss of snow on the fire, the whine and moan of the wind, and the distant howling of some sort of beast followed. In it, Will could almost read the other man's thoughts. And when Farrel said, "We'll die if we go on." Will had his answer ready.

"Those are storm-runners howling out there," he said slowly, "the ones some people call dires. And whatever you want to call them, they're leading a big storm in this direction."

"How long?" Farrel asked, sounding every bit as hungry and exhausted as Will felt. "How long before it storms, wizard?"

A blister broke on his right foot as Will stood, pulled his coat collar up and his hat down, but he didn't have time to worry about his own small pains. Maggie, the brides, and the rest of the captive women were out in the same cold, facing the advent of the first killing storm of winter. As long as there was breath in his body, it was Will's job to try and rescue them.

"Wizards are supposed to be able to read weather," Farrel said, getting to his own feet, "so, tell me, how long have we got?"

Taking a deep breath of icy air, Will tasted it before he turned his face into the wind to snatch at the secrets it held in its terrible teeth. "The storm is a bad one but it isn't moving real fast right now. If it doesn't decide to take off, we'll have five days maybe, six at the most," he said finally, "six days until Maggie and the rest of the women at Cordelia's castle perish in the cold. You can stay here if you want, but I have to go, have to try and get a message through to Wizardholm. We need help, and we need it quick."

Expelled breath clouding the icy air, he was already beginning the long, desolate walk that separated them from the ranch house and his magical supplies before the last words were out of his mouth. Even though both men knew they could never do what had to be done in time to save the women, Farrel wasn't a half a stride behind Will when he left the shelter of the rocks.

Chapter 23

"I'LL NOT STAY IN here and die alone!"

Hanging in the air, almost as palpable as the thick smoke, Jane's words refused to be dismissed. Even after the actual sound had died away, the simple declaration was still strong enough to pierce his battle rage. It halted his leap over the fire and into the tunnel to engage the dires in a death struggle, a long and bloody struggle designed to save Jane if not himself.

Sojourner crouched, his snarl still in place, and risked a quick look back over his shoulder. If he had ever thought her to be one of the shrinking maids of his old world, he would have been totally in error. Perhaps Jane Murdock was from another world where women lived almost peaceful lives, lives not fraught with primal danger, but he knew now that she was a battle maid, a warrior with midnight eyes, all flashing fire and pure courage.

"I would not have you dead," he said, forming the words in a cat's mouth, sending them straight to her mind where they spoke to her in a man's deep voice.

"Nor I you," she answered, seemingly not a whit daunted by his killer-cat visage or the pack of dires that howled just without. She came up beside him, careful not to touch him, and took a large burning brand from the wind-scattered fire. "If you are determined to go out and fight them, then I'm going with you. I will not stay in here, cowering in the corner, and allow someone else to die for me. So, the way I see it, we go together or we don't go at all. If you're going out there and die, then I'm going with you. We can die together. It's probably easier that way anyway because I, sure as taxes, cannot make it back to Farrel's ranch alone."

Pride, love and fear almost choked him. She was his One True Love, his woman of fire and night, and her bravery and honor were without peer, but he couldn't allow her to go out to fight the dires. It would kill him to see her fall. Above all else, she had to be protected.

Holding her flaming torch in one hand, the light revealing every smudge of dirt, every remaining abrasion, every weary line of her face, she glared at him and demanded an answer. "Well, what are we going to do?"

"Love," he said softly, "you must stay. The dires are fell beasts, they show no mercy. I will not permit you to..."

Tears had run through the smoky grime on her face, making whiter tracks down her cheeks. Her eyes were rimmed in red, but they were harder than obsidian, unyielding as oak. She looked at him squarely and her voice was flat and hard when she said, "I may love you, Sojourner, but we need to get one thing straight right now. I will not allow you to tell me what I can or cannot do. If you go out, I'm going too. That's all there is to it."

The wind eased. The dires howled louder, howled loud enough to reverberate inside the cave and he could see the gleam of one pair of eyes well within the tunnel. What remained of the fire snapped, leaped high, and then died down to a mass of white-hot coals.

Sojourner looked at the bed of coals and then looked back at Jane, hesitating just a moment before he asked, "And if they jump the fire and come in?"

Her voice shook just a little, but he could neither see nor hear any other sign of fear when she said, "We'll fight them together."

"For this small time, love, it shall be as you wish. I shall remain at your side," Sojourner said, hoping he had not made a mistake, hoping he had not condemned her to certain death.

In some uncanny way she seemed to know what thoughts lay so heavy in his mind, what new guilt he was ready to assume.

JANE SAW THE tense set of his muscles, the lash of his tail, and knew he wasn't totally convinced he was doing the right thing. Whether it was right or not didn't really matter. She wasn't going to be left behind to battle winter, a trek out of the canyon, a pack of dires, and heaven alone knows what else just so he could go dashing off and play hero.

"There's still a little bit of wood and some other stuff we can burn. Maybe enough to keep the fire going until morning. If morning isn't too far away. Is it?"

"I would think not, but..."

Even though his voice came deep and soft inside her head, Sojourner was still a cat to her seeing, a cat who hadn't relaxed one iota. A great black cat who was ready to do whatever needed doing to prolong her life. Well, she wasn't going to permit any such silliness on his part.

No, indeed. She was Jane Murdock, and Jane Murdock did what had to be done to save herself. And she might be trapped in a cave by an idiot wind and bunch of howling wolf-things, but that didn't make any difference.

The wind died completely. Or maybe it was only a lull in the storm, sort of like an eye of a hurricane, Jane didn't know. But she did know the smoke, while still thick enough to choke a fire-breathing dragon, was starting to drift out through the tunnel, if only in a trickle, thus giving them a little more breathing room.

And fire building room.

Fully aware that he was watching her, his silver eyes wary and somehow amused but proud. Jane had no idea what had caused any of the emotions, and she had no time to waste in trying to find out. Kneeling, but still holding her torch in one hand, she began to scrabble around, finding small pieces and short limbs, leftovers from the fire's gluttonous banquet. There wasn't much fuel, but it, along with whatever else she could find to burn, had to be enough to see them through the night. At that moment, she was perfectly willing to let tomorrow handle its own set of woes. All she had worry about was how she was going to get there, how she was going to keep the dires away from her door until daylight drove them away.

"Jane, it would be better if I go..."

Battle was never better than guile, Jane knew that even if Sojourner had a protector complex. She shook her head in the middle of his mental communication. "You may have been born to privilege, but I've..." suddenly she wanted giggle, not because anything was especially funny, but because what she was about to say was true, "I've been keeping the wolf away from the door most of my life. It's what my aunt taught me best."

A terrible commotion, yips, snarls, and horrific growls came from the tunnel. Sojourner tensed, readied his muscles for a battle, but Jane, after brief glance in his direction, ignored both him and the dires. Focusing her entire attention on the fire, she used a longer stick to rake all the embers into one pile. Placing it in the tunnel entrance, she began to add her fuel, bit by careful bit, building it into a formidable fire in very short order.

Tossing her torch onto the blaze, using the fire as her light source, Jane began to forage for new combustibles among the salvage she had carried up from the stream banks the previous day. The clothing they would probably need, and a goodly amount of the spell-kept food, but the rest could be pitched on the fire.

Sojourner, wavering between man and cat, came close, saw what she was doing and objected. "We will need the food, Jane, you must not..."

"If the dires get in and gobble us up, we will need nothing," she said, going right ahead with her rather slow-motion sorting and pitching. "If we can keep them out tonight, we're going to have to try and get back to the ranch just as soon as you are strong enough to travel. True?"

"We must go whether I'm strong enough or not," he said slowly. "Winter is coming all too soon, it must not find us here."

"When we go," Jane said, still not looking at him, but determined to have her say, "I will be able to carry only so much, so the rest will just be wasted anyway."

"That much is true. I will have to go as a cat, I won't have much choice in the matter, especially if we...if the dires track us down and attack. Love, I am sorry not to help you carry the burden, but I cannot fight encumbered."

Jane looked at him then, saw only man, bronze skin darkened by smoke, silver eyes darkened by worry, and she smiled. "That's what I just said, Sojourner. So, what does it matter if I burn some of Will's food packets? The magic spells on them won't explode or anything, will they?"

"Ah, love," he said, a small chuckle adding warmth to his deep voice, "'tis you and your great wisdom that should be a cat."

"It would certainly make our travels easier, wouldn't it?" she answered, coughing a little as she breathed in a new whiff of smoke.

Sojourner didn't answer, perhaps he had no answer to give on that particular subject. He did ask, after what seemed an eternity of silence, but was probably only five minutes are so, "Are the wolves on your world so prone to attack humans?"

"What?" Jane asked, trying to switch her thoughts from fire to home and finally dredging up something of a reply. "No, I've never actually seen a wolf, what I said is just a saying. It means I was poor and the wolf, in this case bill collectors, hunger, eviction, and whatever else goes with poverty are the metaphorical wolves. They aren't real animals. In fact, I think most of the real wolves are dead, or else they've retreated back into the high country."

"Retreated from what?"

Sojourner sounded as if he wanted an answer, but Jane

suspected he was only talking to keep her mind off the dires that were still growling and snuffling about on the other side of her roaring fire. She answered him anyway. "People, I suppose are the worst offenders. After that, all the things we can't live without." She tossed two bundles of some sort of bread onto the fire.

The cat masque flickering around him, but Sojourner was still a man to Jane's seeing; and an unclothed one at that. He watched the tunnel mouth attentively, but there was a hint of sharpened interest in his voice when he asked, "Which are?"

"Houses, roads, dams, power plants, airports, sewer systems, all the trappings of an industrial civilization that take away habitat."

"Tell me," he said, never once looking away from the tunnel, "tell me about your world, your life there."

She paused in her sorting and flinging long enough to wipe away some of the sweat that was beading on her face. "Why?"

"I would know you as a child, a maid, and a woman. If my past misdeeds hadn't destroyed what was to be, we would have a lifetime to learn and know each other, but now? Perhaps we have this night, certainly not much more, and then the young wizard will return you to your home world and I will go on alone."

Jane didn't know why that bare statement of fact, completely devoid of self-pity, should cause a painful clot in her throat, an ache behind her eyes, but it did. She swallowed hard, took a moment to make sure her voice was as calm as his, and said, "My parents died when I was very young. My aunt raised me. She was strict and demanding, but she taught me how to survive in a world geared for success."

"Did she love you?"

"I was a skinny little girl with black hair and eyes and she..." Jane tried to think back, to remember, but her aunt had died when Jane was barely eighteen and just graduated from high school. "No," she said finally, "I don't believe she loved me. I think she finally liked me and she certainly did her best to make sure I could take care of myself, but love? No, Sojourner, Grace was far from well and lived on a pittance, barely enough to pay for her own needs let alone those of her dead sister's child, so I imagine she resented me more than anything else."

"Did you love her?"

It wasn't a question she cared to answer, but Jane gave him the truth. "Yes. I loved her and I hated her when she couldn't love me."

"I'm sorry that..."

"It doesn't matter now. Aunt Grace gave me something far better than love. She taught me to take care of myself."

Sojourner looked at her then and his voice was soft with sorrow when he said, "Nothing is better than love, my Jane. Nothing."

A question tore at her mind, tried to escape from her lips. Jane worked faster and harder, but she did not ask it, did not say, "Did your mother, did Lizan ever love you?"

Instead she asked, "Do you think Will and Farrel managed to rescue Maggie and the others from the fair Cordelia?"

Watching the tunnel again, Sojourner said, "I would not want to guess, love. Will is young and untried. Cordelia is powerful and angry."

"And if Will lost the duel or whatever it was he was going do, what then? Will he return for us?"

"I do not know for sure. He deems me his friend, but I believe he loves your Maggie. Love is very powerful, and it usually rises above mere friendship."

That wasn't something Jane wanted to hear. Even if she knew it wasn't likely, she wanted him to say Will and Max Farrel and a host of waddies were going to ride in like the cavalry and carry them out of the cold and danger. Perhaps some of that longing was in her voice when she said, "But Will said he would come..."

"Perhaps he will." They both knew what Sojourner left unsaid. They both knew he should have added, "The young wizard will come for us, will keep his promise, if he is able."

WORRY DOGGING his every limping step, Will plodded along behind Max Farrel with his head down and thought only of Maggie and the rest of the women, women in desperate need of being rescued from Cordelia. For her crimes against nature, her storm magic that had disrupted the common courses of the seasons, putting a whole section of the world in jeopardy, the scorned wizard would be judged by the Wizardholm Masters. That is, she would be when and if Will could reach them, alert them to the problem.

Someday soon he would mourn the loss of Sojourner, but not now. He couldn't afford to weep or suffer a bout of melancholy, not when every bit of his energy had to be directed toward defeating Cordelia before she could...Could what? Will didn't know, and that's what was scaring him silly. Her powers were strong and, as she had proved, she had no compunctions about using any and all of the arcane spells; even the forbidden ones.

"Wait!"

Farrel's warning wasn't quick enough to keep Will from bumping into the other man's body. A body that had been moving forward a moment before and had suddenly come to an abrupt halt.

Flailing his arms and doing some rather fancy footwork in order to keep his balance, Will managed to gasp out, just before he went down on one knee, "What is it? What's wrong?"

Max gabbed Will's upper arm and pulled him up. "Look, down there in that hollow."

Will looked, narrowed his eyes, squinted through the darkness and the fitfully falling rain-mixed-with-snow, trying to see what had alarmed the unicorn rancher. Finally, he saw a pinpoint of light, reddish-orange light that might or might not be a campfire, and a fairly large one at that. "Who? Some of the waddies? The ones Cordelia vanished with her spell?"

"Maybe, but..." Farrel stood there a moment before he added, "I hope that's who it is, but I've got a feeling that its..."

"The posse?"

"Maybe. Maybe someone else. Whoever it is, we'd better go in slow and easy. I don't like surprises and Cordelia has more tricks than a pet goose, most of them bad. And all of them directed straight at me."

Although the very thought of a fire and, maybe, something to appease the growling in his stomach were terribly appealing, Will had to agree with Farrel. Caution was the only weapon they had at the moment, and caution wasn't the strongest shield against sabers.

They stumbled forward, moving over rocky, uneven ground, for almost an hour; or so Will's wizard-sense told him—before they were close enough to see the huge fire, the men huddled around it, and smell meat roasting. But they hadn't crept more than a hundred yards closer before they heard a sound behind them.

Weariness surrendering to need, Will snapped fire on his fingertips and whirled around. He wasn't quick enough to do much more than try to duck back and away from the blow aimed at his head by a man he'd never seen before—a huge, bearded man that wasn't to be evaded.

The blow landed. Will went down in a shower of stars, and he stayed down.

Chapter 24

SOJOURNER CAUGHT her arm with a hand that was too hot, held it until she turned away from blazing fire to look at him. He released her and said, his voice gentle inside her head, "There's no need to burn any more of the food right now, the dires are gone. First light must be near."

Trembling with fatigue, Jane looked at him blankly, dropped the spellset package back onto a surprisingly small pile, and rubbed at her sleep-starved, smoke-irritated eyes with the heels of her hands. She hadn't swooned, or keeled over, or whatever it was over-tired maidens did, but it certainly wouldn't have come amiss.

"The dires are really gone?" she asked, feeling stupid, hungry, grumpy, and irritable enough to take on a pack of dires single-handedly. Jane yawned twice and rubbed her eyes again before she could summon up enough sense to question him. "Just because its morning or do they have some other plan in mind, like waiting outside the tunnel and nabbing me when I go out to start gathering some more of that blasted wood?"

"You need to rest," he said, touching her cheek with his forefinger, tracing a curve down to the corner of her mouth.

"I need lots of things," Jane said, wanting to pull away from his touch. "Rest is way down near the bottom of the list, somewhere after something to eat, a bath, and some clean clothes. It's well after I make sure we've got enough wood to last through another night."

Sojourner's hand left her face, dropped down to her shoulder, where it felt like a coal from her watch fire, and he started to say something more. His concern for her well-being was obvious, but it was no greater than hers for him. Jane was quicker in voicing her take on the subject, "Besides that, if anybody around here is going to get some rest, it's going to be you. Right after you take some more aspirin. Your fever is up again."

"Yes, love," he said, with way too much meekness and just a hint of a chuckle in his deep voice. He waited until she found the pill bottle in the purse she still wore on her shoulder, poured two tablets onto her palm, and frowned at the half-empty bottle before she returned it to her bag.

"It storms without," Sojourner said after he had taken the medicine without the benefit of water, grimacing a little at the taste. "I know you must go out, but you will need to dress warmly. It is an icy rain laced with snow."

"How do you know?"

"To all seeings but yours, love, I am a cat, nothing more, and cats, especially great cats have a very well developed sense of smell."

"You know it's storming because you can smell it?"

"And hear it."

It was a ridiculous conversation, or it would have been if it wasn't so serious, so deadly serious. Too tired to be afraid, Jane said, "Now that we have that settled, what does it mean? Is it just a passing storm or what?"

"I fear it is the beginning of a terrible winter. The woman wizard, the one who dislikes you so because Farrel, a wise man indeed, finds you attractive, has disarranged the weather patterns in her efforts to bring about your demise. It is a serious thing she has done, one that could, quite easily, prove deadly for many living in The Great Northwest, perhaps those even further afield."

"Can't anything be done?"

"Yes, wizards with sufficient power can bring back harmony and order. It will take a time and a time to get the weather patterns realigned if they are left alone. Which they will be, unless, of course, Will realizes what has happened and calls for help."

"Will he?"

Sojourner shook his head. "I do not know, love. I know only that we must leave here before the real snow begins, otherwise we will be among the first to perish."

Suspecting him of being overprotective again, Jane bristled. "Why in the hell didn't you tell me sooner? Don't you think I have a right to know if I'm in danger of being flash frozen by a jealous witch?"

His hand brushed back her tangled, matted hair and he said, "I did not know until now. The fever dulls my perception. I beg your pardon, love, for being remiss. It will not happen again."

"It better not," she muttered, wanting to lean against him, to rest her head on his chest, close her eyes, and let him put his arms around her and take care of her until the end of time. But she didn't dare; there was too much that had to be done before night came again, bringing its pack of man-eating ghosties and goblins to howl and slaver outside their cave door.

RAIN, COLD AS ice and grainy with snow pellets, peppered down on his upturned face. Rocks, or something large and sharp, poked him in the back, making him want to shift position. Groaning, more than a little groggy, totally disoriented, Will tried to sit up.

It was a mistake of great proportions. Pain rampaged through his head, making him think, for just a moment, before his memory returned to tell him the truth of things, that he had been kicked in the head by a unicorn.

"It must have been Clyde," he muttered, "Cleo would never do..." And then he remembered enough to make him take cautious stock of his surroundings, to try and figure out who had knocked him in the head and why.

"Farrel?" The words were out of Will's mouth before he could swallow them back, and he was glad he hadn't when the unicorn rancher said, from somewhere very near, "Take it easy, Will. The marshal's deputy was a little scared and he hit you a little harder than he intended and..."

"It's the posse?" Will struggled to a sitting position, fighting off the waves of dizziness that threatened to send him skywest and crooked. "Have they got some extra riding 'corns? We have to get back to the ranch so I can..."

The marshal, carrying a flaming torch came into Will's field of vision. "Whoa up, wizard. Traveling ain't something we be wanting to do afore morning."

"But, the women are...Tell him, Max. Tell him the brides and the rest of the women are in real danger, that Cordelia is..."

"I be knowing all that," the marshal said. "And it be a hurty thing. My own wife be one of the women and I would..." The lawman paused, cleared his throat, and waited a minute or two before he added, "The thing is, wizard, storm-runners, dires you be calling 'em, do be out in packs this night. The fire be all that keeps 'em from tearing out our throats."

Will wasn't ready to concede. "But, we have to...I need to send a warning to Wizardholm about the..."

"Boy," the marshal said quietly, "all that be true, or so Farrel be telling me. But we ain't be breaking camp afore dawn. We can't. They don't be showing themselves now, but they do be out there, and I ain't be taking me no chances. The storm-runners already got two of the 'corns and one of my men tonight. Savaged them real bad afore they killed 'em. I ain't be a-wanting to lose me no more."

Urgency was driving Will, not sense. He wanted to argue, to tell the marshal that he, along with Farrel, had walked through the night without incidence, but his thinking was fuzzy, almost incoherent, and he couldn't seem to bring his words into any sort of focus. All he knew was fear, fear for Maggie, whose face haunted him, whose eyes begged him, and grief. Not just for Sojourner, but for Maggie and the rest of the women as well. If something wasn't done soon, they would be lost also. Lost like Sojourner and Jane, and Will wasn't at all sure he could live through the terrible pain of that additional loss.

"We have to..."

"Ain't no use a-talking it to death. Come on, boy," the Marshall said, "let's be getting you to camp and get some grub in your belly. From the looks of you and Farrel, a good bait of grub wouldn't be hurting you none neither. 'Sides all that, to my thinking, it ain't long 'til morning. You and Farrel do be appearing a mite tuckered to my seeing, a rest'll be making the going easier."

Seeing he had no real say in the matter, Will nodded agreement and took a wavering, unsteady step in the direction the marshal indicated and practically fell on his face.

"Better be a-giving your tame wizard a helping hand, Farrel, from the looks of him he ain't going to be going far on his lonesome. Iffen what you told me about the weather be true, I'm a-thinking we do be needing him right bad."

Evidently, the unicorn rancher needed no persuading in the matter. He was at Will's side, offering himself as a crutch, almost before the marshal was finished talking. "Come on, Will," he said, "it's not more than thirty steps. You can make it."

Leaning on Farrel's shoulder, Will allowed himself to be led around a rock pile and into a smallish hollow backed by cliffs on three sides and ringed by blazing fires on the fourth. Unicorns, all saddled and ready to be ridden, were on a picket line near the cliffs; men, at least thirty or more, were standing, in small groups, between the riding beasts and the fires. They made room for Farrel and Will beside a smaller cookfire, one that was surrounded by cooking pots and some battered plates.

Thankful he had been able to make it that far, Will took a seat on a boulder and tried to catch his breath, slow the racing of his heart. The smell of blood, death, and fear was heavy in the night air, but it was the odor of bacon and beans that clutched at

Will's empty stomach, tickled and teased his hunger, made him more than ready to grab a tin plate and pile it high. One of the men, Will thought he was one of the bridegrooms, brought two plates of food and was handing them to Max and Will when Cordelia made one of her overly dramatic appearances.

She crisped the steaming plates with a single word and derisive gesture, causing the man to yelp in pain, drop the plates, and start blowing on his burned fingers. Cordelia tossed back her wealth of pale hair and laughed. It was not a euphonious sound.

It rang in Will's throbbing head, traveled down to twist in his lank stomach, twisted hard, making him fight back the urge to be violently ill. Pushing back his headache, his own physical weakness, Will stood up. "Do you have any idea what you have done? Wizardholm will strip you of your powers and turn you into a wart-ridden bog rat for using forbidden magic to..."

Acting as if Will had never been born, didn't inhabit the same universe, had neither voice nor breath, she looked only at Max Farrel. He hadn't moved from his perch on the large, flat-topped boulder that had also served as Will's resting place. She smiled at him, and it was a vicious, ugly smile, one that had no place on the pure beauty of her face. And her strident words made Will, and every other man in his range of vision, shudder with loathing at the utter vileness of their content. Perhaps Will was the only one who really wanted to weep. Or perhaps other tears were hidden in the falling of the rain.

"Your whore, and the wizard's cat, are dead, smashed to bits by fire and water, and soon, very soon, the women will join them in the grave. Is that what you want, Max?"

His face white beneath its mask of rain-streaked grime, Farrel shook his head. "You know it isn't. I never wanted anyone dead, or even vanished, I just didn't want to marry you, Cordelia. I didn't love you and I..." His voice caught and he took a deep breath before he even tried to continue, which he seemed unable to do.

Will put his hand on the rancher's shoulder, giving the other man all the support he had to offer.

"But," she said, "I loved you, Farrel, and the world knows I made you an honest proposal of marriage. You gave me nothing in return but scorn. Whatever has happened, whoever dies, it's your fault."

"No, ma'am, it ain't," the marshal said slowly, coming over to stand on the other side of Farrel. "If you be doing the doing, then the fault be yours for the deed. That's what the law be saying, and the law don't be a-caring if you be a wizard or something else. You be taking the women. Now, you be admitting to killing a woman and the wizard's familiar, I do be a-thinking, you must rightly be a-paying for them crimes."

Waving her hand, almost absently, she spoke three words in the language of magic, smiling as a sheet of crackling orange destruction shot across the hollow, mowing down men, unicorns, a marshal, and another wizard. Or at least that's what it was designed to do before Will, drawing on the last energy he possessed, did a little hand-waving and magic-talking on his own. He changed the orange to the green of growing and health, which gave each creature it touched the equivalent of a good night's sleep and warm breakfast.

Every creature except Will. All it gave him was lifeless legs and even more pain in his head. Both of his hands were gripping the outside of his skull when he went down, feet plowing forward, body sliding down the side of the boulder, ending in a limp huddle on the cold, rain-wet earth. The pain in his head was almost all-devouring, but he managed, somehow, to stay conscious, to listen to what the other wizard was saying. Not that it made him feel any better, or lessened his fear for Maggie and the rest of the women.

It certainly didn't do that.

"Love," she spat out the word as if it were bitter in her mouth. "I loved you, Max, and I would have given you the world, all the worlds, if you had wanted them, but you didn't even want me. You didn't love me. So, if I asked you again, would you tell me yes? Would you say, 'Cordelia, I love only you?' Would you become my dear husband?"

Max didn't answer, he just stood there, like a man stricken dumb and looked at the dainty wizard. Will, even in the midst of his pain, knew the rancher wanted to say yes, wanted to save the other women, even if he had to do it with a lie, but couldn't force the words out of his mouth.

The silence was not entire, the screeing of the frightened unicorns and the distant howling of the storm-runners made sure of that. No one in the camp spoke until Max finally found his voice, finally managed to say, "If that's what you want, Cordelia, then I am willing to give it to you."

He hesitated for a moment before he added, "But, you have to know that I have lodged a formal complaint against you at Wizardholm and I did not act alone. Stealing humans is not lawful, neither is the interdict you placed around The Great

Northwest."

"Poor, poor Maxie," she cooed. "All this because I killed your skinny whore?"

"I have no whore, Cordelia," Farrel said, sounding far more dignified that she did. "The woman you killed was an off-worlder, brought here by your spite, and whatever she was, she wasn't a whore. And I would be gravely remiss if I neglected to tell you that Jane Murdock was far more of a honest and giving woman than you'll ever be."

"Paaah!" Cordelia's screech of fury almost stampeded the unicorns. But, after a single outcry, she laughed. "I have decided to refuse your offer of a loveless marriage, Max, and go ahead with my other plans. As to the old boys at Wizardholm, they can do nothing. They have no power to equal mine."

She made a few passes in the air and slowly faded from sight. "Look, Max Farrel, and you, too, little wizard. See what you have ordained, watch and know your true guilt."

A huge window opened in the cloud-choked sky and every man in camp, including Will, had to look, had to see the horror Cordelia was showing them. Had to see the captive women, huddled together for warmth, exposed to wind and rain, gaunt with hunger, eyes swollen from countless tears. They looked until the sky-vision faded, and perhaps only Will saw Maggie's face, perhaps only Will heard her say, "Please, don't give up hope. Will will save us. I know he will."

But everyone heard Cordelia's parting words, heard her laugh, and say, "Will can do nothing. His cat is dead, Maggie, and so are all of you. Dead of Max Farrel's scorn."

The woman's mad laughter was still assaulting Will's aching head when the marshal came to where he had fallen and hauled him to his feet. "We do be in your debt, wizard, and we do be doing the paying. You and Farrel get some grub down your gullets while we break camp. We'll be riding at first light. We'll be getting you to the ranch in right smart time, wizard, and we do be doing anything else we have to to stop her from killing the women. Iffen that's what you be wanting."

Still weak from the magical backlash, Will nodded. He would save Maggie and the rest if it took his last breath, or so he told himself.

And he reminded himself of that again when he tried to mount one of the unicorns, failed, and told the watching posse. "Flop me over the 'corn's back and tie me on like a sack of meal if you have to, but get me to Farrel's before sundown. If I can't reach Wizardholm by spell and scry, then the women are truly lost."

Farrel and the marshal gave each other a quick, worried look. Will saw nothing but truth in their eyes when they nodded and the marshal said, his voice both grave and determined, "We do be getting you there, boy, or we do be dying in the trying."

Chapter 25

THE FIRE LEAPED high, bounced light off the mica-flecked ceiling and walls, revealing, in shadowy clarity, the less than overwhelming fruit of Jane's day of hard physical labor. The tree limbs, chunks of silvery driftwood, and a few more bits and pieces from the remains of Will's splintered wagon were stacked in an untidy, slightly tipsy pile well away from the watch fire. A much smaller pile of combustibles she was closer to the firepit, making it handy fuel for the night fire.

Icy rain, holding a good admixture of snow, had fallen all day, but she had toiled from first light to twilight, scouring the canyon for every available cache of any kind of burning material. The resultant pile was neither high nor wide. It would last three nights at the most, and then...

If he had been a man at the moment, Sojourner would have shaken his head. He didn't know what came after the and then. It was there his worry was the greatest. He didn't have to draw in the night scents to know what was coming, to know a storm was approaching fast, a storm of mammoth proportions. One she would never survive in the canyon, or possibly not out of it either.

Sojourner could hear her moving around behind him, but he didn't turn to look. When the light started to fail, Jane had come in with a final load of wood and tossed it on the stockpile before she knelt and began to coax a new watch fire into existence. It had taken a lot of coaxing, and since Jane was not a patient woman, a lot of fiery language, to bring it into being.

But now, the fire, after its feeble beginnings, burned bright and hot, warming a goodly space around it. Beyond that circle of heat, the cave still held areas of chill in its many nooks and fissures, but that hadn't dissuaded Jane from the course she had chosen.

"I'm soaked to the skin," she had said, the cold and wet of the day adding hoarseness to her tired voice, "and I have to get dry and warm, but I'm so dirty I can't think. I'm going to take a bath even if it's only a small one, almost a pretend..."

Shivering, she had spread the dripping quilt she had worn for a cloak on some rocks, making sure it was just beyond the fire's reach. Then she had stood there a moment, watching the steam come up from the quilt and from the clothes covering her own tall, lean body. She sighed and fetched a kettle of water from the small spring at the back of the cave and sat it in the coals.

While her bath water heated, Jane had set about doing other chores that had been left undone. Sojourner, a cat to even his own seeing, had been helpless to give her aid during the day. And, even if he could have done the small domestic jobs, he probably wouldn't have had the strength to dig through the spellset food and trigger the packages into heating. Which she had done at intervals during the day, insisting the food, along with the pills she had given him, would give him back some of his strength.

He had done as she wished, but only to please her, to make her think she was aiding in his healing. He knew it was not true, knew neither food nor medicine would heal the malady that was his alone, his bane, his curse. Although he had eaten of the man food and had napped, off and on, the whole day, the wanderlust still tore at him like some bloodsucking worm, took his energy, his strength, and taunted him with the knowledge that all he had to do to regain what strength he had lost was to go a-wandering.

His eyes closed. He soaked up the warmth emanating from the fire, absorbing it into a body that was already burning hot. A small sound from the tunnel brought him instantly alert, even though he knew it was nothing threatening. Still, he tried to peer through the leap of flame, to be sure he wasn't mistaken. Caught securely in the heart of the fire, Jane's face stared back at him and he could look no farther. Sojourner knew it wasn't real, knew it was just a memory, a memory of another time, another place. He didn't want to live it again, not here, not now.

But, regardless of his wants, the memory played itself out, complete with Old Derna's voice giving him the prophecy. And another voice reciting the doom tacked at the end.

His muscles tensed. His lip lifted in a silent snarl. Sojourner's lean body readied itself for flight, to leap across the fire, and run out into the night, but he couldn't. He could do nothing but endure until the memory ran its full course.

First the face, the incredible face with midnight eyes, parted lips of rosy coral, ebon hair tipped in gold, high cheekbones bearing only the faintest blush, the face in the heart of the fiercely burning fire. Sojourner drank in the memory, knew the incredible wonder, the return to innocence and delight, fell in love all over again. He heard Old Derna say, her soft, sweet voice a chant, an invocation, "Woman who walks through time and space. Woman who wears love's true face. Woman of fire, woman of night, woman of dreams and perfect sight."

The old woman paused to take a breath.

And in that other time, a young Sojourner, blood pounding in his ears, leaned closer to the hearth fire, looked deep into the heart of the flame, his gaze tracing every contour of Love's beautiful face. And his voice was soft with first love, only love, when he asked, "What is her name, Derna? Where can I find her?"

Like one waking from a sleep, Old Derna rubbed her eyes, looked around the room before looking at Sojourner again, before she said, "I know not. I only know she is your destiny, your One True Love, and in time she will come to you and share your life. She will..."

"Break your heart."

The face in the flames, Jane's face, grew brighter and then began to fade. Sojourner watched until nothing of Love remained, and not even then did he turn to look at the new speaker, the doomsayer who had come into his bedroom unannounced.

Not that it mattered whether he acknowledged the speaker or not. Whatever he did, he still had to stay and listen to the prophecy, had to know what his future held. "She would never break my heart," the younger Sojourner said, not allowing any taint of doubt touch his voice.

"Oh, yes, she will. She will love you more than you can ever know, almost as much as you will love her. She will love you and her love, given without stint, will make you whole again. But the wholeness is only a sham, a promise that can never be kept. In the end, if she walks away, and she will because what you will become will give her no choice, you will be left alone to die of a broken heart."

Gray of beard, stooped with the weight of his years, the wizard, young Sojourner's teacher in matters arcane, shuffled closer, touched the boy on the shoulder with a gnarled hand, and said, "My vision is true, lad. Forget the woman conjured of fire and night and..."

"And if I cannot?"

The old wizard patted Sojourner's shoulder and sighed, "I will fast once more and cast the runes, perhaps you can change your destiny."

The outcome of the rune casting was something Sojourner never learned—the old wizard died that night and the old woman disappeared out of the boy's life.

Those were sorrows long past, but nevertheless, he let out his pent breath in what was more than a sigh, less than a sob, and stared into the cave fire's empty heart. The old wizard had seen true. Sojourner had found his One True Love and their love was doomed, could never be. And when she left, went back to her own world, as surely she must, then he would, just as surely, know nothing but terrible loneliness and heartbreak beyond measure, heartbreak great enough to stay his seeking and bring his death.

"Sojourner? What is it? What's the matter? Are the dires out there already?"

Jane's voice came from behind him and the fear it held was more than enough reason for him to banish the memory, at least for that brief moment, and return to the problems the present held. "No dires," he said, "but it grows steadily colder without."

Knowing he was doing a foolish thing, one that would only add to his sorrow, knowing, too, her closeness would be a temptation, he still did what had to be done. "I would not ask it otherwise, but I think you must join our beds together this night and place them close to the fire. I have rested through the day and can keep the fire if you are touching near. I would have you sleep as much as you are able, for I fear we must leave this place and very soon, possibly on the morrow."

She didn't question him, just did as he asked. And when the mattresses were dragged nearer to the fire, the bed was made, and her kettle of water was steaming hot, Jane took it into the back of the cave and made her own preparations for the night. From the sounds she was making, Jane was also planning for the journey they must take as soon as possible.

He prayed, to all the old and forgotten gods, that they would go soon. He did not know how long he could keep to the path of rectitude, resist his fated love. But, he had to; and it was his own acts that had made it so, had made all love between them forbidden ground. They were acts so terrible that he could not bring himself to dredge the horror from his memory, had to go on bearing the guilt but not knowing the fullness of the deeds.

Cats don't feel guilt, he told himself. Perhaps they didn't, but men did; and Jane had returned his manhood to him, had made him whole once again. And it was the man who loved her, needed her, and adored her. The cat would live on, he knew that, knew, too, that it was the man who would die when she was gone.

But, as long as there was a shred of honor left in his soul, he would protect her and keep her safe—even from himself. For her own sake, if not for his own, she had to return to her own world unsullied and unclaimed. But the destiny was there, declaring Jane was his One True Love.

Fevered, his mind in turmoil, Sojourner sat on the side of the bed nearest the fire and tried to find some solution, some plan that would allow her to stay, allow them to be together for all time. But there was none, and the future was nothing but bleak, empty, cold as the winter that was coming so rapidly.

He would take Jane back to Will, if he had the strength for the deed. Then he would vanish, bid her farewell and walk away, never allowing her to know the fate that waited for him, the heartbreak that would change him completely, take away all the man, leave only the cat. A wild and raging cat that knew nothing but pain.

Her bath scant but strangely satisfying, Jane, still shivering with cold and weariness, marveled at the smell of her skin, the silkiness of her hair, both washed with warm water and the partially melted bar of soap she had found in the treasure chest her purse had become. With more than a little longing, she remembered the luxury hotel where she had stayed in Seattle. A hotel that furnished shampoo, soap, and a host of other amenities. A few of which she wished she had at the moment; such as the bath robe of thick terry cloth and the thick towels.

"And the room service," she muttered as she dried herself on a petticoat and pulled on one of the thick, warm, high-necked, long-sleeved nightgowns she had brought with her from the ranch. She saved the last of the clean drawers and one of Will's shirts for the next day's travels. She was icy cold, weary beyond the telling, but still she lingered, oddly reluctant to join Sojourner in their shared bed.

It wasn't the man she feared, or not exactly. She was too bone-tired to worry about or even to want the fulfillment of destiny. Not that it was ever going to be fulfilled. There was no future for them and they both were hurtingly aware of that fact.

On every level of her consciousness, she trusted him without doubt, with her life, and with her heart, but the dreams waited in the bed as well the man, a man only she could see and feel. And it was the dark knowing held in the dreams she wanted to avoid, to cringe away from, but knew she couldn't, knew she had to learn all they had to teach her.

And like bushwhackers in some western movie, the first of the nightmares ambushed her almost before she murmured a brief good-night, an order to wake her if he needed her and, snuggled down under the fire-warmed quilts.

"Sleep, love. You've earned your rest," he whispered, his fingers brushing a brief caress across her cheek. She slept, but there was no rest in it, only ugly images of a world torn apart by horror and betrayal, hate and death. Sojourner's world. A world that saw him cursed and cast out.

And Jane could do nothing to stop what had to be—what had already been. But someone knew she was there, knew she watched and hurt and relished her pain, took pleasure in her tears, and ignored all her pleas.

IT WAS COLD, terribly cold, colder than any winter in the history of her world, cold enough to freeze a land and its people.

And Jane knew the cold and the place and the dream, but she couldn't escape its clutches, had to live through it one more time. But she didn't have to like the dream or the cold. But, she knew, as she drifted into her place on the stage, that even the light would be cold, murky, bluish, glacial where it fell on the horde of too silent watchers.

Faces pinched, eyes empty, they stood, rank on silent rank, and they neither shivered nor stove for warmth or life. Ragged, dirty, somehow beaten, they, men, mostly old, all infirm, women with babes in their arms, wee ones clinging to their threadbare skirts, other children huddled close, waited in total, absolute silence—but there was no sense of expectancy, anticipation.

Or even dread.

Jane remembered the dream and wanted scream, to demand, at the top her voice, to be set free, to shatter the thrall that held her. But she couldn't. There was nothing within the dream, including herself, that could break the terrible quiet, no wind, no bird, no beast—even the dark border of evergreen trees stood without a murmur or tremble. Even the low-hanging blue-black clouds were without form or movement; all of their rain-tears frozen, silent and unshed.

And it seemed that she had to follow the same path, do the same things she had done before. She couldn't change that either; even if she was fuming and swearing, she was doing it without sound, and without changing, in the slightest, what she had done before.

Drifting out of the sheltering trees, to the edge of the crowd, Jane knew, this time, that it was more than just a nightmare of cold and silence, that was not a picture drawn from some horror hidden deep in her own mind. She knew that this had happened in some other time, in some other place; not that knowing it was true made the watching any easier. It didn't.

As in her previous visit, Jane wasn't afraid, not of the silence and the cold, but, as before, her fear came when the movement began. And this time, her fear was even greater because she knew what was going to happen and was powerless to stop it.

Once again the man, cowled and cloaked in deadly, unforgiving night, hooded, faceless with in its icy shadow, walked, soundless but with a fearsome grace, through the bluish-gray, low-lying ground fog that spread across the village square, making it writhe and roil, like agitated wraiths, at his every step.

And he wasn't alone.

Before it had been a nightmare with a sense of reality around it, that had changed. This time Jane knew it was real, knew it was some re-enactment from Sojourner's past. She would have preferred it to be a dream, but even asleep, Jane's mind wouldn't allow her that way out of the terrible reality. It was so overwhelming, so strong that Jane stood as still and silent as the other watchers and, scarcely daring to breathe, waited for what-would-be.

The man, his black-gloved hand a steel-hard prison around the woman's fragile wrist, led her toward the small, black stone, windowless building that cowered, alone and forsaken, in a barren space at the bottom end of the squalid village square.

Her richly embroidered, gold-on-green gown ragged and thin as any beggar's, the dream woman, her sun-bright hair tangled and fallen, her eyes too full of grief and pain, stumbled along beside the man on bare and bleeding feet. The Black Opal Crown of Seeting, her badge of royal office, still rested on the queen's bowed head, but now it mattered not.

Its gold was blood-tarnished, its opal heart-fire banked, nearly extinguished, leaving only a hint of sullen smolder at the center of each black polished stone, nothing more. The power was gone, gone like her throne, gone like her country. Gone.

Even Jane's knowledge that the fallen queen was Annette, Sojourner's sister-in-law, couldn't change the dream from its set path. It was a path she seemed doomed to travel to its bitter and inevitable end.

It was something Jane did not want, and she moaned, tried to escape into waking, but even as Sojourner's hand touched her shoulder, his deep voice murmured soothing nonsense, Jane dropped back into the horror of the dream.

Chapter 26

FOR A BRIEF, lucid moment, Jane knew she was safely in bed, with Sojourner warm at her side, firelight dancing on the cave walls and ceiling, but the moment was all too brief. And when it had past, the nightmare was the only reality that remained.

All around her, the air grew colder. The ice-blue light shifted, hid the hooded man in even deeper shadow, outlined the captive queen, called attention to who and what she was. Barely able to draw the frozen air into her lungs, feeling the band of winter tighten around her, take her warmth and life, Jane looked at the crowned woman. Jane knew, with full certainty, that she was Annette, the beautiful, young princess who had married Sojourner's brother.

With the knowledge, sorrow rose within her, filled her soul until Jane wanted to weep. And the need was even greater when she looked upon the bright-haired, pregnant queen, and, once again, knew her time was hard upon her, squeezing her swollen belly in an iron-hard grip of pain.

"No," Jane tried to whisper, the feeble word of protest unuttered, frozen fast to her tongue.

Nonetheless, the shadow man, suddenly aware of her existence, turned toward her, stared at her with unseen eyes. Unable to do otherwise, she stared back and wanted to wail, to whimper, to cringe before the faceless void, the black nothing, that lurked inside the hood.

He assessed her with his gaze, and she knew he smiled, a strange cold smile of recognition and disdain, and knew, too, his tongue, like an adder's forked tongue, flicked across his thin lips in some sort of dreadful anticipation.

He said nothing. But there was something about him that was familiar. Something she didn't dare give a name, didn't dare acknowledge; even to herself. But the fear was there and growing, fear that the hooded man might be Sojourner, that the coming events were his terrible deed. She couldn't quite believe it. Not yet. Not without more evidence.

Jane wanted to move, to run away, to wake up, but the dream held her fast, froze her with its icy agony, as the man led the silent, unprotesting woman into the house of dark stone. Jane, because she could do nothing else, waited with the other watchers for what might have been hours or only minutes.

Tears froze on Jane's face when the black-clad, faceless man came out alone, the Opal Crown of Seeting dangling from the bronze-skinned fingers of his left hand. It was just the spoils of war, a bauble without life or meaning. Seeting was no more.

His voice deep, tolling like a great iron bell, a death bell, he pulled a naked babe from beneath his dark cloak, held it high in his right hand, and said, "Your land is destroyed. Your queen is dead. Her babe yet lives!"

The watchers, all except Jane, went down on their knees, moaning out their grief and fear.

The man lifted the child higher, his black-glove hand a horrible blemish on the small, white body. "It is demon get," he said, knelling doom in both the tone and the cadence of his incredibly beautiful voice. His grip slid to the babe's heels and he swung it in an arc, up, up, and then down, hard, against the stones of its mother's crypt.

The terrible frozen silence returned and one by one the mute watchers lay down in the blue-gray fog, let it cover them like grave soil, until only Jane was alive, only Jane remained standing.

Jane and the dark, foreboding figure of the man.

The dead babe discarded, lost in the sheltering veils of vaporous cold, his black cloak swaying with each gliding step, the man came toward Jane. She couldn't move, not even when he stopped in front of her, and held up the crown before her face. It came to life, the stones of polished black blazed with cold, inner fire, dazzled her with explosions of reds, greens, and blues. She wanted to blink, but couldn't.

Lowering the Opal Crown of Seeting, he reached out with the gloved forefinger of his other hand, his killing hand, gently touched the frozen tear on Jane's cheek. Then, he walked on, vanishing into fog and trees before he had gone more than a step or two.

And this time, as little as she wanted to, Jane had to follow the cloaked and hooded man, had to live the nightmare until it dragged her through all its manifestations of total horror and reached its terrible conclusion.

She tried to say, "No," and perhaps she did, perhaps Sojourner's arms held her, and perhaps his deep voice said, "Nothing will harm you, love. I am here."

But that, too, might have been part of the dream—a dream of unbearable sweetness with no relationship to the terror and grief that was growing inside her sleeping mind. On some still functioning level, she hoped it was true, hoped Sojourner was at her side, holding her body in a warm embrace, but whether or not it was true made no real difference.

Nothing could stop the nightmare's headlong rush into what-had-been. Jane, helpless in its cold claws, couldn't even fight against its ice-hard will. Faintly, but not far away, a mocking laugh sounded. A voice, cold with enmity and malice said something Jane couldn't understand. She didn't know what the words meant, but knew they were a threat, a promise of something evil yet to come. Again shivers ran down her entire form, inside and out, and her chest tightened around her pounding heart.

Gasping for breath, Jane fought against the force that pulled her forward, demanded she see the tragedy through to its bloody end. Her struggles were in vain—indeed they seemed to amuse the unknown watcher to the point of new laughter. Laughter that held not a single hint of mirth or joy. Laughter that brought tears to Jane's eyes and an ache to her heart.

But she didn't cower. Even in her dreams, Jane wasn't a whiny, sniveling, catch-me-I'm-going-to-faint maiden who paled at the sight of blood and squealed at spiders. She was Jane Murdock, and Jane Murdock took on the world on its own terms and, more times than not, she beat it at its own game.

In this place, she was only a wraith, a less than visible visitor in a strange land, but whatever the dream had to offer, she would take straight, without flinching away. That much she knew. Or at least she hoped that would be her reaction.

But she wasn't sure, could never be completely sure again. The Jane she knew, the Jane that she had always been, no longer existed. Love had changed her, made her less sure, more vulnerable. And it might be that love would be what would destroy her.

"Love."

The single word was followed by a bark of laughter and Jane was flung into the midst of a storm of horror-saturated pictures. One by one, faster and faster, groaning, screaming, pleading, bleeding, and dying, they rushed at her, through her, and were gone before she could even throw up her hands to ward them off. Nor could she cringe away from the terrible onslaught, or weep with the pity wrung her soul.

And then they were gone, leaving behind an incoherent history in Jane's reeling mind. It was a history of a slaughter, a world gone mad, lands and people falling to ax and bow, sword and stone, fire and plague, and finally hunger, terrible aching hunger that took the least of them first, but was never appeased, even by the strong.

A world destroyed by the man cloaked in darkness, his face hidden from her. A madman. A butcher.

A man she thought she knew, was afraid to name, especially after the cruel laughter sounded again and her dreaming self was pushed through a curtain of mist and haze and into a cave, or dungeon, or some other rock-lined room befouled with greenish, stinking slime. Rank and disgusting, it oozed down walls, spread across the uneven floor, touched her bare feet, crept up her ankles, but Jane scarcely felt it or the ache of cold that was the slime's dear and constant companion.

The light was uncertain, but it held the yellow-green of the slime and something of its stench, enough to burn her eyes, snarl in her nostrils, make her cough, almost choke. She stood there, an animal trapped in the light, and she wouldn't raise her hands, couldn't wipe away the tears that blurred her seeing.

With a clink of metal against metal, the rasp of chain across stone, something moved, slowly and painfully, on the far side of the small room. Something that might have been a man, might have called her name, might have said, "Love," in the warm darkness of her mind.

Something, perhaps a hand between her shoulder blades, pushed her forward, toward the moving figure that resolved itself in a cloaked and hooded shape. And within the shadows of the hood was a face, a bronzed skinned face with silvery eyes. Sojourner's face.

The whisper, coming from behind her, was anonymous, without face or gender, but it spoke with viper's tongue. "Blood stains his hands, lies live his mouth. He is the betrayer, the scourge of worlds, and worse. His curse is thy curse. His doom, thy doom. Renounce him and live."

"No," Jane shouted, pushing the explosion of sound through numb lips. And her wild denial brought her to the topmost peak of sleep, almost to waking, near enough to feel Sojourner's arms enfold her, lift her up, cradle her against his beating heart. To feel his breath warm upon her cheek. To know he was real, if naught else in that nightmare place was. It was knowledge to keep, knowledge to sustain and feed her—and it was her destiny. And his. A destiny of love beyond measure, a doomed destiny that would never know life.

"*Kai mahal intropec be!*" His softly spoken words of command resounded, echoed, and called a magic into being where none had been before. As soon as they were uttered, she entered a haven, a refuge, a warm, spicy-smelling place where no harm, not even dream harm, could touch her.

He was her sanctuary, her rock in a cold and bitter now. It was a refuge she couldn't accept. "You must release the spell and let me find out who the bad guys are and fight through this on my own. Otherwise, they will win. I can't let them do that."

"Owner of my heart, I do not know your dreams, but I fear them greatly for they are..." He paused, held her a little closer and then continued, his voice warm and comforting, but more than a little troubled, "Dreams paths can lead you far astray, can be more than real, can...I would not willing let you walk into that danger without me at your side."

Her eyelids were far too heavy to open, sleep and dreams waited within easy reach, but still Jane lingered just on the far side of waking. "I must go alone," she finally said, the words rasping across the surface of her dry tongue, almost hurting her.

"Love, please. You cannot know what you ask. There is magic here, evil magic. I can smell it. It means you some sort of harm, grave harm."

"I know," she said in return, and it was true. She did know, but not enough, not nearly enough.

She wasn't exactly ready to learn more when he did as she had asked and released the protective spell. She plunged, like a jumper from a high window, back into the seething mass of festering ugliness and raw, implacable hate that was masquerading as something as innocent-sounding as dreams.

HER BREATHING WAS shallow and quick. Sweat beaded on her forehead and upper lip, glistening like small sunstones in the firelight. Holding her close, looking down at her sleeping face, Sojourner ached for her, wanted to take her dreams, fight the magic that was waiting to fell her, but he could do nothing. The woman of his destiny had to fight her own battles, just as he had to fight his. Even if that meant he had to protect her from himself, his need to be her hero.

He looked down at Jane's face again, saw innocence and trust, and his need to care for her, to keep her safe, rose high, almost strangled him. She had to get out of the canyon, had to go back to her own world, even if the thought of losing her was almost more than he could bear.

When she left, the prophecy would come true. Her departure would break his heart, leave him alone and lonely. No one would ever see him as a man again; he would be nothing more than an animal, a great cat who was forced to wander alone. Always alone.

But if she stayed? She was born to an easier life, one of soft beds and warm houses. Even if she wanted to, determined as she was, as wise and willing to tackle new experiences without a whimper, she couldn't go with him on his endless travels, couldn't sleep in caves, in brush piles.

The fire was burning down, but he didn't really think it mattered except to keep out the growing cold. A small outrider, a foretaste of what would be, a snow storm had arrived and was clothing the canyon in white beyond the end of the tunnel. It was not the best of news, but the dires were gone, running before the ice and cold that were coming fast on the heels of this small storm.

"Young wizard," Sojourner sent the thought hard and far, "winter comes too quickly and we must go out from this place. Help us if you can."

Almost as if he was dreaming his own dream, he brushed his lips across Jane's forehead and returned her to the bed, covering her with care. Then, he turned away to add more wood to the fire, to see it burning hot, before he could again hold her in his arms and try to protect her from what attacked her from within. But he was growing steadily weaker; the wanderlust tore at him, every minute making him less able to resist its terrible lure.

Jane had demanded to be free from his protective spell, and his other magic was almost as weak as he was, but he had to try. "May sweet dreams guard your rest, my dearest love," he said, and it was more than a wish—but far, far less than the truth.

"WILL? BE YOU ready for some grub, lad?"

The voice, Will thought it belonged to the ranch foreman, came out of the shadow-filled gloom of the hall beyond his bedroom door. His head ached. His body was sore from too much riding. And his brain pure slop from hours spent in magical communications with Wizardholm, he knew he had to eat, had to get his strength back in order to travel with the others to rescue the women. But all he wanted to do was drop back on the bed and sleep for hours. He would have if the thought of Maggie hadn't intruded.

She trusted him, and he couldn't let that trust be destroyed. After Sojourner, he couldn't stand another loss. But he wouldn't allow himself to think of that now. The great cat had saved his life, been his dearest friend, his only family, and now Cordelia had...Well, she had to be punished for her misdeeds before he could allow himself the luxury of grief.

Some time in the early morning hours, he had fallen on the bed fully clothed, even to his boots. It might not be done in the best circles, he thought wryly, but it certainly makes dressing a whole lot easier. Crawling, almost literally, out of the bed, he managed, with the help of the bedpost, to get to his feet before he staggered to the washstand, washed his face and ran wet fingers through his wild hair.

The hasty toilet didn't help much, but he was feeling only a little less than human when he entered the lamplit dining room and faced the men seated there. Most of the posse that had brought them to the ranch were in the bunk house, but the marshal was at the table with Farrel and they were both watching him with expectant eyes.

"Let him get some grub in his belly first," Coodie, the cook, said as Will slumped in one of the vacant chairs. His next order was directed at Will. Sliding a plate of bacon and eggs in front of the wizard, he pointed at it, and said, "Eat."

Will ate, and as he ate, he listened. What he heard was both good news and bad; and all the bad could be laid at Cordelia's door.

"It be snowing some," the marshal said. "Ground be white, but likely it won't stay."

"Not this time," Will said, the food he was trying to chew suddenly too big for his mouth. "There's another storm right behind..."

"Eat," Coodie said again, taking up a position at Will's side and folding his arms.

"The waddies Cordelia magicked away have been coming in one by one," Farrel said. "As far as we know, there's only one dead and three hurt bad. The rest are scared and mad and..." He shook his head. "The unicorns are scattered over half of The Great Northwest, but we've managed to round up enough to get us where we're going."

Neither man asked the most important question until Will, eating with a coming appetite, had emptied his plate, filled it again, and was making deep inroads into that. Then the marshal said, "Be they coming?"

Will didn't have to ask who they were. He knew. He had spent the night chanting spells, using magic, telling the Master Wizards at Wizardholm of their plight.

"Yes," he said. "Three will be here by midnight. It will take their combined strength to undo what Cordelia has done to the weather, but they can only do that after Cordelia has been subdued, judged, and..."

"Can we..." The question was almost out of Farrel's mouth before he caught it back and said, "I didn't want this to happen. I just didn't love her and..." He got up abruptly, his chair toppling to the floor behind him, and hurried out of the room.

"Love do be making a man's life hell, don't it?" the marshal asked.

Thinking of Farrel and Sojourner and his own hopeless love for Maggie, Will could only nod in agreement.

Chapter 27

EVIL AND DARK, magic tainted the air, but it was old beyond knowing and crumbling into decay. Bits and pieces of it fell free, eddied and roiled in the restlessly moving air. They were but darker motes in the uncertain light that came from everywhere and nowhere, pale light that leached all color, all life from the large, high-ceilinged room.

A throne room, Jane guessed. It wasn't much of a guess, not when the room was, more or less, identified by the two dusty, time-stained ebon thrones setting, slightly separated, on a raised dais at the far end of the room. Once the walls had had hangings of snowy silk, tapestries in bright hues, and bright banners, but now there was only mold and tatters to reflect that former glory.

Fully aware of herself, the dungeon slime drying on her ankles, the voluminous white nightgown, with its trim of lace and pink satin ribbons that tied at the throat, Jane was equally aware that she was dreaming. But for some reason, the dream time had shifted from what-was to what-is, from the *then* to the *now*, as it were. And in the *now* she had to meet, face to face, with the person who sat on one of the thrones. A person whose cackle of laughter would have done full justice to any Ozian wicked witch, especially the one who was bent on stealing some ruby slippers and disposing of their present owner by any means at her command.

Jane didn't have any ruby slippers; she was unshod, walking across the grimy stone floor in her bare feet, or maybe stalking describes what she was doing in clearer, far more precise terms. She didn't like what was happening to her one little bit and was very close to making her dislike known to all involved.

Her fear was all behind her. She was tired, and she was mad. Damned mad. And when Jane was mad, those who knew her, even slightly, knew enough to speak softly and stay out of her way.

Evidently the person on the throne did not know Jane at all.

That changed rather rapidly. It was Jane who brought about the change. "Why are you doing this? What in the hell do you want from me?" she snapped, wanting to draw back her upper lip and snarl like a great cat, like Sojourner, before she attacked with fangs and claws.

The seated figure reached up, pushed back some of the folds of black, funereal black, that had swathed her from head to toe, revealing her face and a few wisps of her yellowish, dead-looking hair. It was an old face, withered, skin stretched on bone until not much more than mummified skull remained, that and silvery eyes, dulled now and dark with bitterness, old bitterness that still rankled and burned.

"You know me, don't you?" the papery old voice asked.

"Lizan." Jane's answer was terse, flat, almost expressionless, and it betrayed nothing of her true feelings, which were almost all devoted to fury; with only a small bit left over to know pity.

"I knew you would come. I saw you long ago in the flames. You are his One True Love, his destiny, and destiny cannot be turned aside lightly, if at all. But it can be circumvented, so I waited for you."

"Why?"

The old woman smiled, her teeth white and long against the wrinkled, leathery skin of her face. It was a predator's smile, one that told Jane she was, in all likelihood, the prey of choice, the special of the day.

The smile did not make for pleasant viewing; in fact, Jane was hard put to repress her shudder of distaste. But she did. Even if her pity shrank a little, took on an overtone of revulsion, not to exclude a growing animosity holding within it a strong seasoning of fear.

It's a dream, she told herself, she can't actually hurt you. Just listen and learn. Her dream-self wasn't convinced of the truth in that, but she took a step forward, stopping at the single step that led up to the two thrones and the old woman.

"Why?" she asked again, taking in only shallow breaths of the fetid air as she waited for the old queen to answer.

"He killed my son. He must be punished."

Jane didn't flinch away from the hatred in Lizan's voice, she just stood there and waited. It was important, it had to be, or else why was she here? Why was she dreaming this dream? But she said nothing, did nothing to fill the silence that followed the woman's words.

It wasn't a long silence, but it was the queen who broke it. The queen who pointed a gnarled finger at Jane and said,

"Someone must suffer for his crime, but he has forgotten almost everything. I will not have it so. If the changing took his memory, then you will suffer in his stead. And that will hurt him even more."

"What was his crime?" Jane asked, sounding reasonable and calm past all understanding.

"He murdered my only son." It was a wail of sorrow, laden with age-old pain, pain the years had not lessened.

The words made no actual sense—even if it was a dream. Jane frowned as she asked, "Who are you talking about? Not Sojourner? He's your son, too, isn't he?"

"His crimes are unforgivable. He has no name. No mother. No land. No people. He is an anathema, and we have cursed him. Cast him out." She leaned forward, stared into Jane's eyes, looked deep, and then she said, her voice hard, cold, "But the changing took away more than a man. It took his memory of his punishment. That cannot be. Someone must know and hurt, hurt until the grave claims them. Only then can my poor murdered son find his rest."

Jane lifted her chin, looked down her nose at the old woman, and said, quite calmly, "You're crazy, lady, and I have no intention of hanging around in this stinking dump and listen to you spout crap."

Smiling sweetly, sweetly for Jane anyway, even if it did hurt her face, she added, allowing nothing of her anger to show, acting as if the whole dream were just a chance meeting in the ladies room, "It's been interesting," as she turned and started to walk away.

"So!" It was hiss of contempt. "You, who carries the twin to his soul, think you can escape the consequences of what he has wrought? Watch and learn, fool."

Between one step and the next, Jane crossed over into another time, a different dream. This time the throne room was relatively clean if somewhat faded, but, as before, only one of the thrones was occupied. Only now, Jane wasn't alone with the queen; a queen whose grief-twisted face was only just beginning to bear the mark of years.

Stripped naked, a man with bronze skin and silver eyes, a chained man with the mark of whips on his back, was being forced to his knees before Queen Lizan's throne by three other men. He had been beaten bloody, but he was far from defeated.

Fierce love rushing up, pounding in her ears, making her blind and deaf to all except the man, Jane ached to run forward, hold him in her arms, tend his wounds, destroy the woman who had brought him to such a pass. But even if they were invisible, the bonds that held her were as strong as his chains. Strain as she might, she could do nothing but watch and listen as Sojourner's mother repeated the terrible spell, the forbidden spell that turned a man into an animal. The spell that fairly burned itself into Jane's brain, her memory, and perhaps even into her soul.

Tears ran down her face, clogged her throat, but Jane couldn't turn away; she wouldn't have if she could. He was Sojourner and she would stay with him until the end.

A woman wrapped and veiled in deepest mourning, Lizan stood, looked down at the chained man. "Why?" she asked, her voice venomous with hate. "Did you hate him so much because he was my favorite? Is that why you killed Damian, the child of my heart, my only son?"

Sojourner's head was unbowed, but his voice was low, husky with weariness when he said, "Damian was mad, Mother. I told you that, so did his wife. But you wouldn't listen to what we..."

"Silence!"

Several more black-clad men, Jane supposed they had some sort of function at the court, stepped forward as if they intended to make sure the queen's slightest command would be obeyed. Lizan waved them away and moved a step closer to her son.

"You are the child of my body, conceived by force, nurtured in hate. You are your father's child, but I am not your mother. I have never been your mother. You are nothing to me. Less than nothing."

"I am sorry to have caused you sorrow, Mother, but Damian killed his wife, his child, and then he burned and savaged the land of her birth. He was a mad dog; someone had to stop him. I did it the only way I knew."

"Why? Why did you kill your brother?"

"Because I loved him," Sojourner said, anguish giving truth to his words. "I did not want to see him suffer any more."

"Fool!"

"Perhaps, but Damian believed the all lies someone spread throughout the court, believed his wife loved me, that the child she carried was mine, but it wasn't so, was it, Mother?"

"Annette and her dear little baby." She laughed and took another step in his direction before she threw back her mourning veil and lifted her hands, began moving them in precise patterns as she recited words that forced their way into Jane's heart, crawled in her mind and took up permanent lodging. All while it added a world of new tears to her life, tears that could never be shed. Tears for knowledge that could never be shared.

The words of the changing weren't harsh, they were almost gentle, and would have been if they had been given with love, but the curse that followed had no gentleness in it.

"I curse you," Lizan said, lines of force going out from her hands, curling around Sojourner in a web of power. "From this time forward, you have no land, no people, no family, and only one hope. You are doomed to wander alone, endlessly and eternally, never resting in one place until you find That Which Was Lost, until you find the Black Opal Crown of Seeing."

She gave a final twist with her hands and smiled coldly as the chained man shimmered, took on the aura and semblance of a great black cat, a silver-eyed cat who still wore the chains of the man.

And then Lizan looked at Jane and said, her voice inaudible to all the others, "Watch and remember. Know in your heart and your mind that this is what he has forgotten, know it and suffer as he has made me suffer."

Lizan reached behind her, and took the Opal Crown in her own two hands, and began breaking off the nine opals it contained. One by one, muttering inaudible spells over each one before she threw it in the air, she watched them vanish.

Her breath caught in her chest, aching there, Jane watched, too, until Lizan lifted the last of the sullen, barely flaming opals. It was the ninth and largest. She showed it to both Jane and the cat before she dropped it on the stone of the dais, stepped on it, and ground it to powder under the sole of her shoe.

"No!" Jane's scream echoed in the high reaches of the room, but no one even turned in her direction. No one but the queen, a very old queen who, once again, sat on a throne in a tattered, moldy room, a room filled with old rotting magic and bitter hate. And with madness taking all humanity from her silver eyes, she smiled at Sojourner's One True Love and said, "Now you know. Will you tell him what you have seen? Will you tell him all his searching is in vain? Will you tell him That Which Was Lost can never be found? Jane Murdock, will you tell him that he will never walk like a man again?"

The old woman's laughter was wild, ugly, and so was her voice when she said, "Cry as I have cried, ache as I have ached, and know that nothing can change it. Nothing!"

Abruptly, with no transition, the dream, if that's what it

was, vanished, ceased to exist, but it did not take with it the memory of what had been done. And it did not take the tears, the terrible wracking sobs that shook Jane's whole body, that made her shake and cling to Sojourner when he woke from his doze, took her in his arms, and tried to soothe her.

"What is it, love? What has frightened you so?" he asked before he said, "Tell me, love, talk about it and it will go away. It was just a dream, it cannot follow you here."

But it had. *It had.*

"Tell me, love. The telling will ease the fear, the pain, take away its sting."

The old woman's words still echoing inside her brain, Jane clung to him, but only for a moment. And, not now or ever could she tell him what caused her terrible pain. Jane Murdock would never give that evil old woman that particular satisfaction.

Instead she wiped her eyes and said, "It was nothing, just a dream about dires or something like that. It's all but forgotten. I'm sorry I worried you, but we're going to leave tomorrow, we'd better get some rest." She freed herself from his arms, turned her back, and murmured some sort of answer to his protests.

The quilts warm around her, Jane closed her eyes, forced her body to relax, but sleep stayed just beyond her reach. She liked it that way. Sleep held dreams, and she hadn't the strength to dream any more that night.

THE RANK SMELL of evil magic lingered around her, like a miasma of decay. Sojourner didn't know where Jane's dream walking had taken her, but he was sure it hadn't been into Cordelia's sphere of influence. This magic was old and real, and there was something about it that tugged at his memories, reminded him of some unnameable something.

He sighed, but he couldn't remember, couldn't do whatever was needful to protect his One True Love. He thought with a touch of wry, she didn't like it much when he tried.

Knowing full well she wasn't sleeping, but not quite sure how to tell her so, he wanted to...to...He wasn't sure what—whatever he did, it would only make parting harder.

Sighing again, he turned his back to her still form, reached out, picked up another stick of wood, and threw it on the watch fire. Then, he mouthed a spell of protection, let it settle around her, and hold back all things arcane; if only for the moment.

Chapter 28

HER BACK TIGHT against his, Jane woke first. Still drowsy but savoring the moment, she smiled before memory smote her a heavy blow, memory of Lizan and the terrible future she had given Sojourner. Jane tried to squirrel the memory of the curse away in some hidden recess of her mind, but that wasn't possible.

Wanting to weep until her eyes bled, she knew she couldn't, knew, too, she had to conceal the terrible knowledge from him forever. She could not and would not cause Sojourner any further hurt. But it wasn't going to be an easy thing, and that was exactly what his mother knew, the reason Lizan had told her the truth. That Which Was Lost could never be found; Sojourner could never regain his man shape. He would search forever and would always be a cat; except to her seeing, to her every touch.

Jane stared into the darkness, forcing her much vaunted reason to take hold. And when her smile was firmly in place, she wiggled around in their rumpled bed until she could sit up without waking him.

What she saw didn't give her all that much pleasure. The fire was dead out. The cave was lit by a pale light, early morning light magnified by the night's snowfall and seeping in through the tunnel like a wan ghost of summer. And it was cold, so cold that she dreaded jumping out of the warm bed and going in search of the garments she had laid out for the day; the day she knew they had to leave the cave.

Her teeth were chattering, but she was fully dressed—in a pair of Will's pants, one of his heavy shirts, thick socks and kidskin slippers— when she had her first setback of the day. The wood was piled and ready for the touch of flame, but the cigarette lighter wasn't being cooperative. Swearing under her frosty breath, Jane spun the wheel against the flint again and again. It was as dead as autumn leaves, without even a spark to show it had ever lived.

"So much for the comfort of civilization," she said, throwing the poor dead thing against the cave wall.

"Love?"

Sojourner's soft question came out of the darkness behind

where she knelt on the sand before her unlit, unlightable fire. She bit back another unseemly word and, remembering something Will had told her, said, or rather demanded, "Teach me how to snap fire from my fingers before we both turn into ice cubes."

He hesitated for a moment before he said, "Magic is for wizards. I do not know if you..."

"Hog wash," she said. "I read Cordelia's primer. Magic can be done by anyone who can read and do a few hand gestures. I suppose, like cooking, that practice makes for a better product, but I don't care about that. I'm cold and I want to get warm."

Chuckling, he said, "You, my dearest love, are a wise and determined woman," before he gave her the words and explained the exact nature of the doing.

Her first try yielded a flicker, a brief whisper of light and heat. So did her second. For her third, Sojourner left the warmth of the bed and came up behind her, putting his arms around her, his hands on hers, to give her aid if it was needed.

His slightest touch seemed to give her added strength, if not added expertise before she felt him shiver with the cold and remembered he was unclothed. That forced her to focus entirely on the matter at hand. She tried again. Flame, yellow-bright and dancing, fairly leaped from her fingertips into the waiting wood, instantly igniting it into a fierce hot burning.

But it was the flare of light from her magic-making that sent her matched opal rings into their own dance of flashing fire. And seemingly for the first time, Sojourner saw them, knew them for what they were, and the tremble of hope in his deep voice almost broke Jane's heart when he asked, "Where did you get them, love?"

"My parents."

"Where did they..." His hands closed tight around hers, held for a long moment before he released them and turned her so she faced him. "Where did they get these black opals, love? Please, I have to know."

"I don't know for sure," Jane said, refusing to shed the tears that burned at the backs of her eyes. "My aunt said they got them on their honeymoon, in Nevada, in a place called the Virgin Valley."

"On your home world?"

Unable to speak, she nodded.

"There are more opals there?"

"I don't know. I think there are mines and..."

He laughed and reached toward her. For a second, Jane thought he was going to lift her up, whirl her around, but he didn't. Instead, he said, "She would not put the rest there. Not even in her madness would she hide them all in the same place, but still like seeks like. The Virgin Valley of your world will have its counterparts on many others."

She didn't have to ask what he was talking about, she knew. She knew far more than he and could never hurt him with the telling. Scrambling through the chaos of her mind, Jane tried to find something to say, something that would not reveal what the dreams had told her. Finally, she asked, "Who was mad?"

"My mother." His happiness dwindled, was almost gone when he said, "After my brother was born, she thought...She believed her second child was the child of demons who entered her bed chamber and took her by force. It wasn't so. It was only that giving birth made her..."

Jane had never had a child, or even wanted to, but she did know of the ills that beset women. "It's not uncommon. On my world they call it Postpartum Depression. Once it caused women to do and say terrible things, but now..."

"Her madness infected my brother."

It was a statement so bleak, Jane shuddered before she managed to say, "But it didn't touch you."

"Did it not? Oh, my dearest love, did it not? Did it not touch us both, destroy all that might have been? Did it not make me less than a man and unworthy of your love?" Before Jane could answer, he gathered her close to his heart in an agonized embrace, whispered a grief-torn, "I'm sorry. So terribly sorry."

Then, Sojourner released her and moved away, became a great black cat just before he leaped over the fire and vanished into the snowy world outside the cave.

And Jane, blinded by the sudden scald of her own tears, could neither contradict him nor call him back—she was sorry too, sorry that love could cause so much pain. All she could do was stand there and ache, for him, for herself, for all the lives his mother's madness had touched and destroyed.

IT WAS MID-MORNING when Sojourner returned. Jane had added wood to the fire twice, triggered the heating spell on one of the packets of food, ate the contents because she had to, even if it did taste like ashes. Then she put together a bundle of clothes, quilts, and food that she thought they would need on their journey out of the canyon. That done, she had dumped her purse, dug through the mass of wet and not so wet objects that tumbled forth. Saving her apartment and office keys, her billfold with its cash and credit cards still intact, the bottle of aspirin, and the pepper spray canister, she returned them to the bag, leaving the rest heaped in a corner.

Opening the book of magic, she read through several spells; one rather nasty one to do with snakes and spiders, she thought, with a grim bit of humor, she would like to try on Cordelia. Jane was paging through the rest of the magic book when she heard Sojourner coming back. After a moment of indecision, she closed the volume, returned it to her purse, and was standing when the great cat once again leaped over the fire and into the cave.

Making no further mention of his mother, or madness, he stayed carefully away from Jane, retained his catness, and said, the words soft and contrite inside her brain, "You are the owner of my heart, my only love, and I would ask your pardon for my acts causing you any disquiet."

"You didn't," she said, and every word she uttered was true, if not exactly all the truth. "I saw your pain. My only worry was for you."

"Love, I..." He sighed once before he said, his voice already holding a foretaste of impending loss, "I wish we could stay in this place, away from all hurt and harm, and learn more of the wonders of love, but we can't. The dires are gone, but a storm comes on their heels. We, too, must be gone and rather quickly if we are to win our way back to Farrel's ranch."

There was no other course open to them, and Jane knew it—even if she didn't want to believe it. However, "I'm ready," was all she said as she looped her purse around her neck and shouldered the small, rather awkward pack she had made ready for their journey.

And, after she had scattered the still burning fire, she stepped across the smoking embers and followed where he led. It was a long, cold trail, with patches of snow still in the shadows, and steep slopes, huge rocks, and flood wrack to be crossed. But the storm drove them, coming out of the cloud-dark sky, gradually growing colder and darker, and they had no time to stop and rest, no shelter against the increasing snow.

Sojourner ran as a cat, scouting ahead, but always staying in sight. Jane's long legs were tired and her hands were scratched from rocks and brambles, but by the time the light was close to fading into a darkness, they were out of the canyon.

Walking together, they made their way slowly through wind-driven snow toward the flood ravaged campsite that Will had chosen to keep them safe.

"There's no one here," Jane said, new worry jumping onto the horde she was currently nourishing. "Cordelia might have...Sojourner, Will told me once that you talked to him. In his mind, I mean. Would you know if something happened to him? Something really bad?"

The great cat, his lip drawn back in snarl, the hackles on his neck standing high, crept toward their original camping place but only after hissing, "There's magic here, stay back." He took a single step forward, seemed to relax a trifle, and said, "Will's been here, love. The magic is partly of his making, but..."

He vanished.

Throwing caution to the winter winds, Jane ran toward where he had been and plunged into the same arcane trap—one set by Cordelia using Will's spellset message as the bait. Jane knew that just as soon as she fell out of the sky with a rather painful thud. She landed a short distance away from the limp, sprawled body of a great cat, with the wind knocked from her lungs and confusion reigning in her mind.

It should have been dark, but it wasn't. There was a reddish glow, a dome shape that encircled them, covered them, and Jane had no idea what it was or why it should be there. She just lay there, flakes of snow falling on her face, gasping for breath, and wondering what was going on and why people were screaming and carrying on all around her and the cat.

Dazed, she sat up, shook her head, and recaptured about sixty-three percent of her wandering senses. The screamers and criers were all female, women and children. Hollow-eyed, hungry-looking, dressed in dirty rags, they were huddled together like a herd of freezing sheep that edged away from Sojourner with little whimpers of fear.

Jane wanted to order them to be quiet, but words wouldn't come out of her mouth. A goodly portion of her brain was doing some shrieking and crying of its own, and it didn't want her to edge away from the fallen cat; it wanted her to rush to his side, to...She knew better, knew she didn't dare turn him into a man. The catness of him was all that was keeping him safe from Cordelia, and she couldn't take that meager protection away from him.

"Maggie?" Jane said, when she had enough breath to speak. "Is Maggie here?"

Hair snow-wet and lank about their gaunt faces, the nearest of the women looked at her with blank eyes and, after what seemed an eternity or two, moved to one side, creating a lane among the crowd of freezing bodies, and yielded up a half-frozen, bedraggled Maggie.

And if Maggie was less frightened by the big cat than her companions, her tears were just as heartfelt, if for a different reason, when she hurried to Jane, dropped down to knees. She extended her arms, hugged Jane so tight it hurt, and said, her voice husky from the cold and hunger, "Thank goodness you're safe, Ms. Murdock. I knew Will would take care of you, but..." She looked around, peering through the thickening snow. "Where is he? Didn't he come with you?"

Bewildered by her entrapment, her fall, Jane stared at her secretary for a moment before she shook her head, tried to push the younger woman away. She couldn't see beyond Maggie's shoulder, had to ask a question of her own as she tried to escape from both her secretary and the awkward pack of quilts and food that was hindering her motion, "Sojourner? Is he hurt?"

"Who?"

"The cat," Jane said, trying to be calm and reasonable; not an easy task given the givens.

"Who cares about a cat?"

"I do, damn it, and you'd better do a little caring to if you want to get out of this mess." Getting to her feet, Jane pushed Maggie to one side and ran toward the silent cat, finding just enough sense to stop short of touching him.

"Maggie," she said, straining to sound like an in-command boss and not someone who was ready to faint from fear, "see if he's still alive."

The watching women had fallen silent as they tried to hear what was being said between Maggie and Jane, but now their chorus started again.

"No," someone cried. "No, Maggie, don't. He'll kill you."

Maggie came to Jane's side, looked down at Sojourner, and said, "I'm afraid to... He's wild, Ms. Murdock, and I..."

Unable to still the tremor in her voice, Jane whispered, "Please, Maggie, I have to know. I...Oh, please."

"Forget your begging, whore. The cat is as good as dead and will be as soon as I give you a few lessons in..."

Cordelia would do exactly as she said. Jane knew that and fear for Sojourner almost overwhelmed her, but only for a second and then it gave way to love. It was love, total and absolute, that made Jane strong. Cordelia was spoiled, selfish, and, in the name of love, had done more harm than anyone should be allowed to do, and it had to end. Right then and right there. If Cordelia intended to murder Sojourner, she was going to have to blast Jane first.

Jane had already been blasted one too many times. Turning toward where the beautiful wizard stood, not more than three paces behind her, Jane said, "I am not a whore, nor do I enjoy being called one. You, on the other hand, are nothing more than a spoiled bitch and a trouble-maker, who well deserves everything that's going to happen to her."

And as she spoke, Jane reached inside her purse and pulled out the pepper spray and the book of magic. She had had time to read but not practice any of the spells; however, she had always been a fast learner.

"Love, no!" Sojourner's shout reached Jane's mind just as Cordelia, her face red with anger, raised her willow switch and started to bring it down across Jane's face.

THE WIND WHIPPED snow into blinding swirls, beading it on their hair, their eyebrows, and every other exposed surface, but the company of wizards and the unicorn riders that plodded along behind them, heads bent against the storm, didn't dare call a halt. There was too much at stake—and not just the lives of Maggie and the rest of the women.

Trying not to breathe too deeply of the icy cold, Will used a gloved hand to wipe his eyelashes clean and tried, for about the hundredth time, to see where they were, to know if they were anywhere near Cordelia's castle. But it was impossible, the night and the storm had seen to that.

But they had to get as close as possible before they spellset their capture nets and wrapped Cordelia up tight before she could do more harm. Only then would the Wizardmasters be able to begin the tedious task of quieting the weather, sending it back into its normal paths. If they failed, the whole land would suffer and thousands would die, the weakest of the ice and snow, the strongest of hunger that was bound to follow crop failures and even more storms.

Max Farrel and the marshal urged their weary mounts forward, flanked Will on either side. "The castle lies just beyond the rise," Farrel said, "but I'm afraid we..."

His words were interrupted by a sputter and a hiss and the awesome sight of a wall of reddish fire rising where no fire could actually exist, shooting flames of a sullen, unhealthy hue that fed on snowflakes and stood staunch against the wind.

The marshal swore, damning Cordelia to every hell known to man. And his lurid anger picked up a chorus from the men traveling in the rear.

"What in blazes is it?" someone asked.

"Some damned wizard trick," another answered.

Will knew it was a wall designed to keep them, and their own brand of wizardry, out until Cordelia had reason to invite them in, but he saw no reason to share his knowledge.

Gordon, the oldest and presumably the strongest of the trio of Masters, reined in his unicorn and looked at the flames for a moment before he dismounted and began to rummage through the saddlebags behind his saddle.

Sheila and Beau followed suit, with Will, who hadn't the slightest idea what it was they intended doing, making a tardy fourth.

A short, very plump, and truly powerful wizard, Sheila wasted no time informing him, not bothering to subdue her voice, announcing their intent to all the company. "Will, you must know that Cordelia isn't strong enough to withstand all of us. We will join forces, breach the wall, and go in for the capture."

Climbing down off his own unicorn, the marshal gave voice to Will's greatest worry. "There be women in there," he said, obviously trying to sound like a man who wasn't a bit frightened, and not succeeding at all.

Swallowing hard, but not ready to give up on what he had to say, the marshal went on, "I'm not be knowing much about the ways of you folks, and I be meaning no disrespect. But, Cordelia do be having my wife in there and I do be having to ask: will this thing you do be planning be hurting the women what that she-devil's took?"

The howl of the wind and the hiss and crackle of the barrier wall were the only answer he got. The trio of visiting wizards gave each other a quick look, but they said nothing at all.

The fear that encased Will's heart, fear for Maggie and for the rest of the young women, the brides he had sworn on his honor to protect, was far colder than the night and the storm.

And there was nothing in his power that would warm it even one degree.

Chapter 29

THE WIZARD'S FACE was red, twisted, and ugly with the force of her anger, and Jane hadn't a doubt that Cordelia meant to dispose of her in some rather nasty, definitely unsavory fashion before she killed Sojourner. Jane had never retreated from a fight in her life, and she wasn't about to start now; especially now when so much was at stake.

Cordelia's conceit, the willow switch she used as her wizard staff, was lifted high. Her thumb on the triggering mechanism, Jane held the pepper canister at ready. Like an action scene in an old movie, everything shifted into slow motion. Jane was totally aware of her surroundings, of the whimpering women and girl children, of Sojourner staggering to his feet, sending her urgent mind messages, of the sparkles, like bits of gold glitter drifting down from Cordelia's weapon of choice.

Fragments of the spells she had read in the book coalesced in Jane's mind and her mouth began to shape the words, but her hands, instead of making the accompanying gestures, were busy with some rather mundane tasks of their own.

Her left thumb pressed down, releasing a cloud of burning, stinging, choking spray full in Cordelia's face. Jane's other hand threw the heavy, brass-bound book, hitting the wizard's willow, knocking it out of Cordelia's hand, sending it in a slow, spiraling spin until it was lost in the snow and the crowd of cold, hungry, frightened women.

Rubbing at her eyes with both hands, Cordelia screamed, partly from rage, partly from pain, and called Jane any number of names that should never have been found in a lady's mouth, even a somewhat dastardly lady wizard's mouth. And if they were there, spewing out like toxic waste, certainly a good washing with lye soap was well in order.

Jane Murdock, who was a self-made woman, had never been a lady, and she had no ambitions in that direction. All she wanted at the moment was to keep Sojourner safe. And the best way to do that seemed to disable Cordelia to the point where she could do no more damage. Jane, still speaking the magic words, gave the screaming, cursing wizard another shot of pepper.

It sent her tear glands into hyperactivity, but it did nothing to slow the stream of venom spurting from her tongue. "You'll spend the rest of your life servicing the men at Jake's, whore. And then you'll die moaning."

Just to be on the safe side, or so Jane told herself with a truly wicked grin, she triggered the spray again. Cordelia screamed louder, so Jane gave her another prolonged shot. White robes fluttering, eyes swollen shut, Cordelia went down to her knees in the muddy dirt of the women's compound, or corral, or whatever it was.

Still furious, still intent on saving Sojourner, Jane was beyond reason or fear. And she spoke the final word of the spell with precision just as Sojourner's, "No, love, you must not," reached her mind. It wasn't the snake and spider spell from the magic book, but whatever it was, it truly worked, worked far beyond Jane's wildest expectations. It worked well enough to silence the great cat and to make the whimpering women back away from Jane just as far as they were able.

"WILL! WILL, look!"

Max Farrel's shout jerked Will's attention away from what the Masterwizards were telling him and he looked. As did everyone else, wizards, unicorn rancher, posse members, and marshal. All looked with fear and awe; all muttered questions that had no real answers.

Light, green, blue, red, purple, white, and orange fountained into the sky over Cordelia's castle, exploded, shot in myriad of fiery zigzags, illuminating the snow, transforming it, making it a part of the light show. Then, the reddish dome started fizzling and wavering and cracking. And, in the distance, muffled by the storm and the night, the watchers could hear screams, screams that held fury and disbelief at their core.

"Cordelia?" Max asked, moving closer to Will and the other wizards. "It sounds like her. What's going on, Will?"

Will hadn't a clue. Still staring at the incredible display, Will shook his head.

The marshal had other worries. "My wife and the rest of the women? Do they still be alive?"

Again Will shook his head. Nothing was making any sense. The display of light had to be magic in origin, but he had never seen the spell that would bring it into being. Sojourner's magic was old and true, he would have had an answer to what was happening, but Sojourner was...

Sadness twisted through Will's body, and he tried to fight it away, but only managed to give a mental wail, one that said, "Sojourner." He sent the cry out into the stormy night just as the dome fell and darkness engulfed the land.

Total darkness except for one bright spot, clearly visible through the falling snow, that seemed centered somewhere very near to Cordelia's castle.

The marshal mounted his unicorn, said, "I be going in."

The Wizardmasters chorused, "Wait until we have time to evaluate...

"I no be waiting."

Before the words were out of the marshal's mouth, Farrel's foreman was in his saddle and ready to ride. Max wasn't a second behind him; neither were about fifteen of the possemen.

"Maggie," Will whispered, running toward his own mount. His booted foot was in the stirrup and he was lifting himself toward the high-cantled saddle when a deep, familiar voice sounded inside his head.

"Young wizard," was all Sojourner said, but it was enough, more than enough to make Will let out a shout of relief and ask a handful of mental questions, all tumbled together and mostly incoherent, "Where are you? Do you need me to...Are you in danger? Jane? Is she still alive, too? Are you hurt? How...Why..."

Both respectful and indulgent, Sojourner's chuckle whispered through Will's mind before the great cat said, answering nothing, bringing new questions into being, "Jane Murdock is a determined and far from common woman, I would not say her nay."

"What do you mean, Sojourner?"

Will didn't realize he had spoken the words aloud until Farrel, reining in his skittish unicorn, asked, "Sojourner? Your familiar? What about Jane? Is she still alive, too?"

Nodding an answer to the rancher's question, Will asked Sojourner, "Where are you? Do you need us to come?"

"It would be for the best," the cat said. "The women, except for your Maggie, fear us both greatly, and they are in need of care." After a moment, he added, "And judging from what has happened here, what Jane has brought into being, Cordelia would not find your presence greatly amiss either."

"Mount up," Will shouted, suiting his own action to his words. "The women are safe. Jane and Sojourner are at the castle."

It wasn't quite that easy. The wizards from Wizardholm were a suspicious bunch, and they took their suspicions very seriously. Even if they did know who Sojourner was, they still feared a trap of some sort and demanded the rescuers go in slow and under a magic shield.

Impatience tearing at him, urging him to kick his unicorn into a canter, to rush down the slope like a hero from one of the old sagas, to defeat Cordelia in a duel of magic, rescue the captive women, sweep Maggie up in a wild embrace, and...He knew there was nothing beyond the and; he could give Maggie no future, no home, but even that sobering thought could do nothing to quench his need to hurry.

Need and deed do not always match, as Will well knew. Curbing his own feelings, he fed his magical powers into the shield, rode in his appointed place, and only stopped to stare, along with the rest of his companions, when they rode into the space fronting the castle walls and saw what awaited them there.

Lit, very brightly, from some unseen source, Cordelia hung, head-down and naked, from a line of twisted force that looked very like a snake. Looped around her ankles, it writhed and wiggled and tossed her hither and thither, and she wasn't making a sound in protest. Actually, she couldn't. Someone or something had plastered her mouth shut with a square of silvery-looking material; her wrists were bound behind her with the longer strips of the same stuff.

Will recognized the material as being duct tape, a substance from Jane's home world, and the recognition gave him pause and a worrisome thought, one he didn't quite want to believe. But the belief seemed to grow of its own accord when they dismounted and moved in closer.

"Jane?" he asked, inspecting the scorned wizard, the question directed to Sojourner alone. "Jane did this?" And what was left of the disbelief gave way to awe, a wizard's awe for magic well and truly done, when he looked at Cordelia's transformation, a transformation that left her very little of her former beauty. And then floated a mirror in front of her face so she could contemplate what had been wrought.

He heard someone come up behind him, but couldn't look away from Cordelia. Her hair was less than half an inch long and it stuck up all over her head like the stubble of a newly mown field. Her eyes were swollen to mere slits. Her nose had grown long and hooked. Her naked body was saggy and baggy and covered with muck, mostly ill-smelling. And, even though she deserved a far worse punishment for the harm she had done, Will couldn't help feeling a little sorry for her, mostly because she was, so obviously, suffering the torments of being purely ugly. It was an ugliness that not only offended the eye, she also smelled terrible.

"Why?" he asked, speaking to himself or to whoever had come up behind him. "How could Jane do something like this?"

"I don't know how, Will, but I can tell you why. Cordelia was really mad. She was screaming terrible things and said she was going to send Ms. Murdock to a place called Jake's and then she was going to kill the cat. Ms. Murdock didn't want her to, so she stopped her."

"Maggie?" All else forgotten, Will gulped out her name and whirled to face her. He ached to grab her, hold her close, tell her how much he loved her, but his sense of honor and responsibility returned in time to keep his arms empty and his love unspoken.

Her face was haggard. Shadows were deep beneath her eyes. She was still dressed in her off-world garments, which were soiled, torn, and soaking wet. Her hair was plastered against her head, but she was smiling when she said, "I knew you'd come to get us. I kept telling them so."

"I know," was all Will had breath to say, but he couldn't stop looking at her.

"The others are inside. They are scared silly of Ms. Murdock and that big cat, but they...Will, what's the matter? Why don't you say something?" Maggie reached out, put her hand on his arm, and gave it a little shake.

Finally he managed to say something. "The other brides?" he croaked out. "Are they all right? Did Cordelia harm..." And then he said, "Oh, Maggie," and pulled her into a fierce embrace. She wasn't unwilling. In fact, it was her arms that encircled his neck and pulled his face down for a long, lingering kiss.

THE WIZARDMASTERS were still addressing the problem of undoing Cordelia's magical plight and deciding on more suitable punishments for her crimes when Maggie and Will, followed by the full posse, Farrel, and his waddies, walked across the draw bridge and into the castle courtyard, where they were engulfed by the stream of laughing, crying, happy women who came rushing out of the warmth of the great hall to greet them.

Will barely had time to speak to Jane and Sojourner before

the other wizards, greatly perturbed by their inability to free Cordelia, came to haul Jane off into one of the other castle rooms and interrogate her on the hows and whats of the spell she had used to dangle, disrobe, disarm, and discommode Cordelia.

"Tend to your brides," the great cat said, weariness seeping into Will's brain with every one of Sojourner's words. "They deserve a better welcome to this world than the one they were given." That said, the great cat found an out-of-the-way corner, one where he could watch the doorway to the room occupied by Jane, and stretched out, pretending to doze while he kept watch.

And that much was true, the brides deserved the best he could provide until each one was safely married to the man of her choice. With Maggie's help, he explored the castle, saw to the comfort of the brides and the other women, fetching clean fresh garments, by magic means when it was necessary, making sure they each had a warm bed. Bestirring Cordelia's legion of confused and slightly dumbfounded servants, Will ordered them to prepare food and drink for the entire assemblage.

And the next day the three visiting wizards, after releasing Cordelia from Jane's spell, prisoned her with their own and set about realigning the weather patterns, a very tedious and tiring task which they eased by doing some further research into Jane's rather intriguing way of spelling.

It was also the day the courting began. For the next five days, Will watched, with a sinking heart and smothering sense of depression, the bachelors of The Great Northwest cluster around Maggie. They vied for her attention, wanting to take her for walks, bringing her small gifts, and promising her all manners of impossible things.

He did other things, of course, wizardly things, such as sending many of the stolen women, and their daughters, back to their husbands and sons with as much dispatch as was humanly possible. Greatly troubled, not only by the thought of losing Maggie to some other man, Will watched Sojourner grow weaker and weaker each passing day.

He tried to give the great cat healing potions, but they were all refused. "It is the wanderlust tearing at me, stealing away my strength and my hope. Soon I must go, but I cannot leave until I know Jane is safe. Send her back to her home world, young wizard, I beg you."

But that wasn't possible yet. The Wizardholm wizards refused to let her go and Will wasn't sure he was strong enough to send her traveling by his own strength against their desire.

"Tomorrow, all will be in order," the oldest of the wizards said. "Tomorrow we will have a feast when the sun is high, pronounce the rites for those who wish it, and announce a part of Cordelia's punishment." He gave Will's shoulder a quick pat before he went scurrying off in a flurry of wizard robes to attend to the rest of his rather secret business.

Will found Jane, who was wearing a long skirt, a frilly blouse, and a shawl gripped tight around her narrow shoulders, standing on the castle parapet, looking off into the distance. If she had been anyone other than Jane Murdock, he would have sworn she had been crying.

He started to say something, to tell her she could go back to her own world the following evening, but she spoke first, sounding just as sharp and certainly as mean as always, "Why on earth are you mooning around like a lovesick calf making everybody around you miserable? Why don't you just ask Maggie to marry you and be done with it?"

"I can't," he said.

"Why?"

"She came to my world expecting many things, things I promised her on my honor as a wizard. I can give her nothing. I have no house, no prospects, nothing. What kind of husband would I be?"

Jane's pithy answer wasn't one Will expected to hear, nor was it one he could repeat in mixed company. "A house? You think that's all that matters? Men!" she snorted as she glared at him before she stalked away. "Idiots! Every damned one of you, total idiots."

THE BANQUET, which began at noon, was a total success. It was what happened afterwards that was both surprising and a little disquieting. Not the mass wedding, of course, that went as planned; except Maggie hadn't as yet chosen a groom so she remained unwed, if only for the moment.

"Jane," the three Wizardmasters said, standing at the head table, speaking as one, "come forward."

And when Jane stood before them, one of the wizards, Will couldn't see which one from where he was seated at the end of the high table, handed Jane a scroll of thick parchment. It was the sort of parchment used almost exclusively for property deeds, proofs of ownership. "It has been decided, by one and by all. Cordelia, for her crimes, must forfeit all her lands and goods, as well as going back to Wizardholm and undergoing some further punishment. And you, since yours was the power than vanquished her, have earned those lands and goods as your just reward. The castle and its grounds are yours, my dear, to do with as you wish, no matter what you decide about going back to your home world."

Jane stood there a moment before she smiled. After thanking the trio of wizards, she asked, "Will, does the terms of the contract the brides signed allow the bride to pick the husband of her choice?"

Almost afraid to breathe, to hope, he nodded.

Still smiling, Jane looked at Maggie and asked, "If you had your choice, which one would you make your husband?"

Blushing hotly, refusing to even look in his direction, Maggie said, so low he had to strain to hear, "Will. I would choose Will."

"In that case," Jane said, "Maggie, since you have been such an excellent secretary, I feel it's time I gave you a bonus." She walked to where Maggie was seated before she added, handing Maggie the deed to all Cordelia's wealth and property and giving Will a questioning look, "Or shall I call it a wedding present?"

Will was struck dumb. His tongue was glued to the roof of his mouth and he couldn't say a word, could do nothing but nod vigorously and grin, like the idiot she had called him, when Jane asked, "Well, what's your excuse now? Isn't a castle and land good enough to help you keep your honor?"

Overwhelmed by her generosity, Will stood, kissed Jane on the cheek, and whispered, "Sojourner is right. You are a wise and wonderful woman," before he walked to where Maggie waited, knelt before her, and asked if she would consent to be his bride.

The cheering of the crowd stole her answer, but he didn't need more of an answer than her arms around his neck, her lips seeking his, and the shining happiness in her brown eyes.

BEFORE THEY magically transported the newlyweds to their diverse homes and did their own departing magic, the wizards pronounced the rites for Will and Maggie. With well-wishing and happy laughter echoing through Maggie's castle, Will and Maggie, followed by Jane and Sojourner, walked out of the castle and across the drawbridge to bid the departing guests a farewell. Max Farrel looked at Jane with longing eyes, but had enough sense to keep his sentiments to himself except to say, "If you ever decide to come back, Jane, you know where I live."

And when the last of them was gone, only the sadness of parting remained. Sojourner was so weak he could barely stagger, but he managed to say, "My love, you must go, but I cannot bear to...Young wizard send her quickly, lest I falter in my resolve and..."

He gave Jane one last look and turned and walked away, stumbling along toward the west and the face of the dying sun. He wove back and forth as if he was blinded by his own anguish at their parting, grief at the death of the destined love that had been doomed by his own acts.

Tears were streaming down Jane's pale cheeks when Will touched her arm. He said, as gently as possible, "Jane, you have given us much and I would do anything in my power to do the same for you, but it cannot be. It is his wish that you go back, that you be safe in your own world, and I have given Sojourner my word that it will be so."

"I...I..." She didn't even try to wipe away her tears, she just stared after the departing cat and wept as if her living heart was being torn from her body.

"Sojourner won't die," Will said, trying to give her some small measure of comfort. "It is the wanderlust, the terrible curse, that saps his strength. His strength will return to him as soon as he begins to journey, begins to quest again for That Which Was Lost."

"I know," she whispered hoarsely. "I know everything."

"Evening is coming fast and I have set the travel spell, shall I trigger it now and send you home?" he asked, holding his own weeping bride close against his side as he waited for Jane Murdock's answer.

Epilogue

"JANE?" WILL said softly.

She didn't answer. Wearing magicked replicas of her off-world garments, all her good-byes said, Jane Murdock didn't even glance in Will's direction.

The stricken look on her face, the frozen look of stark sorrow, loss beyond endurance, made Will ache for her, but he had to keep his promise to Sojourner. "The travel spell is set. It's time to go back," he said softly, reaching out to touch her arm.

She still didn't answer; she just stood there, her battered purse hanging from one shoulder, her hands at her sides. She stared at the slowly retreating form of a great cat, a cat that looked old and defeated, all will to live gone, a heart-wounded beast looking for a place to die.

"Please, Will, wait. Ms. Murdock, Jane, needs...She loves him!" Maggie's voice rose, became a wail of grief.

"I know, Maggie." Holding his new bride with an arm that trembled, Will said, his voice holding no lesser measure of grief, "And he loves her. But Jane has to go back to her own world, Maggie. There's nothing for them now. Maybe one day when Sojourner finds That Which Was Lost and becomes a man again, he can go to Jane's world..."

"No!" Jane snapped. And suddenly she was a different woman; the sorrow on her face was replaced by a smile, a very real smile, that smile of a woman who knew exactly what she was going to do. Jerking her purse strap off her shoulder, she dropped the bag on the ground as she called, "Wait for me, Sojourner, I'm going with you."

Her expression grew more and more determined as she walked across the small distance that separated her from the great black cat, but her smile never wavered. If anything it grew, became luminous.

"Oh, my love, you can't. I wish it could be, but..."

Sojourner's soft, sad words echoed within Will's mind, and he thought, without any real surprise, that Maggie was, for the first time, hearing the cat, too, because she jumped a little and her tears came a little faster, but she didn't look away from the drama unfolding before them. Neither did Will; he couldn't. He almost envied his bride her tears of grief, wished he could shed those burning in back of his eyes, clotting in his throat.

"Oh, look," Maggie whispered, awe making her voice soft.

Will looked, saw Jane strip off her clothes, stand tall and proud, reach out and touch Sojourner. And witnessed a transformation, saw what he had always hungered to see, saw Sojourner as a man, a tall, lean bronze-skinned man who said, in a man's deep voice, "I cannot let you do this, love," as he took his One True Love in his arms, held her as if she were precious beyond life.

Her chuckle throaty and warm, Jane said, "Rule one, you don't get to tell me what I can or cannot do."

"I beg you, go. There is nothing..."

"On my world, a very wise woman once said, 'Wither thou goest, I will go. Wither thou lodgest, I will lodge.' It sounds like good advice to me," Jane said. Giving him a truly wicked grin, she began to intone a spell, a changing spell, in gentle, loving tones, a spell that would keep them together for all their days, a spell that would fulfill their destiny, a spell she had heard in a nightmare and would always remember.

"Ohhhhhhh, that's the most beautiful thing I have ever seen." Maggie's words were only a whisper of sound, and she half-turned to Will, clung to him, as they watched what were now two great cats, standing where only moments before a man and a woman had stood. The cats look into each other's eyes for an endless moment, a wondrous moment, before they walked off, shoulder to shoulder, without a single backward glance, and vanished into the brilliant, red-gold light of the setting sun.

~*~

Patricia White

A best selling author, Patricia White, lives in the Cascade Mountains, very near an extinct (she hopes) volcano. Keeping her company is a long-suffering husband, a darling daughter, and three really different cats—who may or may not have been the inspiration for A WIZARD SCORNED.

Formerly a teacher (high school English), she has been published in many mediums, from paper to audio to electronic, and in many genres, from mystery to western to romance to fantasy.

Visit Patricia at: http:// www.patriciawhite.net

Don't miss Patricia's other Hard Shell Word Factory titles!

The Godmother Sanction (Fantasy Romance)
Edwina Parkhurst, Spinster (Western Historical Romance)

Available from your favorite bookseller
or directly from:

Hard Shell Word Factory
PO Box 161
Amherst Jct. WI 54407

Fax: 715-824-3875
Email: books@hardshell.com
http://www.hardshell.com